OCTAVIA E. BUTLER

My Reading

CHI-MING YANG

OCTAVIA E. BUTLER
H is for Horse

OXFORD
UNIVERSITY PRESS

OXFORD
UNIVERSITY PRESS

Great Clarendon Street, Oxford, OX2 6DP,
United Kingdom

Oxford University Press is a department of the University of Oxford.
It furthers the University's objective of excellence in research, scholarship,
and education by publishing worldwide. Oxford is a registered trade mark of
Oxford University Press in the UK and in certain other countries

© Chi-ming Yang 2024

The moral rights of the author have been asserted

All rights reserved. No part of this publication may be reproduced, stored in
a retrieval system, or transmitted, in any form or by any means, without the
prior permission in writing of Oxford University Press, or as expressly permitted
by law, by licence or under terms agreed with the appropriate reprographics
rights organization. Enquiries concerning reproduction outside the scope of the
above should be sent to the Rights Department, Oxford University Press, at the
address above

You must not circulate this work in any other form
and you must impose this same condition on any acquirer

Published in the United States of America by Oxford University Press
198 Madison Avenue, New York, NY 10016, United States of America

British Library Cataloguing in Publication Data
Data available

Library of Congress Control Number: 2023951960

ISBN 9780192862358

DOI: 10.1093/oso/9780192862358.001.0001

Printed and bound by
CPI Group (UK) Ltd, Croydon, CR0 4YY

Links to third party websites are provided by Oxford in good faith and
for information only. Oxford disclaims any responsibility for the materials
contained in any third party website referenced in this work.

The manufacturer's authorised representative in the EU for product safety is
Oxford University Press España S.A. of el Parque Empresarial San Fernando de
Henares, Avenida de Castilla, 2 – 28830 Madrid (www.oup.es/en).

SERIES INTRODUCTION

This series is built on a simple presupposition: that it helps to have a book recommended and discussed by someone who cares for it. Books are not purely self-sufficient: they need people and they need to get to what is personal within them.

The people we have been seeking as contributors to *My Reading* are readers who are also writers: novelists and poets; literary critics, outside as well as inside universities, but also thinkers from other disciplines—philosophy, psychology, science, theology, and sociology—beside the literary; and, not least of all, intense readers whose first profession is not writing itself but, for example, medicine, or law, or a non-verbal form of art. Of all of them we have asked: what books or authors feel as though they are deeply *yours*, influencing or challenging your life and work, most deserving of rescue and attention, or demanding of feeling and use?

What is it like to love this book? What is it like to have a thought or idea or doubt or memory, not cold and in abstract, but live in the very act of reading? What is it like to feel, long after, that this writer is a vital part of your life? We ask our authors to respond to such bold questions by writing not conventionally but personally—whatever "personal" might mean, whatever form or style it might take, for them as individuals. This does not mean overt confession at the expense of a chosen book or author; but nor should our writers be afraid of making autobiographical

SERIES INTRODUCTION

connections. What was wanted was whatever made for their own hardest thinking in careful relation to quoted sources and specifics. The work was to go on in the taut and resonant space between these readers and their chosen books. And the interest within that area begins precisely when it is no longer clear how much is coming from the text and how much is coming from its readers—where that distinction is no longer easily tenable because neither is sacrificed to the other. That would show what reading meant at its most serious and how it might have relation to an individual life.

Out of what we hope will be an ongoing variety of books and readers, *My Reading* offers personal models of what it is like to care about particular authors, to recreate through specific examples imaginative versions of what those authors and works represent, and to show their effect upon a reader's own thinking and development.

ANNE CHENG

PHILIP DAVIS

JACQUELINE NORTON

MARINA WARNER

MICHAEL WOOD

Figure 0.0 Octavia and mare. Photo credit: Leslie Howle. OEB 2273. By permission of Octavia E. Butler Enterprises.

*To everlasting friendships, kindred spirits,
and fellow ungulates that roam the earth.*

PREFACE

For years I had been visiting the Huntington Library and Gardens in San Marino, California to research European accounts of Asian art. Generations of travelers had extolled the splendor of Eastern imperial courts and whetted Western consumers' appetites with descriptions of marvelous substances like porcelain and lacquer. My focus was the China-mania of the eighteenth century, which saw an unprecedented volume of goods, including plants and animals, shipped daringly across the oceans. Considered "white gold," Chinese porcelain was a cutting-edge technology replicated by royal chemists and adored by the aristocracy and gentry; it fashioned their world to the extent that some British women even bleached their skin to match the color of their white, translucent chinaware. Then, as now, life imitates art in unsettling ways. The same European consumers of Asian commodities also ingested the products of Atlantic slavery, such that affluent domestic interiors were filled with things from all four known continents: porcelain held tea, or coffee, taken with Caribbean sugar, in the company of an imported pet monkey, parrot, or lapdog. Such practices were part of the story of how whiteness was made under conditions of globalization.

As a literature professor, I unearth texts that reveal the intense pace of England's mercantile expansion and the newness of the

PREFACE

early modern inventions that are still with us today, for better or worse: vaccines, private property, copyright, the stock market, multinational corporations, banking and credit systems, and the racisms born of transatlantic slavery and exploitation of populations and environments which enabled all this "progress." People usually draw a blank if asked to name an author between the time of Shakespeare and Jane Austen. Yet they do know the work of the Anglo-Irish satirist Jonathan Swift or the dissenting English entrepreneur Daniel Defoe, if only through the diluted versions of *Gulliver's Travels* or *Robinson Crusoe* that have been turned into children's literature and fun-loving cartoons. The historical backdrop to these survivalist adventures was the plantation system that converted others' lands into laboratories for human breeding, resource extraction, and products of incipient biotechnology. Tropical island-stranding narratives, like the first encyclopedias and dictionaries (also published during that time), documented the sense of colonial wonder and knowledge acquisition of white travelers and castaways surviving against the odds, long before reality TV or science fiction. Swift's intelligent horses, the Houyhnhnms, were the first equisapiens, Defoe's savage cannibals, the first Orcs.[1] These books blended human and nonhuman realms; they experimented with genres before that term came into being. This was an age of speculative fictions.

Wholly unrelated to this, or so I thought, in 2008 the Huntington acquired the extensive manuscript collection of the African American science fiction writer Octavia E. Butler. Out of curiosity I consulted the materials related to her 1985 trip to the Amazon. I was already a fan of Butler, and given my interests in travel writing, I wondered how her time in Peru informed her science fiction. Her research notes on the Andean tropics might reshape

PREFACE

my university lectures on *Dawn* (1987), a postapocalyptic novel in which Earth must be populated anew. Amidst the drafts and memorabilia I came upon an intriguing set of her early teenage horse drawings. From there, I uncovered a massive trove of juvenilia. Over the next several years, each time I visited family in Los Angeles, I would call up a couple manuscript boxes. One horse story, diary entry, or scrap of marginalia led to another, until a picture began to emerge of a young Black science fiction (SF) author's equine sensibilities. I did not expect to find myself combing through all of her childhood writings looking for horses, or for these stories to eventually take the shape of a literary memoir. Such is the work of serendipity.

From the archive I have pieced together a trajectory of Octavia E. Butler's development as an unconventional SF writer. There are five decades of materials in the library's collection, and I have only accessed one slice of it. However non-exhaustive and selective my reading, it offers a rare glimpse of Octavia's* life via her youthful writings and adult reflections on her early years. It is hard enough to accurately piece together one's own youth, let alone someone else's. But, not only did Butler's vocation as an author begin in primary school, much of her juvenilia is intact. In pairing images from the archive with my own short essays on her writing, *H is for Horse* is part speculative childhood biography, literary criticism,

---

* Note on Naming: Drawing as much as possible from her own words and texts, I mostly refer to the author familiarly as Octavia, except when studying her earlier childhood. There I take my cue from how she signed her writings. While she sometimes went by her middle name, Estelle, she signed most of her schoolwork Estella. I will generally use Estella when speculating upon her pre-high-school years, and Butler when discussing her professional career or oeuvre from a more academic perspective.

xiii

PREFACE

and personal reflection on the discovery process. It is an exercise in life reading and reading for life.

To stay true to Octavia's practice of researching and indexing the world, or what she called her "dictionary habit," the chapters of this book are organized alphabetically. It seems only fitting that a study of childhood take the form of an ABCs of O.E.B. Consider this a primer on characters, places, and ideas that mattered to her. Twenty-six essays of varying lengths are keyed to letters of the alphabet and to vocabulary oriented toward her coming of age in Pasadena, mere miles from the Huntington Library. The chapters need not be read in order. This format helps me tell two stories in parallel: (1) Octavia's lifelong dedication to experimental storytelling, fueled by her passion for library research and all kinds of shapeshifters, including mixed-race pairings, and plant–animal comminglings; (2) my process of piecing together vignettes of her childhood archive, interspersed with my own memories of growing up as an introspective and bookish immigrant kid who, like Octavia, found sanctuary in the public library.

Going back centuries, abecedaries have helped children learn the alphabet; they have also served as teaching aids for the illiterate, and templates for experimental art and poetry. Letters are shapes and patterns that allow us to see and organize the world. Young-adult fiction author Jacqueline Woodson recalls, in verse, the revelatory childhood moment she first wrote out her full name on her own: "Letters becoming words, words gathering meaning,/ becoming/ thoughts outside my head/ becoming sentences/ written by/ *Jacqueline Amanda Woodson*."[2] In his *Alphabet for Adults*, the Surrealist Man Ray wrote,

PREFACE

A letter always suggests a word, and a word always suggests a book. There are words that are for everyday use and there are words reserved for the more special occasions, for poetry. One may glean from the former those disinherited symbols which by an inadequate association can be divested of their prosaic meaning and finally projected into the domain of greater emotional exclamations. To make a new alphabet of the discarded props of a conversation can lead only to fresh discoveries in language.[3]

It is not a coincidence that we look to animals to teach children how to spell, to see the world anew. Often the abecedary is a bestiary—as in, *H is for horse*.

The A to Z chapters of this book interweave literary and personal musings sparked by the library's archival materials. You can expect periodic departures into poetry, art, or eighteenth-century history which pay homage to Octavia's wide-ranging, time-traveling intellect. My study also includes several field trips around and beyond Pasadena (*"M is for Mother,"* *"V is for Victorville"*), a few equine digressions (*"E is for Equisetopsida,"* *"R is for Rex McDonald"*), and one extended reading of Charles Dickens (*"H is for Horse"*). I wish I had been able to interview Octavia about her childhood when she was alive, but I'm grateful to those who recorded her thoughts over the years, and to others who have spoken to me about growing up alongside her in Black Pasadena and neighboring Altadena at the dawn of Civil Rights.

Having spent most of her life in the Los Angeles area, Octavia E. Butler moved to Seattle in 1999 after the death of her beloved mother, Octavia Sr. In the land of evergreen trees and snowy peaks she spent the next seven years until her untimely death from a fall and heart-related complications. When she died suddenly and tragically, Octavia Estelle Butler was only fifty-eight

xv

years old. Yet if we consider that she began seriously writing at age ten, she'd been an author for nearly five decades. Like many kids, she dreamed of escaping to other planets when her own surroundings felt intolerable. Inspired by the cowboys and space travelers of 1950s and 60s popular culture, she wrote about disabled Black outcasts with superpowers. Often they were horsey. As an ardent reader, scribbler, typist, and patron of the public library, she was prolific by the time of high school.

Octavia E. Butler has become a hero to many, an African American ecofeminist who embodies the freedom struggles of the past four centuries. Whatever their genre (fantasy, science, climate, speculative, or historical fiction), her novels could be considered Afrofuturist, especially when they rewrite the past. Her work is equally attuned to histories of slavery and the ongoing, manifold violence of white supremacy. She was always ahead of her time, even as a child writer. Key to understanding her alternate universes of utopian and dystopian survival are her formative years in Pasadena, where she was a tall, Black misfit girl growing up in segregated, Cold War America. This book explores the young Octavia's otherworldly resilience.

CONTENTS

List of Illustrations	*xix*
Introduction	1
1. A is for Alias	29
2. B is for Bambi	49
3. C is for Character	57
4. D is for Dog	63
5. E is for Equisetopsida	73
6. F is for Flash	81
7. G is for Ganymede	93
8. H is for Horse	103
9. I is for "I am"	115
10. J is for Junie	119
11. K is for Kapok	127
12. L is for Lion Girl	131
13. M is for Mother	135

CONTENTS

14. N is for Notebook 145

15. O is for Ooloi 147

16. P is for Public Library 155

17. Q is for QWERTY 165

18. R is for Rex McDonald 173

19. S is for Sexy 185

20. T is for TV Western 189

21. U is for Utopia 199

22. V is for Victorville 209

23. W is for White Cloud 221

24. X is for Xenogenesis 225

25. Y is for Yearbook 237

26. Z is for Zorro 245

Butler's Works Cited 247
Horse Appendix / Appendix of Horses 249
Index of Names 261
Endnotes 265
Acknowledgments 285
Index 287

LIST OF ILLUSTRATIONS

0.0. Octavia and mare. Photo credit: Leslie Howle.
OEB 2273.   viii
By permission of Octavia E. Butler Enterprises.

0.1. Octavia amidst buttressed trees in the Amazon.
OEB 7249.   4
By permission of Octavia E. Butler Enterprises.

0.2. Detail, Octavia in full plaid.   7
Credit: Bebe Martin-Smith.

0.3. Second-grade class photo, Lincoln School, 1955   7
Credit: Bebe Martin-Smith.

0.4. Grocery bag/book jacket, c. 1985. OEB 1612.   11
By permission of Octavia E. Butler Enterprises.

0.5. Inside view, grocery bag/book jacket, c. 1985.
OEB 1612.   11
By permission of Octavia E. Butler Enterprises.

0.6. Altadena street sign.   18
Photo credit: Author.

1.1. Eighth-grade yearbook cover, 1961. OEB Box 337.   28
By permission of Octavia E. Butler Enterprises.

1.2 and 1.3. Correspondence with Mead literary agency, 1961–62.
OEB 4.   32
By permission of Octavia E. Butler Enterprises.

1.4. Detail, S.S./Silver Star alias with Flash insignia, 1958.
OEB 590.   39
By permission of Octavia E. Butler Enterprises.

LIST OF ILLUSTRATIONS

1.5. Detail, Star the horse with star birthmark. OEB 2472.   41
By permission of Octavia E. Butler Enterprises.

1.6. Senior yearbook photo with Flash and Star insignias, OEB
Box 337.   42
By permission of Octavia E. Butler Enterprises and John Muir High
School.

2.1. *Bambi* movie poster, 1966. Everett Collection Inc/Alamy
Stock Photo.   48

3.1. Writing mantra/Calendar page, 1976. OEB 1514.   56
By permission of Octavia E. Butler Enterprises.

4.1. "Jump, Spot, Jump" from *The New Our Big Book*, 1952.   62
Courtesy of Princeton University Library.

5.1. Pamphlet owned by Octavia E. Butler, *Home Course in Animal
Breeding* (1944).   72
Author's copy.

6.1. "Flash-Silver Star" story page, 1958. OEB 590.   80
By permission of Octavia E. Butler Enterprises.

6.2. Writing schedule, *c*.1965. OEB Box 336.   82
By permission of Octavia E. Butler Enterprises.

6.3. Detail, Flash/Star insignias. OEB 590.   86
By permission of Octavia E. Butler Enterprises.

7.1. "Life on Ganymede," back cover illustration by Frank
R. Paul. *Amazing Stories* vol. 14, no. 10 (1940).   92
© Amazing Stories, the Experimenter Publishing Company.

8.1. Detail, horse drawing. OEB 461.   102
By permission of Octavia E. Butler Enterprises.

8.2. "Palomino," Anna Pistorius, *What Horse Is It?* (Wilcox &
Follett, 1952).   109

LIST OF ILLUSTRATIONS

8.3. "And could this not be Emily as she vows not to come
back unless she is brought back, a lady." OEB 461.   109
By permission of Octavia E. Butler Enterprises.

8.4. Checkout card pocket, Charles Dickens, *David Copperfield*,
*c.*1960s. Boys' & Girls' Department, Pasadena Public
Library.   111

9.1. Writing mantra, *c.*1980. OEB 1517.   114
By permission of Octavia E. Butler Enterprises.

10.1. Birthday card from Octavia Margaret to Octavia Estelle.
OEB 4594.   118
By permission of Octavia E. Butler Enterprises.

11.1. "The Cotton Tree, Freetown, Sierra Leone, 12/22/2011."   126
Courtesy of artist: Daniel Tucker. daniel@pippinhedge.com

12.1. Mowgli and wolf, "The Law of the Jungle" Letter J, flipped.
Illustration by John Lockwood Kipling, from Rudyard
Kipling, *The Two Jungle Books* (1895), 113.   130
Courtesy of the David Alan Richards Collection of Rudyard
Kipling, Beinecke Rare Book and Manuscript Library, Yale
University.

13.1. Gravestone of Octavia Margaret Butler.   134
Photo credit: Wanda Poston.

13.2. Gravestone of Octavia E. Butler.   134
Photo credit: Author.

14.1. Seventh-grade notebook, 1960. OEB 323.   144
By permission of Octavia E. Butler Enterprises.

15.1. Index card on symbiosis, OEB Box 161.   146
By permission of Octavia E. Butler Enterprises.

16.1. Peter Pan Frieze, Pasadena Public Library Children's Room.   154
Photo credit: Author.

LIST OF ILLUSTRATIONS

16.2. Fourth-grade class photo, Lincoln School, 1957.   159
Courtesy of Bebe Martin-Smith.

16.3. 1950s school library checkout card, I.M. McMeekin, *First Book of Horses.*   160
Photo credit: Author.

17.1. Remington Rand typewriter advertisement, c.1957.   164

17.2. Detail, typewriting practice page. OEB Box 325.   170
By permission of Octavia E. Butler Enterprises.

18.1. *Tom Bass and Rex McDonald* (2011).   172
Courtesy of artist: Jeanne Newton Schoborg.

18.2. Detail, Animal–character list, c.1957. OEB 1620.   175
By permission of Octavia E. Butler Enterprises.

19.1. "I ran as I had never run BeFore," Rocket and Silver Star. OEB 2472.   184
By permission of Octavia E. Butler Enterprises.

20.1. Detail, typewriting practice page. OEB Box 325.   188
By permission of Octavia E. Butler Enterprises.

21.1. Topographical map of Star Island, land of horses, c.1958. OEB 2472.   198
By permission of Octavia E. Butler Enterprises.

22.1. "My Hopes and Predictions for the Future," c.1957. OEB 1519.   208
By permission of Octavia E. Butler Enterprises.

22.2. View of Bell Mountain, looking south from where ranches used to stand.   210
Photo credit: Author.

22.3. Highways to Victorville, Barstow building mural detail, "The Mormon Trail."   215
Credit: Kathy Fierro and Main Street murals, www.mainstreetmurals.com.

Photo credit: Author.

LIST OF ILLUSTRATIONS

23.1. Drawing of "White Sun," *c.*1958. OEB 2465.   220
By permission of Octavia E. Butler Enterprises.

24a, and b. Cancer research envelope, *c.*1985. OEB 3013.   224
By permission of Octavia E. Butler Enterprises.

25.1. Title page of John Muir High Yearbook, 1964–65.   236
Courtesy: Bebe Martin-Smith. By permission of John
Muir High School.

25.2. Octavia's senior yearbook photo. OEB Box 337.   238
By permission of Octavia E. Butler Enterprises and
John Muir High School.

25.3. Muir students with Mustangs banner, 1965.   242
Courtesy: Bebe Martin-Smith. By permission of John
Muir High School.

26.1 and 26.2. List of animal names, *c.*1957. OEB 1620.   244
By permission of Octavia E. Butler Enterprises.

28.1. "Preshevalski's Horse." Anna Pistorius, *What
Horse Is It?* (Wilcox & Follett, 1952).   251

28.2. "IF [*sic*] Uria Heep were a Horse he would look
like this". OEB 461.   251
By permission of Octavia E. Butler Enterprises.

28.3. "Donkey." Anna Pistorius, *What Horse Is It?*
(Wilcox & Follett, 1952).   251

28.4. "And who could this be but Miss Murdstone. She
has just the personality for it." OEB 461.   251
By permission of Octavia E. Butler Enterprises.

28.5. "Belgian." Anna Pistorius, *What Horse Is It?*
(Wilcox & Follett, 1952).   253

28.6. "This horse like Peggotty is beautiful in a
different way." OEB 461.   253
By permission of Octavia E. Butler Enterprises.

LIST OF ILLUSTRATIONS

28.7. "Shire." Anna Pistorius, *What Horse Is It?* (Wilcox & Follett, 1952). — 253

28.8. "This could stand for Ham or Mr. Peggotty. It is the largest breed of horse in the world" — 253
By permission of Octavia E. Butler Enterprises.

28.9. "Arabian." Anna Pistorius, *What Horse Is It?* (Wilcox & Follett, 1952). — 255

28.10. "The Arab is said to be the Purest breed in the world. It could represent no one but Agnes." OEB 461. — 255
By permission of Octavia E. Butler Enterprises.

28.11. "Morgan." Anna Pistorius, *What Horse Is It?* (Wilcox & Follett, 1952). — 255

28.12. Uncaptioned [possibly David Copperfield]. OEB 461. — 255
By permission of Octavia E. Butler Enterprises.

28.13. "Tennessee Walking Horse." Anna Pistorius, *What Horse Is It?* (Wilcox & Follett, 1952). — 257

28.14. "I don't know why this horse, the Tenn. Walking Horse, should remind me of Steerfourth [sic] but it does." OEB 461. — 257
By permission of Octavia E. Butler Enterprises.

28.15. "American Saddle Horse." Anna Pistorius, *What Horse Is It?* (Wilcox & Follett, 1952). — 257

28.16. "The American Saddle Horse is nicknamed 'Peacock of the show ring.' I imagin [sic] if David were a horse he would want Dora to look like this." OEB 461. — 257
By permission of Octavia E. Butler Enterprises.

LIST OF ILLUSTRATIONS

28.17. "Pinto." Anna Pistorius, *What Horse Is It?* (Wilcox & Follett, 1952). 259

28.18. "If this pony appears to be looking for something, he is. Its [*sic*] Mr. Micabwer [*sic*] looking for the 'something' that will turn up some day." OEB 461. 259
By permission of Octavia E. Butler Enterprises.

28.19. "Palomino." Anna Pistorius, *What Horse Is It?* (Wilcox & Follett, 1952). 259

28.20. "And could this not be Emily as she vows not to come back unless she is brought back, a lady." OEB 461. 259
By permission of Octavia E. Butler Enterprises.

30.1. Author photo, *c*.1979. Everson, WA, Main Street Rodeo Parade. 281

xxv

INTRODUCTION

"It's ... the ship."[1]

Walls are supposed to be cool, solid surfaces that don't touch you back. But on the fleshly spaceship of Octavia E. Butler's novel *Dawn*, everything is alive, from the buildings to the toilets. The residents inhabit intelligent, tree-like structures, and sentient vehicles run on their own slime. The ship is not really a ship. It is a vast organism capable of loving the beings who grew it into existence. Without this "love," or symbiotic affinity, one of them explains, neither the "ship" nor its inhabitants could survive. Here, paradoxes abound. Cancer is a genetic talent, three sexes must be present for pleasurable union, and memories can be used to fabricate physical objects. When the human Lilith awakes after a 250-year slumber, she finds herself confined to a spartan room within the tree-like space organism. The male being in charge of acclimating her has eerily smooth skin, like a fingernail. His repulsive tentacles can penetrate human bodies to heal and rearrange cells, even stimulate otherworldly, orgasmic bliss. What's natural to the Oankali could not be more frightening to the Earthlings who have been rescued from a nuclear holocaust and brought aboard to breed a new, interspecies population.

Dawn was my introduction to Octavia Estelle Butler and a gateway to all her other novels, most of which do not feature aliens. But, like all good science fiction, they offer alternative versions of the past, present, and future by disturbing, or rather, exposing the natural order of things. They get us to question the sanctity of the human by confounding the basic categories that organize our lives—male, female, animal, vegetable, mineral. Nouns sometimes fail when worlds collide. When writing of other universes, Butler tends to avoid neologisms or ornate description. She lets the stripped down syntax of human–alien conversation do the work of approximating extraterrestrial life.

> "[Nikanj] gave her...a new color. A totally alien, unique, nameless thing, half seen, half felt or...tasted."[2]

Much is left out in the process of naming the new. Yet in the elliptical space of hesitation [...] knowledge takes shape, as does the conjuring of expanded realities.

* * *

In the summer of 1985, Octavia was living in Los Angeles, not far from where she grew up. She had just turned thirty-eight. She'd written six novels and won several prestigious prizes but was still ten years from becoming the first science fiction author to get a MacArthur "Genius" Grant. She needed a setting for her new book, *Dawn*, and decided to make a three-week research trip to South America with a UCLA study group. There she climbed the Andes, visited the ruins of Machu Picchu, and toured Peruvian rivers and lush rainforests. She took note of the giant trees that had survived millennia. The queer, interlinked life forms of the Amazon would be the perfect site for her posthuman civilization's rebirth. Octavia's travels would shape her protagonist's journey, as when Lilith leads a group of select humans into a virtual training ground. Lilith observes, with much relief, a profusion of earthly, *nameable* flora: breadnut trees, cassava, papayas, "bromeliads, orchids, ferns, mosses, lichens, lianas, parasitic vines."[3] A tropical lexicon of fruits and roots gushes forth.

> Liana roots, thick woody vines, hang swing-like from the forest canopy, burrow into the ground, and climb up their host trees. From the French *lien*, meaning "link, bond," the liana is named for how it grows. It bridges trees even as it twists about its individual hosts to the point of strangling them.

I used to puzzle over the novel's listing of Amazonian plants. They seemed oddly specific and out of place, until I learned more about Octavia's yen for research. While in the Amazon, she recorded the Indigenous uses of flowers, barks, and vines. In pocket-sized Steno memo notepads she sketched leaf sizes and shapes and noted the white-ringed trunk of the cecropia, a tree that houses the Azteca ants that both colonize it and defend it from its insides out. *Intimacy across species can take many forms.* In her Amazon files, Octavia's ordinary-looking snapshots capture the life-and-death symbiosis of jungle flora. She trained her amateur camera on lianas entwined in a serpentine embrace, on the dense crisscrossing of overgrown branches and

Figure 0.1 Octavia amidst buttressed trees in the Amazon. OEB 7249. By permission of Octavia E. Butler Enterprises.

leaves, flowering fungi growing on rotting logs, and communal spider webs.

In one picture (Fig. 0.1), she's wearing a lavender sweatshirt and looking askance, nearly camouflaged amidst sun-dappled foliage and a wall of giant kapok trees. *(See "K is for Kapok.")* The kapok is the largest of the rainforest trees. It is so tall, reaching up to 230 feet, it grows massive flared buttresses from its trunk to prevent it from toppling. In daily life, Octavia was a six-foot tall, Black woman who stood out everywhere she went. But here she is a mere creature of the forest. She must have been looking at this photograph when she wrote that Lilith "stood between a pair of buttresses, two-thirds enclosed by the tree. She felt enveloped in a solid Earthly thing." To Lilith, the arboreal growths of this simulated Amazon act "like walls [that] separated the surrounding land into individual rooms."[4]

One tree can be many things. In Malay-Penang the word *kapok* also derives from *kaping*, to embrace, envelop, or wind around,

INTRODUCTION

and *berkapuk*, to clasp someone from behind. The Mayans placed this "tree of life" at the center of the universe. It provided a habitat for plants and animals in its grooves and connected the underworld to the human and upper realms. The home-making of Peruvian flora, Octavia reckoned, is not so different from the intelligent infrastructure of Oankali spaceships. In this instance and many others, she puts distant places and times and species into conversation by transforming her concern for the environment into tales of symbiosis—*"love"*—embedded within larger narratives of collective survival.

* * *

Born in Pasadena on June 22, 1947, Octavia was the daughter of a shoeshine man and a housecleaner woman. In 1947, the Brookside Pool or "Plunge" (now the Rose Bowl Aquatics Center), after years of legal battles, finally admitted all races. And that year, hometown alumnus Jackie Robinson made history as one of the first African American players to enter baseball's major leagues. Today, his picture and Dodgers' jersey are encased in the John Muir High School "Alumni Hall of Fame" just a few lockers down from Octavia's commemorative photo and plaque. *(See "Y is for Yearbook.")* They are celebrated as pioneers of diversity. But through her childhood Pasadena was a segregated city. Elder Black residents still remember how their parents fought alongside the NAACP to end the rule that people of color could only swim in the community pool one day a week.[5] One of Octavia's schoolmates recalls her mother saying, "After they got out, the city workers would drain the water and scrub the pool down for the white public to enjoy for the next week . . . [A]s a child, it was something that was always in the back of my mind."[6]

If you look at historic housing maps, a vertical swath of the west side where Octavia and her peers grew up had been redlined by developers in the 1930s and essentially designated a minority zone of working-class Blacks, Asians, and Latino/as. Since the 1900s, Japanese gardeners had helped sustain the floriculture of the City of Roses. Along with their neighbors of color, they worked as estate staff or groundskeepers for the wealthy, conservative whites in the enclaves to the far west.[7] In addition to the decades of racist housing covenants and deed restrictions that made it difficult if not impossible to own property east of the dividing line of Lake Avenue, Black community members in western Pasadena experienced multiple displacements during the 1950s and 60s. Notoriously, the construction of the 134 and 210 freeways bulldozed entire neighborhoods; redevelopment projects eviscerated additional scores of single-family homes. In the words of one long-time resident, all this "annihilated a good deal of the population" and pushed many families and businesses north into the Altadena highlands, which offered cheaper land and some peace and quiet.[8] In the 1960s white flight ensued, and the Black population of Altadena rose over eighty percent.[9]

The changing demographics incited a racial panic among white families who feared the quality of the schools would plummet. Located at the northwest corner of Pasadena, bordering Altadena, John Muir High was already relatively integrated while Octavia was enrolled there between 1962 and 1965. As the school moved toward being majority Black, white families pulled hundreds of children out and transferred them to the newly opened schools of La Cañada, to the north, and Blair, to the south. By the estimation of one former teacher, Muir's white population dropped in half between 1964 and 1967.[10] Octavia's classmate Bebe remembers a large number of white students leaving

INTRODUCTION

in their junior year.[11] During these turbulent years of housing discrimination, desegregation, and Civil Rights protests, Pasadena was also a bastion of science fiction, with NASA's Jet Propulsion Laboratory up in La Cañada, and Caltech scientist-writers right in the middle. Young Octavia no doubt absorbed this culture of racism and science, backwardness and futurity, while becoming a writer in a white, male-dominated field of Isaac Asimovs and Ray Bradburys.

Growing up is painful. Junior high is an emotionally gangly period that indelibly shapes a person's tastes and implants one's future objects of melancholia and nostalgia. For those who grew up pre-Internet and were expected to entertain themselves, it was possible to be, as Octavia was, both a bibliophile and a television-addict. She devoured radio dramas first, then TV Westerns and astronomy and horse books. At school she was ostracized for being a towering and introverted girl (Figs. 0.2 and 0.3). She found kinship in horses and in the fictional orphan David

Figure 0.2 Detail, Octavia in full plaid.
Figure 0.3 Second-grade class photo, Lincoln School, 1955. Octavia on top row, far left.
Credit: Bebe Martin-Smith.

7

Copperfield; like him she clung to books and impersonated their characters, "reading as if for life."[12] *(See "H is for Horse.")*

At twelve, Octavia had already dreamed up the mixed-species world of her *Patternist* series of five novels she would write between 1976 and 1984: *Patternmaster, Survivor, Clay's Ark, Mind of My Mind, Wild Seed*. Spanning millennia, they unfold sagas of mental battles fought between and among the ruling classes (telepathic Patternists) and Clayarks (primitive, humanoid quadrupeds). The network, or Pattern, can join thousands of minds; virile male rulers attempt to dominate animals, mutes (who lack telepathy), and women. The telepaths can block, inflict, and control the pain of others, often to self-debilitating extremes. At thirteen, Octavia received her first rejection slip from a publisher; by fifteen, she was composing her first novel. She later said, "It gave me a chance to fashion the Patternists' 'transition' from adolescence—my own and other people's."[13]

We might think of all Butler's speculative fictions as "young adult" novels. Across her many writings her characters undergo the disorientations of puberty, whether they are girls, shape-changing healers, vampires, asexual aliens, or grown adults. A Black vampire like Shori in *Fledgling* is still vulnerable to white-male run society, even as she negotiates her way to power sharing through an "Afrofuturist feminist ethic" of mutualism, to borrow a phrase from Susana M. Morris.[14] Often, as in *Dawn*, the character must make sense of how their body is transitioning into a posthuman entity, a compound mixture of human-animal-plant encounters that requires a new taxonomy. *Revolution is evolution*, the late Grace Lee Boggs used to say. In uncertain, catastrophic times, the Black and mixed-race female protagonists of Octavia Butler's oeuvre must lose themselves in order to survive. Amber, Alanna, Anyanwu, Mary, Martha, Keira, Dana, Lauren, Larkin,

INTRODUCTION

Shori, Lilith. Each is in her own way tasked with saving the human race. Together they experience "unspeakable speculative" pleasures and brutalities en route to communal healing and self-discovery.[15]

> In *Wild Seed*, the shape-shifter Anyanwu takes on animal form to elude her captor. In *Clay's Ark*, the mixed-race girl Keira is infected by a parasitic microorganism and gives birth to a quadruped offspring. This future "Clay-ark" species is notably named after a spaceship.

How did the young Octavia imagine freedom from within the stifling confines of white patriarchy and her mother's strict Baptist household? In one of Octavia's seventh-grade composition books, a schoolmate wrote that she seemed to fit the description of an "October" personality—"You are a queer person and love all kinds of bugs and worms and animals. You may turn out to be a natureilest [sp]. You will have a good chance to marry but you will probably not take it"—"This should be for you Octavia! You like things like that!"[16] She never did marry, but she stayed fiercely loyal to both humankind and the creaturely environment. As a Black girl desirous of freedom, Octavia dreamed across species. Horses were her first love, space travel a close second. She read all manner of horse tales—*Black Beauty*, *The Black Stallion*, *Smoky the Cowhorse*, *King of the Wind*—but she didn't simply read them. She refashioned them and inhabited their perspectives. In a sense, horses were her first aliens. They could shoot lasers from their eyes, talk among themselves, and outrun and outsmart any person. These grew into stories about school-bullied girls with supernatural powers, and then intergalactic Martian spy romances. Equine and space-inspired themes would span her career. Even some of the original characters' names persist.

Though the first book she ever bought new was a book about horses, most of Octavia's reading material came from her "second home," the Pasadena Public Library.[17] She loved being surrounded by books. Young Octavia spent so much time at the library amidst the fiction and reference materials that a concerned family friend thought she would make herself "sick with all the books."[18] What could be further from the truth for a literary kid who professed to love dictionaries? Octavia's attraction to the nonhuman and penchant for classifying things extended well beyond natural history. She was fascinated with the study of words. In high school she wrote a tenth-grade essay on the pleasures of acquiring a "dictionary habit." "Once you acquire the dictionary habit," she typed, "you will find that the study of words can be an interesting and fascinating pastime."[19] Later on, she admitted to being "addicted" to specialized dictionaries of science, religion, history, medicine, law, and names.[20] One of her unfinished works was a massive "Thesaurus of First Names." *(See Index of Names.)* It drew on baby name books (Figs. 0.4 and 0.5), school yearbooks, and specialized dictionaries like her trusty *World Book Encyclopedia Dictionary* (WBED) to organize male and female first names from dozens of languages— Urdu, Greek, Chinese, Igbo. She filed them according to their etymologies and categories such as: Colors, Flowers & Plants, Animals, Time, Minerals, Emotional States. In such a tome, she hoped people might find names with related meanings across different cultures. She believed, like a true onomatologist, or lover of words (from the Greek, "to name"), that etymology might forge kinships.

INTRODUCTION

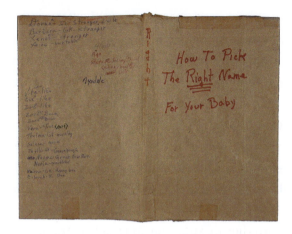

Figure 0.4 This artifact is a book jacket made from a grocery bag. It protected one of Octavia's reference books, Marion J. McCue's *How to Pick the Right Name for Your Baby* (1977). Grocery bag/book jacket, c. 1985. OEB 1612.

By permission of Octavia E. Butler Enterprises.

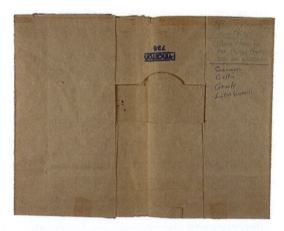

Figure 0.5 On the cover's outside (Top) and inside (Bottom) Octavia jotted notes on German, Celtic, Greek, Latin, and Igbo etymologies for her "Thesaurus of Names" project. OEB 1612.

By permission of Octavia E. Butler Enterprises.

Names are especially important if, like Octavia, you share a first name with a religious mother who raised you as a single parent, against countless odds, and a middle name with your even more formidable grandmother. The junior must naturally find ways to distinguish herself from the senior. *(See "J is for Junie.")* Octavia was also dyslexic, which made her both a bad speller and someone keenly aware of the value of seeing askew and questioning the order of things. She made a lifelong habit of building her vocabulary, amassing hundreds of index cards and notes on everything, from Slime Molds to Slavery and Seventeenth-century Shipping and Sea Life. For her, a name was also a time machine that could carry meaning across centuries and continents. She collected words like they were specimens. *Paramorphism, neoteny, auxotroph, cyclomorphosis.* I realized, in reading through her notebooks, she was drawn to organisms that change or retain their shape in unexpected ways, or that coevolve with humans and animals. In one of her notebooks she wrote, "What animals—or more likely plants—might hitchhike from one world to another."[21]

Taxonomy, the science of classifying, seems a cold and pedantic endeavor bent on dividing up the world. And yet, it assigns a special place for outliers. One exception asks us to rethink the validity of existing groups—it might even warrant a new class of thing. We could track the origins of the "Thesaurus of Names" to Octavia's school days, when she first became a keen observer of human differences and commonalities. Always an outsider, she responded to bullying by classifying her bullies into character types (i.e., haughty girls fall into one of three categories.[22]) Just as she relished etymologies, she catalogued all kinds of knowledge. She kept handwritten lists of people and animals and copied

INTRODUCTION

out the lyrics of TV shows. She wrote self-inspirational mantras to name her desires and rouse them to action: *So Be It! See To It! (See "I is for I am.")* From a young age, she made inventories of her stories as well as her sparse household belongings. Sometimes survival depends on good account keeping.

Traditionally, taxonomy manifests a drive to order and dominate nature. Naming a thing treads the lines between appreciation, understanding, and mastery. *What is it? Is it a tree or a spaceship?* Even learning the scientific names of backyard life forms can be an achievement; one finds mystery, and multitudes, in the mundane. For a person of meager means, the indexing impulse might provide a bit of certainty when things seem to be always on the verge of falling apart. Far from dominating nature or fixing categories into discrete impenetrable boxes, Octavia's vocabulary and alphabetized name lists helped her invent worlds and integrate lives across race, nation, gender, and class—criteria that identify us and too often divide us.

Dictionaries, like encyclopedias, are not ordered chronologically, but rather by topic or theme, according to an alphabetic guiding principle. Even though they follow a highly ordered scheme, they are not linear reading experiences. Far from dry, they allow for spontaneity and discovery. In the Reference Section of the library, one could take off to hither and yon. So too will this book loop back and forth in the chronology of Octavia Butler's life and career to link far-flung moments of her equino-centric thinking. Because the archive is not organized chronologically, the experience of opening any box of her manuscripts was itself like time travel. I might go in looking for 1980s Amazon notes but end up immersed in a supernatural animal story from the 1950s. It's a curious, proleptic reading process when you

13

glimpse the future in the past. Childhood reverberates across the pages.

I take my impressions of Octavia's youth from her adult records along with the prolific body of writing done between ages five and eighteen. Octavia might have been a cataloguer and self-indexer, but her papers were in a supremely disorganized state at the time of her sudden death. She had promised her materials to the Huntington Library, but she didn't have time to discard or withhold anything. And so two large filing cabinets and thirty-five cartons of unsorted materials were shipped off to California to became part of today's collection of 8000 items and over eighty boxes of ephemera. In the archive you can find grocery lists, receipts, birthday cards, diaries, address books, correspondence, random scribblings, outlines, and manuscript drafts of her twelve published novels and one volume of short stories.[23] The librarians spent over three years cataloguing it all. They tried to use her own subject headers when possible to maintain her thought process.[24] But her notebooks were impossible to index because of the sheer range of personal reflections, story and character plots, and sundry ideas. She kept newspaper cuttings on everything from Reaganism to cancer research, race relations, and Cold War budget cuts. *(See "X is for Xenogenesis.")* She was a self-professed news junkie and "histo-futurist," as interested in current events as in the past and the possible.[25]

Inside the library, you can read from Octavia's life works alongside centuries' worth of the Huntington's other holdings, which include fragile tomes of botanical drawings, world maps, and travel writings. When you step outside the climate-controlled building, you immediately catch whiffs of the flowering sage,

INTRODUCTION

myrtle, and willowy grasses that pronounce the manicured privilege of the surrounding gardens. Here in the San Gabriel Valley, thousands of rare books and manuscripts are kept amidst statuesque lawnscapes. In more ways than one, the Butler collection was meant to end up in this rarefied place. The eighteenth-century satirist Jonathan Swift once wrote: "Such order from confusion sprung/ Such gaudy tulips raised from dung."[26] Octavia was drawn to spaces of contradiction between the beautiful and the grotesque. She wrote of sanctuaries that double as slave plantations, and desert outposts where alien, carnal desires overtake familial bonds. Always, the picturesque has its dark side. For centuries, Western colonial expansion has reproduced itself in part through the enclosure of indigenous botanical specimens in luxurious parks and libraries. Here, the expertly tended plots of cacti, bamboo, and roses attest to this legacy. Utopias take work.

This book is about the persistence of childhood across existential, historical, literary, and political registers. Highlighting a selection of her unpublished drawings, short stories, photos, and inspirational notes, I explore how Octavia continually revised her youthful compositions about equines and Martians; teenage angst shaped her creative genius in profound and unexpected ways. Across her life she kept her childhood memories alive and working. Like a ficto-prospector, she mined her past for stories. In 1981, she reconnected with one of her teachers, who was shocked at how much Octavia remembered of her elementary school days. "Writers remember," Octavia remarked. "We dig through our memories the way miners might dig through a gold mine ... I people the world I create with mix 'n match combinations of the people out of my past. I even use my childhood tendency to

15

mispronounce names to create names to my extraterrestrials or people of the distant future."[27]

From the archive, we have only snapshots of experiences and reconstructed memories, but they are enough to establish Octavia was a child genius with a gift for bridging the human and the animal, the personal and political. Children are agile at learning taxa, and at drawing outside the lines. They take this for that: a kitchen cleaning brush can be a clown's hat, or a saxophone, or a stethoscope. In young Octavia's hands, a pencil became a tool of self-construction. She concocted alternate realities out of everyone she encountered. Reveling in category crisis, she mixed and matched things that normally don't belong together. She found beauty in what the poet Gerard Manley Hopkins praised as "all things counter, original, spare, strange."[28]

We are all products of our environments. As someone of Asian descent who grew up in small white towns of the Pacific Northwest, I did not know how to name the racism my family experienced until I moved to California. I hadn't realized I spent my childhood longing for community. Having now dwelled in Los Angeles and Philadelphia, I have an even greater appreciation for community organizers and the lived solidarities, as well as ongoing erasures, often not acknowledged in mainstream conversations about race. I am a scholar of history, which means I have a deep respect for people who have struggled together across generations of dislocation and diaspora, under systems of patriarchy and capitalism. This might explain the jolt of pleasure when I see the name of a character like "Jorge Cho" appear on one of the pages from *Parable of the Talents* (1998), sequel to *Parable*

INTRODUCTION

of the Sower (1993). The postcatastrophe novels are testaments to Octavia's coming of age in the mixed-race environment of northwest Pasadena. In *Talents* the spiritual leader Lauren Oya Olamina travels by foot northward along the West Coast in the year 2032. She describes her "Earthseed" community this way:

> We're you name it: Black, White, Latino, Asian, and any mixture at all—the kind of things you'd expect to find in a city. The kids we've adopted and the ones who have been born to us think of all the mixing and matching as normal. Imagine that.[29]

In the archive looking for the young Octavia, I have felt our paths cross when considering the places we both lived or passed through, including the Pacific Northwest, Peru, Los Angeles, and the San Gabriel Valley. I have identified with her vegetarianism, love of animals and the environment, struggle with being her mother's daughter, belief in racial justice, and the Pacific Coast orientation that led her to include Asian characters, and Black and Asian pairings, in her writings. Such is the power of her ability to connect with her readers through all *her* mixing and matching.

I was never a horse girl per se, though I did grow up in a remote Pacific Northwest border town, minutes from Canada, going to dairy farms, county fair livestock competitions, and logging shows. Once I rode in the Main Street parade. Mostly, I had only impressions of horses from watching TV Western re-runs of the same shows Octavia loved growing up in the late-1950s: *Zorro*, *Bonanza*, *The Lone Ranger*. Like many working-class children with nowhere to go after school, I relied on the public library for

Figure 0.6 Altadena street sign.
Photo credit: Author.

sanctuary. Seated against the brown-bricked walls, I had access to quiet words and fictional places that transported me beyond the smallness of daily life. I could spend hours there, absorbed in books and forgetting about the violence lurking at home. It was a tiny place right off Main Street that an eight-year-old Chinese girl could walk to with her two little brothers and feel safe. At home, reference books offered adventure as well as solace. I can still feel the heft of the precious, mocha volumes of the *Encyclopædia Britannica* that my parents saved up to buy, one at a time. They spent their days and nights running the Home Plate Café, the only Chinese American restaurant in an otherwise white town, Population 898. Thumbing the pages of the encyclopedias made me feel rich. I liked to open to a random page and discover what strange word my parents couldn't fathom or pronounce. This was my version of a dictionary habit.

As a literature professor I used to balk when people asked me my favorite author or book. Which qualities or historical era to prioritize, how to choose? But once in a blue moon, you find a writer who seems to speak to your soul. They capture your sense of what's beauteous and wrong about this planet, how it could be better. You must read everything they've written. This is Octavia's

INTRODUCTION

work, for me. Her writings became a lifeline when I least expected it. When my mother was diagnosed with acute myeloid leukemia, I spent a year and a half with her in Alhambra, just south of San Marino. In the first stage of a crisis, there is no time for reflection, only putting out fires. When we become caregivers to our parents, we lose our childhoods, even as those ties dictate every act of filial service. As the months went on and my own stamina flagged, I eventually found my way back to the library, all this time a mere fifteen-minute drive away. I re-immersed myself in Octavia's writings, now gravitating toward her cancer-related research, closeness to her mother, adolescent struggles, and escape into books and fictional lands far removed from her own.

Reading through decades of Octavia's handwritten promises to herself I found an anchor when I was most at sea. As a child she vowed to one day cure cancer and run a horse ranch for girls *(See "V is for Victorville")*; as a young adult, she determined to buy a house for her mother, and be a bestselling Black female author. Her stories ranged from unfinished fragments to titled works sent out for publication. She doodled, drew, and wrote about everything and on everything—lined and unlined paper, envelopes, grocery bags, recycled stationery, receipts, cassette tape cases. With heartbreaking honesty, the pages upon pages evidenced a practice of writerly resilience. Even as she struggled with self-doubt, she embraced her alienation, liana-like, and put it to work in symbiotic fashion. My time in the archives no doubt mirrors the experiences of many readers, especially Black people, women of color, and queer and non-conforming folks, who see themselves in her characters or find a kindred spirit in Octavia's understanding of herself as an outsider and writer whose mission it was to envision new forms of relating. She has been called

19

a "long-lost friend," "a north star," a Black speculative fiction "matriarch," and "someone to look to for long-haul advice."[30] There are many stories to tell. In *H is for Horse* I contend that Octavia's pursuits of human–alien symbiosis stemmed from her empathy with animals from an early age on. These connections spurred her experiments with species crossing and shapeshifters that would become the hallmark of her SF writing.

An equino-centric view of Butler's oeuvre reveals the impact of her girlhood fascination with animals' lives—their quiet, emotional intelligence, their ability to adapt to a given situation, bear witness, or bear the brunt of human cruelty. Getting inside their heads requires an introvert's powers of observation. Octavia loved animals in general, and the horse in particular. It was tall, strong, majestic. It could take to the road without wheels. It seemed to come from another time. Just as equine nobility embodies the untamed spirit of human resilience, the plight of the horse resonates with the human experience of chattel slavery and its ruinous legacy. Like her ancestors, these creatures were kidnapped, branded, and whipped. They were bred for labor and forced to toil alongside people on the plantations and the sharecropped fields. Yet there is no animal equivalent to the word dehumanized. This would have puzzled the young Octavia.

To be horse-like is to be at once a beast of burden and a symbol of earthly transcendence. This Black science fiction writer, who is at heart a horse writer, intuits the interlinked experiences of racism, gender nonconformity, disability, and historical trauma. In bridging past and present, horses, were, for Butler, good to think with. They are material and metaphorical. When they appear in her novels, even briefly, horses foreground the racism, ableism, and speciesism that plagues the planet. Their

INTRODUCTION

presence—and the solidity of their form—helps mark the changes and the disturbing continuities between the antebellum and postbellum eras. In Butler's writings, the experience of time travel is not always liberating. It takes a toll on the body and mind, or "continually threatens disablement," as Sami Schalk has noted of the character Dana's disability in the novel *Kindred*.[31] As a child, Octavia knew the costs of being different. She made a habit of scrutinizing the traits of others, understanding what distinguished one thing from the next, and when these qualities amounted to a type. Her efforts in learning the assorted breed names of horses epitomize her quest for knowledge of the biosphere and her attention to the zoological (and botanical) vocabularies that she would continue to collect throughout her life.

In the 1950s, horses were everywhere in popular culture. The library, where Octavia spent much of her free time, would have been stocked with children's horse literature, or pony books, as they were called in Britain. Some libraries even had equine sections. In the stacks Octavia could read about girls having outdoor adventures with their equine companions. She later referred to this as the "The Girl and Her Horse" genre.[32] But at the time she only knew that these scenarios were much more appealing than the usual places where females were pictured. She could see herself on a ranch or working a well in the desert before she would be confined to a suburban kitchen or secretary's desk. At the same time, the TV shows she watched religiously featured mostly men doing things. Yes, she fell for the cowboys of the small screen. They were tough, swarthy, and dashing on horseback. One even wore a mask *and* a cape. Across the selection of networked shows, these frontiersmen—whether outlaw or law enforcer—taught

21

her the power of mythmaking. She would come to understand these characters to be nationalist, whitewashed performances of masculinity. Even as the American cowboy exercised through his horsemanship his power over land, family, community, and ethnic identity, ranching culture was originally transnational, as Laura Barraclough reminds us in her study of the Mexican cowboy, or charro.[33] It makes sense that TV Westerns became the ground for Butler's postapocalyptic science fiction. Early on, she absorbed the patriarchal plots of the American master narrative of Manifest Destiny, adopted their conventions, and pushed back against the norm by writing girls into the lead. Her experiments with genre and gender went hand in hand.

For Butler, horses were also living, breathing beings that could be seen around Altadena and Pasadena. In talking with long-term residents of the area, I found that everyone has a horse story to tell. Whether they rode or kept a horse, or knew someone who did, their anecdotes are portals to a slower time and pace of life along the streets that young Octavia traversed. *(See "R is for Rex McDonald.")* Horses were a reminder of their parents' and grandparents' migrations from the Southern U.S. to the Los Angeles area. As remnants of rural living in industrialized spaces, and as the precious property of wealthy equestrians and working-class cowboys alike, horses manifested class warfare and urban development. Today, when I see a young Black horse rider crossing a bridge over a freeway in Philadelphia, I am alerted to the forces of segregation and privatization that make it hard to live off the land. I see the "postmodern blackness" that Madhu Dubey identifies in her study of 1970s urban planning and its resonances in *Parable of the Sower*, a novel about the "multiracial underclass." Reading Butler allows her to diagnose the ongoing struggles of those who attempt to

INTRODUCTION

maintain community amidst displacement and must stay on the move in order to survive, even while "longing for spatial permanence."[34]

Home can be hard to find. At one time Altadena was a hub for Black equestrians seeking refuge from Pasadena urban development, and some of the horse-riding families that moved there in the 1960s remain. Octavia eventually moved there too, purchasing a house in 1995, likely drawn to the wilderness of the foothills, arroyos, and canyons, perhaps even to the presence of horses on the streets and the historic equestrian trails.[35] Today West Altadena is basically still a "country town with no sidewalks,"[36] where some Black families maintain their original half an acre of land and cherish the "solitude and openness" of a dead end cul-de-sac.[37] You will still see a horse every morning if you go walking near the Arroyo Seco[38] (Fig. 0.6). Today, there is a vibrant culture of Latinx Charros, riders who follow the centuries-old tradition of Mexican equestrians.[39]

In this book the horse is thus also a memory device for collective and individual histories. An equino-centric view on Octavia's early life's work is as much a journey through library archives as it is an occasion for us to relate to her personal remembrances of growing up feeling out of place. When she looked back on her childhood horse character Silver Star, it reminded her of being an ambitious Black girl who challenged herself to understand human and nonhuman animals by learning their shapes, the way they walked and talked. When she drew them, or captioned their thoughts on paper, they offered her escape from traumas big and small, and encouraged her to reinvent herself. She was less interested in riding horses than in picturing them unharnessed,

23

as if to conjure a riderless world.[40] The young Octavia is a cosmic dreamer and an on-the-ground pragmatist, a humanist and anti-humanist—a resistance writer. She is guided by the dream of running wild and escaping social strictures, even as she knows what it means to struggle under captivity, to be perceived as bestial, or less than human. *(See "B is for Bambi.")* Her understanding of these things pushes her to explore unlikely affinities.

Childhood is itself an archive of discrete impressions that accrue narrative arcs through our acts of continual reconstruction. Try as we might, we never quite leave our younger selves behind. In an essay titled "The Monophobic Response," Octavia noted our tendencies to scapegoat "aliens" for the social ills of our own creation. All around, she saw self-absorbed adults who behave like children, needing to be rescued, denying their past traumas, recasting sibling rivalries and family dysfunctions. Just as aliens, for Octavia, were never simply creatures from outer space, childhood was not a terminable stage of human development. "The child persists. And it's lonely," she wrote.[41] Despite its hold on us, childhood is also an ephemeral time of irrepressible curiosity about the world and heightened sensitivities to joy, shame, and neglect. Octavia was typical in her desire for knowledge and need for love. But she was exceptional in her ability to transform her everyday experiences into imaginative universes that reconceptualized our relations to illness, authority, and community, and our uniqueness as a species.

I hear resonances of her creative spirit in poems about Black girls finding their places in the world: Eve Ewing's Black girl flying a magical bike over the mean streets of Chicago,[42] Jacqueline Woodson's future girl-author who transforms the sounds

INTRODUCTION

of grownups talking in Greenville.[43] With emotional precision Gwendolyn Brooks conveyed a girl's wayward longing for more than she has been given:

> I've stayed in the front yard all my life.
> I want a peek at the back
> Where it's rough and untended and hungry weed grows.
> A girl gets sick of a rose.[44]

The young Black women who speak their truth while navigating the obstacles of urban poverty and homelessness are the creative vanguard whom Aimee Meredith Cox calls "shapeshifters," borrowing from SF the concept of bodily transformation and the abilities to problem-solve and choreograph space.[45] For Black feminist scholars working in the archive, girlhoods reverberate across history and geography. Christina Sharpe has shared the contemporary stories of Black girls who are not allowed to be girls because they are criminalized, just as their ancestors were once enslaved.[46] Saidiya Hartman describes her young subjects' "wayward lives" as "beautiful experiments" in the art of living. In defiance of the forces of criminalization, these are Black girls who define themselves and their environments as they move through urban places.[47] Their voices may have been marginalized, but still they ask to be heard.

Tracking Octavia's youthful love of animals can lead to queer and unexpected junctures . . . close encounters of the horse kind. I have chosen to take seriously Octavia's early writing as a formative part of her oeuvre. Through scrutinizing the details of her unsure cursive, typed out drafts, and marginalia I have come to appreciate her lasting manner of introspection, a mindset at once erudite and forever young. From the paper trail she left behind for us, we can glimpse snapshots of a Black girl-author shaped by a specific place and time, 1950s and 1960s Pasadena, California, where she was, as she said in one interview, "in love with horses and living in the middle of a city where no horses were available."[48] Ironically, in neighboring Altadena, there have been stables for decades. Octavia would surely have seen them ambling along the trails or making their way on surface streets down to the Rose Bowl. The horse is always closer than you think.

Among the photos of Octavia's many travels, one stands out (Fig. 0.0). It is from 1999, taken at a stable outside Seattle, near the Olympic Peninsula. The middle-aged, dark brown woman in a buttoned-up, flowery shirt leans into a chestnut mare. She tentatively holds its harness. Their heads touch ever so slightly. Together they pose for the camera against a bright blue sky and Pacific Northwest evergreens. She is smiling, she looks happy, free. Horses helped Octavia picture freedom and subjecthood. In her mind she unleashed them from their domesticated states of being.

The touch of the horse is many things: how we relate to each other across texts, times, and backgrounds, how we understand our shared condition of living captively under the oppressive structures of racism and capitalism. Encounters with animals, trees, and literature can exercise our imaginations, expand our kinship circles, maybe even in small ways, help us reshape the world around us, from A to Z.

Figure 1.1 Eighth-grade yearbook cover, 1961. OEB Box 337.
By permission of Octavia E. Butler Enterprises.

CHAPTER 1

A

IS FOR ALIAS

At the top right of the eighth-grade yearbook cover, the name "Karen Adams" is penned in blue cursive, and underneath it, in red: "(Estella Butler)." Did she, or even her mother, add her real name as an afterthought, perhaps at a later date? Lest we doubt her intention of claiming her dual personality, we can make out some suggestive blue and red color coding below (Fig. 1.1). She used a blue pen to sketchily fill in the big "W" for George Washington Junior High. Red pen colors in the school's mascot, a bear. The student designer of the cover art has fitted the bear's body delicately and awkwardly into the shape of the W. Whether it stands trapped within the vertical zigzag or rests snugly in its letter frame, the two are entwined. It is as if Estella (red) identifies with the animal (red) as her hidden self; while Karen (blue) is the outgoing public school persona (blue W) to which she aspires.

Every serious writer needs a good pen name, especially if you are unconventional by virtue of being female. Under the guise of James Tiptree, Jr., Alice Bradley Sheldon issued her feminist science fiction in the 1960s. The Victorians had Acton, Currer, and Ellis Bell (the Brönte sisters) and the two Georges (Sand and Eliot). I think of the inscrutably initialed H.D. or P.L., and the singly-named Ouida and Sapphire. Octavia E. Butler would one day become the country's most famous Black science fiction writer, but in her youth she had plenty of reasons to hide behind a series of human, superhuman, and nonhuman alter egos: Karen Adams, Lynn Guy, and S.S., or Silver Star (a horse with supernatural powers). For all her talent, throughout elementary and junior high her grades were pretty abysmal, mostly C's and D's. She was called "backward" and "slow." In her fifth-grade progress reports, one teacher commented, "Estella's most grievous fault is her slowness . . . . She dreams a lot and has poor concentration." Her grades improved drastically once she got to high school. But in the preteen years, she only seemed to show an interest in "Book reports." While her seventh-grade home economics teacher Miss Peters was encouraging, the others appear not to have realized she was an undercover writer in their midst.[1]

> Yearbooks can be a sleuth's best friend. Poring over people's comments—and Octavia's own annotations—I tracked down classmates who shared their memories of her from sixty years ago. (See "Y is for Yearbook.")

The signs were all there. At school she went by Estella, a variant of Estelle, the middle name she shared with her maternal grandmother.[2] Though painfully shy, she stood out. With her masculine voice and stature, she towered above her peers. When she walked, she leaned to one side; she spoke with a lisp, and wore thick clothes even in summer weather.[3] She was a gawky, dyslexic kid with serious literary aspirations. Several of her schoolmates remember that she carried her pencil and notebook with her everywhere, even in elementary school. After class, she would attend Bluebirds. To the chagrin of her troop members, she'd be scribbling away furiously, working out her ideas. Among her compositions were short stories like "The Leprechaun's Revenge," at least one television series, a "novelette," and a "novel."[4] Attempts to turn her attention to the group project were mostly futile. As several of her classmates recalled to me, "she always had a story in her head." In high school, she was still that quiet, loner girl who carried around her grey-blue binder of stories. Now and then, a kind, outgoing girl would sit next to her at lunch or in line. She'd share her writing with them. It would strike people as lofty, salacious, thrilling, or opaque—in any case, strange and ahead of its time.[5]

It is one thing to write under a pen name, another to adopt an alias. Each allows a different form of freedom through subterfuge. With a pseudonym, you can publish anonymously without the burdens of biography. You enact a paper self, and keep work separate from life. An alias presumes a trickier balance of living out multiple and embodied lives. In superhero fashion, you perform a persona for strategic ends. You live for and by inscrutability. The cause could be national security, criminal enterprise, or on a smaller scale, the expression of desires no one expects you to have. Some of us go by another name to get things done when our given names or faces prove to be impediments. Some of us have more need to be our own secret agents.

Children dream up imaginary friends and alternate universes all the time. Few work at it with the intention of being a published, paid author. In May of 1961, fourteen-year-old Estella

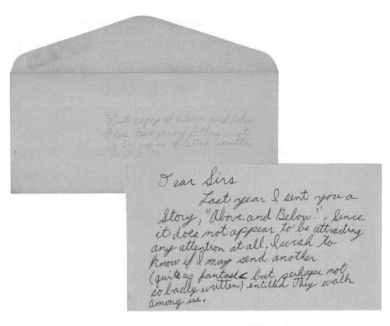

Figure 1.2 and **1.3** Correspondence with Mead literary agency, 1961–62. OEB 4. The envelope reads: "First copy of above and below Plus two proof letters, not carbon copies of letters. Written to D.S.M."
By permission of Octavia E. Butler Enterprises.

began corresponding with the Mead Company literary agency in New York.[6] She submitted "Above and Below," a story about thin-skinned, sightless beings who live in darkness beneath the Pacific Ocean (Figs. 1.2 and 1.3). One adventurous soul learns to exist among the surface-dwellers. After a year it didn't sell. She next sent them "They Walk Among Us" in hopes of publishing something she considered "quite as fantastic but perhaps not so badly written."[7] In this story, Vivian, an alien in disguise, feels "[t]he pain of looking like a human and walking among them but still not being one of them!"[8] One day, Octavia would develop this story into her novel *Clay's Ark* (1984). For now, she wrote of snake creatures who passed as Earthlings. They planned to propagate their race by impregnating unsuspecting women, who would then die after giving birth. Again, the Mead agents found the work promising but in need of professional editing. They asked a whopping $30 fee for their services.[9] Though always scraping by to make ends meet, Estella's mother paid this much, and more, to try to help her realize her dream.[10]

It would be ten more years before her first short story, "Crossover," appeared in print. It came out in a 1971 Clarion Writers' Workshop anthology of speculative fiction alongside the work of her mentors Harlan Ellison and Samuel Delaney. But Octavia never left behind the trove of unpublished stories written during her junior high and high school years (1958–1965). In them she explored the hidden lives of everyday people—and undercover girls—with supernatural talents. They were often untitled, rambling, or unfinished; some were typed, others written by hand. They are a fascinating glimpse into the development of a science fiction oeuvre built upon Black girl power.

* * Karen Adams * *

Karen is a recurring secret agent character of the early stories. She lives in Pasadena, Victorville, or another Southern California town. Bullied at school and misunderstood by her mother at home, "Karen" longs for a different life. Along comes a charismatic Martian named Flash, who speaks to her using telepathy. He inducts her into a Martian spy community embedded on Earth. Though raised as a regular girl, she eventually realizes she is half-Martian. In some versions of the story, a Martian queen comes to capture an Earthling as a gift to her king. Our girl volunteers because she "Just feel[s] like going somewhere."[11] She subsequently acquires the name Star. Alternately, the girl learns her birthname was Silver Star, given to her by her human mother. By some counts, her mother is Mercurian, her father Martian.[12] In other iterations, Star is assigned to pass as a human to learn their ways. She is, however, by birth "Martain" (a variant, pointedly explained by the narrator, of the Earth word "Martian.")[13]

Estella would live with dyslexia her entire life. Her deliberate misspelling of "Martains" strikes me as a cheeky rebuke of society's intolerance toward disability. Even at the level of orthography, she worked to re-order the ways of the world. She shared the postwar American public's fascination with the possibility of extraterrestrial life—from Ray Bradbury's *Martian Chronicles* to Walt Disney's *Mars and Beyond*. She also came of age during the atomic era of Cold War paranoia. An older generation of superheroes, Captain America and Flash Gordon, was joined in the early 1960s by new, mixed-gendered rescue teams like Marvel's Fantastic Four and the X-Men. At home Estella collected Marvel comics and absorbed the paranormal TV horrors of the *Twilight Zone*. In public, the movie theaters screened countless disaster spectacles of invasions from outer space and under-the-sea. Low-budget SF flicks titled *Teenagers from Outer Space* or *Devil Girl from Mars* no doubt got her thinking about aliens and alienation in her own adolescent dystopia. But she wasn't content to simply copy the mainstream.

Not surprisingly, Estella's school essays called out the postwar climate of McCarthyism. She titled one assignment *"Masters" of Our Minds*. Submitted for eleventh-grade Physiology, it denounced the media's Pavlovian brainwashing of U.S. citizens in the wake of World War II and the Korean War: "People are conditioned to believe what they hear—and hear and hear and hear. Children are most easly [sic] influenced by this."[14] Neither did she believe in an easy or bottom-up solution to the pervasive xenophobia, because people were fundamentally self-serving. *(See "U is for Utopia.")*

Space travel did promise a freedom that Estella longed for, freedom from the constraints of everyday Pasadena life. As an adult, she often told the story of how her SF writing was inspired by her dissatisfaction with *Devil Girl from Mars* (1954). Watching this black-and-white, British, B-movie at the age of twelve, she realized she could invent something better. I wonder what she found the least appealing. Was it the tea-drinking misfits gathered at a Scottish inn on a rainy night, the romance plot between an escaped convict and a barmaid, or the ineffectual professor and reporter investigating a meteor crash? Was she at all charmed, as I am now, by the stoic, man-averse Nyah, played by an arch Patricia Laffan? Nyah descends in a flying saucer garbed in black latex mini-skirt, helmet, and cape, and armed with laser gun and hypnotic power. On feminocentric Mars, males are in short supply. She has come to gather Earth men, whose semen can be mixed in machines to help repopulate the planet. As if not threatening enough on her own, Nyah is abetted by a giant, silver, refrigerator-shaped robot assassin. Her spaceship also has powers of "organic, self-repairing metal" that might just prefigure the living Oankali ship in Butler's future novel, *Dawn.*

As much as she scorned the theatrical antics of *Devil Girl*, it's clear that Estella appreciated the idea of a superior race of intelligent aliens. For years after, she composed tales called "Silver Star," "Flash," "Flash or Silver Star," and "Into Infinity" with recurring characters and elaborate backstories of intergalactic war-espionage intrigues.[15] In a nineteen-page, typewritten iteration from December 1, 1962, the narrator Karen reveals to her mother that for eight years she has allowed Flash to access her thoughts to "spy" on earth. Her mother accuses her of betraying the United States amidst the Cold War with Russia. When Karen is awakened at 3:00 a.m. by someone calling her "Star," she allows herself to be teleported to Mars. She is an ideal mate for Flash because of her immunity to the deadly "Cla-ark" sickness and her exceptional strength ("she was mentally the strongest girl on Earth.")[16]

In a letter penned to her own mother in one of her spiral notebooks, Estella wrote in wobbly cursive, from a "Karen" perspective:

> To my Mother When they come for me.
> The Night it's Done
> Where We live at The Time
> In any City weare in

> Dear Mother
> In this letter I can not possably tell you everything I'd like to. If you would like to know more Read the story that bears this ⟨ℱⱰ⟩ sign. I will give you a Vaage Ieda of my futaure though a good deal of it is fiction.
> What happened This night (or today) is something I have been expecting for a long time.[17]

The character of Karen is no Dorothy stranded in Oz, longing for Kansas. In fact, she has no qualms about leaving her family and human society behind. She finds freedom in foreignness. In another story, Karen has been raised on Earth until the alien ruler Coranse comes and takes her to a space ship where she learns she is part of a race of telepathic, bodiless Protectors.[18] Star, as she is now called, is placed in an underground room on Mars for three years while learning the ways of the Protectors. Using her newly acquired mental powers to fight to death twelve other girls, she earns her place as one of seven undercover agents assigned to each of Earth's continents.

Across her writings, Estella's ostracism and loneliness are palpable. Often solitude is a matter of life and death. Her adolescent aliases performed versions of herself as a healer seeking connection to others and an exceptional outsider who yearned to be rid of maternal discipline, the cruelty of her peers, and the limitations of her own body. In a story called "The Search" (1962), a half-blind woman seeks the realm of sight. All around her the blind people mock her quest. Her mother cannot help her. As she climbs up a mountain, alone, she realizes she will die if she does not cross out of the darkness. The diary entry on the back of the page, dated August 29, 1962, gives us a glimpse into the basis for the allegory: "In 12 days I will return to school. I think it may be easer [sic] for me this time. I must find a friend. This must be the person."[19]

Even as adults, we can conjure that mixture of dread, hope, and determination that marks the end of summer and start of class-bound days. Over and over Octavia likens school to earthly social captivity. In marvelous, sometimes rambling narrative experiments, misfit girls hide and unleash their secret superpowers at will. In "The Freak" (1958), Joetta is an outcast at school. She keeps under wraps her ability to shoot red rays from her eyes (like Star the horse) and douse people with water. She can send and receive mental messages with lifesaving foreknowledge—*the gym is on fire!* But no one believes her until it's too late. The school burns. Though she does lead people to safety, she is fed up with their small-mindedness. She plants a warning in everyone's head to appreciate "those of my kind."[20]

Girls might not always speak out, but they often prove to be the most lethal undercover cops. In "The Toy," begun in 1963 and revised over the years, a part-human "toy" named Rand is bullied on a bus by telepathic humans. They control his mind and make him say offensive things against his will. In this instance a powerful Sector Head (Sec) intervenes, and secretly reveals to Rand his true identity: he is in fact not a toy, but a Sec in training. Rand looks around trying to guess which passenger has been mentally calling the shots on the bus. He realizes with surprise that it's an unassuming, plain-looking girl whom no one would guess holds so much power.[21]

*　*　Lynn Guy　*　*

Under the name "Lynn Guy" (Guy was her mother's maiden name), Octavia wrote stories of existential crises with titles like "Incident," "Death!" and "Alone."[22] In "Alone" aliens have taken human form everywhere on Earth, echoing the *Invasion of the Body Snatchers*, and the narrator is betrayed by a seemingly nice, seemingly human girl. From that point on, her own mother cannot be trusted. She believes she is all alone, until she realizes she, too, is turning into a monster.

The pseudonyms and undercover human–alien characters also allowed Octavia to try on different bodies and even genders. Take the character of "Adam Lynn," who seems to be a combination of her pseudonyms Karen Adams and Lynn Guy. He sometimes appears as an enigmatic friend of Star and rival of Flash. In an instant, Adam can move from the body of a "ragged ... tramp" into that of an "Oriental Earthling."²³ This character will eventually become Doro, the godly, power-hungry shape-shifter in Butler's novels *Wild Seed* and *Mind of my Mind*. Even in this early phase of her writing, Adam can penetrate minds. While eavesdropping in the character Karen's head, he wonders if he could be falling in love with her. "Perhaps I had been Adam Lynn for too long," he thinks, "I decided then to change identities soon."²⁴ As I read the manuscript, I noticed that Octavia had crossed out the "He" pronouns and inserted the first-person "I." Not only does she make Adam's feelings more relatable; the "I" also bespeaks her own desires to be someone else for a bit.

A glance at some of her title pages reveals Estella's love of doppelgängers. Her authorial selves keep good company with one another and with the audience. She sometimes includes a fictitious translator alongside different versions of her name.

Figure 1.4 Detail, S.S./Silver Star alias with Flash insignia, 1958. OEB 590. By permission of Octavia E. Butler Enterprises.

On the cover of a seventh-grade composition book, her name appears as Estella Butler, with S.S. (Silver Star) next to it. But inside, she goes by Karen Adams in her responses to a chain survey she designed for her classmates to answer.²⁵ It was sometimes challenging to decide who to be at a given moment.

One of my favorite Karen-authored stories has nothing to do with space but plenty to do with the entanglements of fantasy and reality. It's a steamy workplace romance Estella wrote at age twelve called "Let's Go," "By Karen Adams," in which a character, also named Karen, is a twenty-three or twenty-four-year old actress hired onto the James Michener TV series *Adventures in Paradise*.[26] Set in the South Pacific, the show aired when Octavia was in junior high. It starred some of her favorite actors, James Holden, playing Clay Baker, and Gardner McKay as Captain Adam Troy. She also writes TV Western heartthrob Lorne Greene into the episode. (*See "T is for TV Western."*) In "Let's Go," the cast is at work shooting an episode about island cargo trafficking. Behind the scenes, unbeknownst to their co-workers and the director J.P., Gard and the character Karen are having an affair filled with "soft caressing kisses." After they marry, she tells him she's pregnant, and conflict ensues when he doesn't believe the baby is his. Eventually, they make up.

Not all twelve-year-olds compose such racy stuff. As fan fiction before fan fiction, "Let's Go" writes a woman protagonist—desired by two men—into a show known for its white male stars (who are abetted by numerous female guest stars and Asian extras.) Even in this syrupy soap opera, Estella experiments with secret lives and embedded stories. It exercises the dialogue and interpersonal conflict that would become her signature style. She wryly states in the preface: "the story you are about to see is true the names (except for one) have not been changed to protect the innocent scence [sic] there are no innocent Lets Go (alright)."

To me, her refusal of the very category of innocence is tinged with a world-weariness beyond her years. Perhaps her narration models itself after the serial television programming she watched on a weekly basis. As if talking to herself, the narrator also ropes us in when she remarks on her process of storytelling

A IS FOR ALIAS

and TV commentary. She concludes, again with a razor wit, "If The End Seems abrupt that's because it isn't the End, it's only the beginning." Just as Estella inhabits the aspirational worlds of adult lives through the character and pen name of Karen, she also can't resist revealing the precocious girl behind the woman. She signs off, "Karen Adams A Estella Butler."

* * Silver Star * *

Little known fact: the equine origins of Octavia's science fiction. Long before Silver Star was a Martian in a girl's body, she was a magical white horse named after the birthmark on her horse mother's shoulder (Fig. 1.5). As early as 1957, Estella began initialing her horse alias—S.S.—near her name (Fig. 1.4).[27] For years, she doodled stars on the margins of her notes. Onto her high-school yearbook photo she even inked a bolded star tattoo on her left shoulder (Fig. 1.6). On her right shoulder she inscribed her secret

Figure 1.5 Detail, Star the horse with star birthmark. OEB 2472. By permission of Octavia E. Butler Enterprises.

symbol for Flash, a backward percentage sign. (*See "F is for Flash."*) At one point she compiled a list of her characters and their superpowers. She included three "Stars" in her expanding fictional universe: Silver Star—girl, Silver Star—horse, Star—%Martian-ized girl.[28] The latter two Stars, she notes, are proficient in telepathy.

Figure 1.6 Senior yearbook photo with Flash and Star insignias. OEB Box 337.
By permission of Octavia E. Butler Enterprises and John Muir High School.

The star icon was less a public persona than a cipher. It conjured her inner horse worlds—the imaginary universes that coexisted with the unpleasant humdrum of hallway lockers and chalk-boarded classrooms. Perhaps more than any of her aliases, Estella's horse identity reminded her of the powers of self-transformation. When she was sixteen, in bed at night she fondly reflected on "an old friend of mine Silver Star."[29] She found that her horse heroine stood the test of time. Silver Star stayed with her through many shapes and characters.[30]

* * *

Star Island was the name of the place where horses ruled and roamed free. Like Wonder Woman's Paradise Island, it existed in a remote but findable location. *(See "G is for Ganymede.")* Extant story drafts date back to 1958. The twenty-page episode entitled "Silver Star: Orfon" is written in pencil and big, loopy cursive on wide-ruled notebook paper. It essentially rewrites *Bambi* and *The Black Stallion* into equine science fiction. *(See "B is for Bambi.")* Unlike in Bambi's case, Silver Star's mother does not love her. In fact, the mother dies by violent suicide: "She hated me so that she jumped into the ocean and dowered [drowned]."[31] The death of the mother only encourages the foal's independent spirit. She fights to become queen of the horses and eventual mate of the dashing stag, Rocket. The leader of the herd, he shares her white coloring, cosmically inflected name, and a love of fighting. Together they fend off wolves and rival horses such as the King and Queen of the Black Islands. Silver Star's superpowers include emitting heat rays from her eyes and breathing fire out of her nose and mouth. She also telekinetically raises the ceiling of a collapsing cave to help a colt escape. She is the co-protector of the 1000-horse community.

At one point a boat of men attack the island hoping to capture a fast horse for a championship in The Land of People. Ever competitive, Star challenges Rocket to a race and wins. Estella's line drawing of the two horses running neck and neck is labeled, "I ran as I had never run Before." (*See "S is for Sexy"*) In another episode, she lets herself be captured to prove her prowess. While abroad, though she participates in racing culture and mingles with domesticated horses, she hates being lassoed and harnessed. She tries to get "free" of the saddle. The page labeled "The Pento [Pinto] thought she would win the Race," shows a brown-and-white patched Fanny and Silver Star, one above the other. They are tied to a railing that is meant to be a close-up of the interior of the stall to the right. The attempt at perspective, as with her spelling, is all off. Shakily drawn, the horses have been copied from a book, likely the first Octavia ever bought for herself. (*See "H is for Horse."*) The drawings' captions add another register of storytelling to the body of the text, a bragging, conversational voice that aims to please. Not only is Star free, but she is also a storyteller who ultimately controls her own destiny. When she returns to Star Island of her own accord, she narrates her adventures to the others. *The horse is an author.* (Next to her name on the title page, "Octavia Estella Butler," appears a small circle with two S's inside, an icon of herself as Silver Star.)

Though horses eventually disappear from Octavia's stories, their existential situation—resisting captivity—persists. Remarkably, many of the characters and concepts from the early horse and Mars stories reappear in Butler's *Patternist* series of five novels written between 1976 and 1984. In one notebook she remarked, "Doro's been hanging around in my head since I was about 12 or 13. The Patternist series is something that I've been playing around with for a long time."[32] Star and rocket doodles show up on her 1975 notes for *Mind of My Mind*.[33] Even *Wild Seed* (1980), the most historical and least futuristic of the novels, bears vestiges of the Silver Star horse stories. That novel retells the transatlantic slave trade through Doro, a Nubian "ogbanje," or reincarnating evil spirit.[34] Over his 4000-year life, he has collected and bred people with supernatural traits in order to achieve the perfect species of telepathic humanoids. In the 1600s, he uses his heightened mental and physical powers to rescue fellow Africans from European slavers. He ships them to North America, where he plans to cultivate their talents over the next several hundred years. The name of the vessel: *Silver Star.* The text describes "Doro's own ship, the *Silver Star,* small and hardy and more able than any of his larger vessels to go where it was not legally welcome and take on slave cargo the Royal African Company had reserved for itself."[35]

Why would Octavia name a tyrant's slave ship after her beloved horse-Martian moniker? Perhaps, as a way of acknowledging the perpetual tension between freedom and power. One person's freedom does not mean liberty for all. Masters come in all colors and shapes—"*There are no innocent.*" However utopian or dystopian Octavia's alien and animal spaces, they were always tied to her lived experiences. As a girl who understood suffering, she identified with the captors as well as the desperate and downtrodden. That is, she comprehended the paradox of the horse: at once a symbol of untrammeled freedom and of subjugation. Her horse stories were shot through with abuses of power and human frailty. They staged what she would later call "speciesism as racism."[36] For Octavia E. Butler, humanity should not automatically be preserved at the expense of other life forms. The same hubris that divides species, divides races.

*　*　*

In her first year at Pasadena City College, Octavia won her first writing prize of fifteen dollars—beating out more experienced writers—for a short story submitted under "Karen Adams."[37] Fittingly, the story, "To the Victor," featured a championship boxing match between two men who fight "psionically" with their minds instead of their hands.[38] The body is only a shell for much more potent inner strength.

Karen Adams and Silver Star were more than pen names, they were surrogates that got Estella through tough times. Silver Star morphed from being a horse queen, to a girl adopted by Martians, to a vehicle of the Middle Passage. Each iteration conjured different modes of transport across time and space. Stars help us navigate the globe. They connect outer space to the watery earth. Gazing up at them, we see patterns, which for millennia have engendered stories of human-animal symbiosis. As an adult, Octavia re-read her childhood notebooks and continually revised and adapted her early Star writings. They mapped the way for her mature science fiction. Octavia's email address, even up to her death, was: butler8star@qwest.net.

Figure 2.1 *Bambi* movie poster, 1966. Everett Collection Inc/Alamy Stock Photo.

CHAPTER 2

B

IS FOR BAMBI

Octavia had waited ages for this moment. In Spring of 1966, Disney's re-released *Bambi* was playing in town as part of a limited Easter run (Fig. 2.1). As a child, she devoured all of Felix Salten's original forest world novels, but she'd never seen the film. Her mother disapproved of public movie theaters. All these years, *Bambi* had stayed with her. She wrote in a diary entry on April 5, 1966, "Mild cramps today. No problem accept (sic) that I didn't dare go out to see Bambi at the Crown. Luv you know how long I've been wanting to see that. If Disney left any of Sallie [Salten] in it its too good to miss."[1]

Luckily Pasadena City College was on spring break. The next day, free from work and classes, Octavia felt well enough to head over to the Crown Theatre on Raymond Avenue, in the commercial heart of Old Pasadena. There was always something happening around here. Just four blocks away, at the Friendship Baptist Church, Coretta Scott King was scheduled to give a concert later in the month. Octavia's Muir classmate Bebe remembers the excitement of attending that event as well as prior visits to the church by Reverend Martin Luther King, Jr. She and her fellow youth choir members sang for him the gospel favorite, "We've Come This Far By Faith," which she still knows by heart.[2] It is hard to forget the hymns one learns early on. This was certainly the case for Octavia, who also grew up Baptist and accompanied her mother's singing on the piano at home.[3] She kept pages of written and typed out lyrics, sometimes noting the key changes, to spirituals like "Rock of Ages," "Just a Closer Walk with Thee," "Go Tell it on the Mountain," "Deep River," and the songs of Civil Rights luminary Mahalia Jackson.[4]

On this spring Wednesday, April 6, Octavia was ready to escape the religion and politics of the moment and indulge her younger self. *Bambi* had three daily showings on a double bill with *The Hallelujah Trail*.[5] And though she probably didn't stay to see Burt Lancaster, Lee Remick, and Sioux Indians fight it out over a wagon train of whiskey, the epic-comic Western might have satisfied her penchant for cowboys and horses. The odd jobs she worked during weekdays—dishwashing, taking inventory, answering telephones—helped pay for her night classes and her consumption of Westerns, comic books, and science fiction.[6] One of her revered childhood pastimes was watching Zorro on the small screen. *(See "Z is for Zorro.")* In her diary just the day before, she lamented both her cramps and the news that dreamboat Guy Williams had shaved his Zorro moustache for his latest role in the TV show, *Lost in Space*.[7] The past Friday, April 1, she had cashed a check for $3.44 and headed over to the new second-hand bookstore to peruse the freshly arrived batch of comics.[8] Gone were the days when her mother censored her reading materials, even ripped some of her comics in half. (Back then, she had managed to keep stashed away her prized issues of the popular and countercultural *MAD Magazine*.[9])

Of late, Octavia was becoming more interested in developing what she called "an Afro story," while "keeping SF as a sort of second."[10] The Watts Rebellion had occurred in South L.A. shortly after her high school graduation in 1965. As she entered Pasadena City College, the Black Power movement began. She partook in Black Student Union activities even as she kept a distance from some of the more macho radical types. She took notes on Black nationalism and attended meetings of the Pasadena Afro-Relations Club.[11] In her final year in 1968, she experienced the assassinations of Martin Luther King, Jr. and Robert Kennedy during midterms and finals.[12] The world was in flux. Even the school curriculum was changing to reflect the freedom struggles of these revolutionary times. Before Octavia arrived, there were no specialized literature classes at PCC, and by the time she left two new offerings included English 48, "Oriental Literature" and English 50, "American Negro Writers."[13] Her final year, she was working full-time during the day, but luckily she could take the Black literature class at night with an African American woman professor visiting from Cal State Los Angeles.[14]

She was most keen about "Short Story Writing," her first writing class ever. She signed up for it repeatedly in order to have her writing critiqued and read out loud.[15] While at PCC, in addition to winning a prize for her short story, "To the Victor," she also published a story called "Loss" in the student literary magazine, *Pipes of Pan*. It was an "Afro story" of sorts, though not in the manner of what would become, a decade later, her "neo-slave narrative," *Kindred* (1979), which was set between 1970s Pasadena and antebellum Maryland.[16] Instead, "Loss" drew on Octavia's familiarity with the public transportation systems of Pasadena and Los Angeles. The main character, Tod Everett, steals five dollars from his mother's purse and uses it to ride the bus around the city all day to escape the fighting at home. So many things weigh on him: his mother, her drunk boyfriend, their hardscrabble life. At one point he gets off the bus and joins a line of kids outside a movie theater: "The show was made up of several old cartoons and a Walt Disney film."[17]

* * *

Often cinematic adaptations of our favorite books disappoint, but not this time. Octavia wrote on Wednesday, April 6, 1966: "Saw Bambi today. Good. . . Sad. . . with just enough of Sally left to keep me from walking out on it."[18] Likely the darker elements of Salten's forest world kept her in her seat. Animal fables have never been innocent. Aesop, after all, was a Greek slave. When Felix Salten wrote *Bambi* in the early 1920s, he was a Jewish Austrian in exile, fighting anti-Semitism, and highly active in the early Zionist movement. (It's no wonder Hitler banned the novel.) After Disney bought the rights to the book, they marketed the cherubic cartoon animals to children, despite the traumatic forest fire and the murder of the fawn's mother by "Man" the hunter. Behind the pathos of the woodland creatures was a complicated history of human longing for a homeland.

Knowing all this, including the propagandistic uses of sentimentalized nature, I was still unexpectedly moved to tears when I read for the first time the 1928 English translation of *Bambi* by Whittaker Chambers. Far from cute, the talking animals and plants plainly articulate their existential angst; they are helpless yet transcendent in the face of the guns that invade their pristine environment.

Octavia clearly identified with the allegory of persecuted wildlife. As a high school student, she penned her own Bambi poem on ruled paper:

> The Deer
> I run swiftly in the morning sun—
> Through the tall sweet meadow grass I run
> My heart pounds within me [in] with awful dread
> The speed leaves my legs, My body is lead
> Yet like a mad thing I run toward the trees
> There is a sound like thunder. I fall to my knees
> I struggle to rise though I know I cannot
> There is a pool about me of something red and hot
> I lie quietly as thoughts of life pass
> I close my eyes. Death takes me at last.
> > Inspired by the three books of Felix Salton that
> > I like best. Bambi, Bambi's
> > Children, and A Forest World.[19]

If we break it down, "The Deer" is ten lines of deceptively simple couplets. It opens with a first-person deer perspective and then imagines the process of dying while fleeing. It is an exercise in animal identification that bespeaks not only the shock of seeing, as a child, the death of Bambi's mother by gun-toting men; it seems to voice the suicidal thoughts of a world-weary teenager who rewrites the deer's story as her own. The experience of desperation and exhaustion, of being brought down after one can run no more, recalls other female-authored poems about hunted deer.

The young contemporary poet K-Ming Chang, for instance, addresses the ungulate directly: "dear Bambi / steal yourself back

/ from their hands. Frisk / & fly away. A man once / hunted you / but all he gave you / was a warning / no one kills a pet. So be / domestic, Bambi / no one kills a pet / So sell your flesh / for fabric, Bambi. Leash / your skin to a lawn / meat yourself."[20] At first hushed, then increasingly distressed, this lesson on feminine survival cuts to the heart. The intimacy of the epistolary form calls to mind the entwined figures of female and deer in the bronze sculptures of artists Kiki Smith and Alison Saar. A full-sized female, prostrate, is being birthed from a doe.[21] A standing female sprouts a crown of antlers from her head and stands amidst a pile of the bones shed and shorn.[22] Woman and beast are one—their hybrid forms bear witness to the violent energies of birth and loss.

There is nothing more terrifying than being hunted. In 1653, the Duchess of Newcastle, Margaret Cavendish penned "The Hunting of the Stag." She too described the manic adrenaline of being chased, the dread and acceptance of death, and the final shift from vitality to thinghood.

> The Stag no hope had left, nor help did 'spy,
> His heart so heavy grew with Grief and Care,
> That his small Feet his Body scarce could bear
>   . . . .
> 'Twas not for want of Courage he did Run,
> But that an Army was 'gainst him alone."[23]

In a companion poem, "The Hunting of the Hare," she again documents the plight of innocent prey. It's hard not to do a double take at her ruthless evisceration of the hunters who eat the bodies they murder: "Making their Stomacks, Graves, which full they fill / With Murther'd Bodies, that in sport they kill."[24]

These men are the ultimate hypocrites, wilder than any wild animal in their killing and filling. The gothic image of their stomachs-turned-graveyards bends the mind. Neither the first nor the last in a long line of feminist animal liberation poems, Cavendish's "Stag" is all sentimentalism and lashing didacticism, not to mention its Royalist sympathies for a dethroned King of England.

The Pasadena girl has a less refined and yet more introspective take on the plight of the animal. She embodies the deer. She tries to see the world from the perspective of a creature untrained in the ways of men. She deliberates on which things should go unnamed (guns, which "sound like thunder" and blood, mentioned only as "something red and hot.") She de-familiarizes the human to approximate animal cognition. She tries on a voice. Later in her adult life she would say, "[Salten] tended to write about animals as though they were human—more accurately, as though they were knowingly, although not always willingly, *subject* to humans."[25]

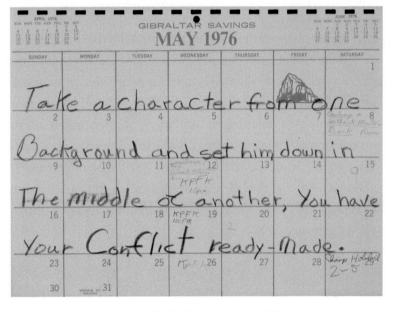

Figure 3.1 Writing mantra/Calendar page, 1976. OEB 1514.
By permission of Octavia E. Butler Enterprises.

CHAPTER 3

C

IS FOR CHARACTER

"Take a character from one Background and set him down in The middle of another, You have your Conflict ready-made." This is one of many writing mantras Octavia devised in pursuit of her storytelling craft. She inscribes it atop a repurposed page of a local Gibraltar Savings Bank calendar (Fig. 3.1). Octavia made the most of her often-meager resources. She turned scraps into grids for philosophies big and small.

The calendar reveals some of the varied interests of her daily life in May 1976. On three Wednesday nights at 10:00 p.m., she tuned into KPFK (90.7 Pacifica Radio) for a series of programs on the dangers of nuclear energy. Octavia would explore the relationship between cancer, nuclear proliferation, and government irresponsibility in multiple novels. These themes preoccupied her through the scandalous deregulatory policies of the 1980s and 1990s. (Gibraltar was one of many thrift banks that would eventually fold under the federal savings & loan mortgage lending crisis.) Two of the L.A. Public Library books Octavia renewed this month (May 8 and 12) speak to her devoted study of Westerns and the history of slavery: *Cowboys North and South*, by her childhood favorite Will James, and *Slaves Without Masters: The Free Negro in the Antebellum South*, by Ira Berlin. One was a French-Canadian writing about ranch life of the American West, the other, a Bronx-born Russian Jewish historian documenting the struggles of African Americans in the Deep South.

In her reading, listening, and calendaring habits, Octavia consistently brought into one frame characters from divergent backgrounds. *(See "H is for Horse.")* Memories of the mixed-race student body of her high school became novelistic fodder for *Mind of My Mind* (1977), which she was writing around this time and considered her most autobiographical novel. Her Black protagonist Mary Larkin is a telepathic young woman who lives in the Southern Californian town of Forsyth, a stand-in for Pasadena. She is raised by her foster mother and grandmother, also active psychokinetic beings (Psis) of the sort Octavia first explored in her Flash and Silver Star stories. A lover of books, the quiet and shy Mary calls the Forsyth Public Library her "second home." She will one day start a Psi colony to help her build a "pattern" of mental energy and vanquish the tyrant Doro. *(See "A is for Alias.")* Each section of the novel features a different member of Mary's blended, chosen family. In early drafts Octavia designated Ada Matsumoto a third-generation Japanese woman who was meant to be "more like Mary than anyone else in the family."[1] Though she would later drop the character's Japanese surname, the interracial connection between the two figures recalls her formative Pasadena school days.

As evident from Octavia's John Muir High yearbooks (1962–65), students of color were among the leaders of the school. The

C IS FOR CHARACTER

senior class president was a Japanese boy, Black students were on the senior class council and winners of leadership awards, and

> "Constructing my characters still helps me to construct myself." OEB 2712.

that year a Japanese girl and Latino boy were voted most likely to succeed. *(See "Y is for Yearbook.")*

At school Octavia was fond of a Filipina girl named Romay, who sat next to her in classes and looked forward to giving her feedback on her stories. Another friend, from her neighborhood, was a mixed-race Black and Japanese girl (whom she'd assumed for years was Latina.)[2]

While at Pasadena City College (1965–68), she took classes on African American and Asian History.[3] Her detailed notes on a Channel 4 history program, on the Japanese in Southern California, list the generations of Issei, Nisei, and Sansei, the racial discrimination the Japanese faced, and the fact that they were only allowed U.S. citizenship in 1952.[4] Adding her own commentary, Octavia speculated that African Americans were only just beginning to embrace the kind of common heritage that other minorities—the Japanese, Chinese, and Irish—could rely on to stay united. She wrote of the need for Black people to stand up for themselves and shed their dependence on the white man. For inspiration, she looked to the Japanese resistance to the Chinese, and called on all African Americans to be adults, not petulant children.[5]

E Pluribus Unum. Out of many, one. Just as she drew on the Civil Rights and Black Power movements to fashion her racially integrated fictional worlds, Octavia based her portraits of childlike adults on the teenagers that attended John Muir. Her adult annotations of her senior yearbook are an exercise in character development. Next to the photos of two white girls she wrote, "Happy-mystic" and "All glittery and perfectly masked." She assigned two Black girls the roles "coordinator" and "Do it all & more." Sometimes Octavia ventriloquized people's outlooks on life, as she wrote next to one classmate, "I don't like People" and another, "I'm gonna get an F."[6] One of the most trenchant yearbook meditations is a three-paged typology of selected classmates. On the back of recycled *Business Week* pamphlets from 1973, she typed out succinct descriptions of people's adolescent behaviors. In the margins, in red ink, she extrapolated their societal roles.[7]

For Octavia, social truths revealed self-truths. Assembling people from different settings, spelling out their conflicts, and establishing their common ground was her specialty. After all, she wrote Black female protagonists into science fiction. She had character.

Figure 4.1 "Jump, Spot, Jump" from *The New Our Big Book*, 1952. Courtesy of Princeton University Library.

CHAPTER 4

D

IS FOR DOG

Animals are like books. They help children escape from the adult world, and they also help make sense of it. Octavia's father, Laurice James Butler, passed away when she was a baby.[1] Her mother, Octavia Margaret Guy Butler, worked cleaning houses. For a time, she and her mother lived in the home of a white employer, where her uncles also worked as house staff. At the age of two and half or three Estella met the family's cocker spaniel, Baba. In a 2002 interview with *Oprah Magazine*, she chose to describe this dog encounter as the "aha moment" of her early life. She recalled looking into the dog's eyes and finding a mutual curiosity between them that made her realize, "he was someone else entirely."[2] This is something akin to what John Berger has described as the self-defining, self-awareness of "*being seen* by the animal."[3] As a first-grader Estella read *Fun with Dick and Jane* for the first time. She found it hopelessly boring, but it reminded her of that picture-perfect white family and their dog (Fig. 4.1). In her head, she assigned each of the book's characters to the family, even Spot, whom she dubbed "Spot-Baba."[4] She was already composing fiction from life, and it captured her race, class, and species disidentifications.

Octavia never forgot the creatures with whom she locked eyes. When she visited a zoo at age seven, the animal gaze helped her further intuit the difference between freedom and slavery. She remembered witnessing children's cruelty toward a caged chimpanzee.[5] Though she was too young to be ashamed of her species, she knew she wanted the chimp to be free. In a separate interview, she remembered visiting a pony riding ring where she noticed festering sores on the horses' small bodies, and realized in horror that they had been kicked repeatedly by all the children impatient to go faster.[6] By the time she was an adult, and a vegetarian, Octavia could look back on these early encounters and realize, "I hated zoos. I still hate them, although people tell me they've changed. They have bigger, nicer, less obvious cages."[7] In her *O Magazine* interview, she turned the example of the zoo into an analogy for the social world: "I learned to hate solid, physical cages—cages with real bars like the ones that made the chimp's world tiny vulnerable, and barren. Later I learned to hate the metaphorical cages that people try to use to avoid getting to know one another—cages of race, gender, class."[8]

Even as a young teen Estella connected the plight of animals to enslaved people across history. In eighth grade she shared with her classmate Sylvia a twenty-four-page story called "Hope," handwritten in a brown spiral notebook. It imagined the persecution of a Jewish family in late 1930s Germany. With some sleuthing I managed to track down a few of Octavia's school acquaintances. Even now, sixty years later, Sylvia vividly recalls reading this story: it struck her as odd that the father of the house seemed more concerned about saving his money and belongings than his family. At the time, she read along and kept that thought to herself.[9]

In the story, a Jewish girl tells of the Gestapo invading her home. One scene of suffering follows another. After they shoot her sister's dog, and then her sister, our narrator seethes, "How could crimes such as these go unpunished." The family is herded into a cattle car. The girl stabs a German officer to death, is captured by another officer, and brought to his mansion to serve him. The story ends with a trade she's asked to make, to be his concubine in exchange for the lives of her remaining siblings. As it dawns on her what he's asking of her, she voices her final words: "I wished I had kept the knife."[10]

Just as Octavia was fighting Nazis in her fiction, I picture her as a resistance writer during those junior high years of being shamed by her teachers. *(See "A is for Alias.")* One of her undercover dog tales, "Man's Best Friend," takes place in a world where, unbeknownst to the humans, pet dogs control their owners' minds.[11] The commanding canine is the Old One, a formidable Great Dane who reprimands his dog subjects when they refer to each other with degrading "human" breed names like collie and fox terrier. His efforts to telepathically eradicate humans of their penchant for fear and discrimination have not been working. The story is told in the first person by the Old One's daughter, a girl who looks human, but in fact is a mixed-species werewolf. Shunned by dogs and people alike, she squats in an abandoned house trying to stay out of sight. The werewolf girl longs to be a dog in her father's community. When he gives her a mission, she can't refuse it—perhaps *she* can figure out why people's minds can no longer be manipulated by the dog race. He instructs her to visit the insane asylum where her mother lives, locate her human relatives, and live amongst them as a spy. The Old One cannot give her the power of human speech so she must pose as a "deaf mute" to complete the operation. *(See "J is for Junie.")*

Decades later, we can find echoes of this early experimentation with animality and disability in *Parable of the Sower,* in which the teenaged protagonist Lauren Oya Olamina suffers from hyperempathy syndrome, an ability to feel others' pain that extends to animals as well as humans. In one episode, Lauren is overcome by the agony of a wounded dog; when she shoots it out of mercy, she must endure its life extinguishing: "I felt the impact of the bullet as a hard, solid blow—something beyond pain. Then I felt the dog die."[12] To be a dog, or look into the eyes of a dog, is to imagine both difference and connection. The werewolf girl of "Man's Best Friend" doesn't belong to any tribe. She puts it simply and painfully, "I have no people. I am not a human because my father is a dog, and I am not a dog because my mother is a human."

In Butler's novels, women tend to lead the fight against people being treated like animals. And yet, Octavia had a soft spot for outsiders who saw themselves *as* animals and refused to conform to traditional expectations of sex and family-making. *Survivor* (1978) is a hard-to-find novel of the Patternist series which Octavia disliked and allowed to fall out of print. It is actually one of my favorites. The protagonist Alanna, an orphaned feral child, reminds me of the dog-girl of "Man's Best Friend." After losing her parents to the alien Clayark invasion of Earth at an early age, Alanna grows up houseless and fending for herself until she is taken in and fostered by fundamentalist Christian missionaries who refer to her as a wild human.[13] Alanna is not only a wildling, she is the mixed-race child of a Black father and Asian mother.

D IS FOR DOG

Having grown up during segregation but in an area of Pasadena where Japanese, Latino/as, and African Americans lived side by side, Octavia was used to people from different groups interacting. The interracial connections of one's youth can resonate well into the future, maybe even in the form of the Blasian romantic couplings that Octavia wrote into several of her novels. In *Dawn*, a tall Black woman named Lilith finds an unlikely soulmate in a small Chinese man named Joseph. *(See "O is for Ooloi.")* Her fifth Patternist novel, *Clay's Ark*, ends with the union of a Japanese man, Stephen Kaneshiro, with Keira, a mixed-race woman born of a white father and Black mother. In one notebook from 1981, Octavia noted that bigots make up most of the real world, especially in the Reagan era in which she was composing *Clay's Ark*, "Yet I refuse to fill my worlds with them."[14] Instead, she peoples her fiction with resistance fighters like the unloved half-breed girl of "Man's Best Friend," who is destined to accomplish what her dog-father could not.

* * *

The summer of my seventh-grade year, I learned to fear dogs. While out walking local forest trails, my friends and I stumbled into a neighbor's backyard and met the growl of a massive German Shepherd-Labrador. It lunged, we turned around and ran back into the woods, but I was the unlucky one whose leg it caught and clamped onto. I had never seen such an intensity of red as the blood that streamed forth. For years after I would freeze when approached by a dog on the street. If I made eye contact, they could smell my fear. Still, one of my favorite animal shows in the early 1980s starred a German shepherd as a good dog. *The Littlest Hobo* was a Canadian, bachelor-dog version of *Lassie*

I watched growing up in northwest Washington State, minutes away from the border. This dog wandered alone, homeless, from town to town, saving humans in trouble. I liked how he ambled along the railroad tracks. He was a dog with no master. *"Until tomorrow. I'll just keep moving on . . . ."* Most TV celebrity animals were rescuers of humans. Lassie the familial Rough Collie, Mr. Ed the advice-giving American Saddlebred/Arabian horse, and Flipper the Bottlenose Dolphin. *(See "R is for Rex McDonald.")* Their helpful actions usually complemented the boyhoods of the humans on screen. Part of the appeal for me, though, was that the animals seemed to escape the confinements of gender. (Lassie was technically female.) They existed both inside and outside of the lily white, Dick-and-Jane families.

When I went to identify the dog at the pound, I found out that it was known for terrorizing children on bikes. The owners were drug dealers who likely abused the dog. Weeks passed before they bothered to retrieve him. It's a known fact that people who are cruel toward animals also abuse other people, especially women and children.

Growing up, Octavia had two cocker spaniels, Sandy and Tory, who no doubt helped her channel into fiction the perspectives of the underdog. She was especially fond of Tory, named for his red coloring (her perhaps ironic nod to the dogged politics of left-wing British conservatism). He lived through her formative writing years of ages ten through twenty-four. At around thirteen, she penned a one-page, unfinished story titled "Torey." It opens with a brown collie named Queen furiously digging a huge hole. Her friend, a black collie named Lassie, observes and wonders what she is looking for (not a bone), until a small cry emerges from below ground. We don't learn what it is, because the next page is a list of types of horses.[15] Sometimes dogs keep their discoveries to themselves.

Years later, in a journal entry from February 9, 1979 Octavia penned an anecdote about her childhood dog that she later typed up and titled, simply, "Tory."[16] She paints a portrait of a lovable rebel who constantly escaped his collar and got into trouble. An audacious small dog with a dangerously inflated sense of his strength, he took on dogs however big. He would come home beaten and bruised, though proud. Octavia spent her babysitting money and allowances bailing out Tory from the pound. Though he had a mind of his own and refused to stay put, "He outfought or outran his enemies and came home to his friends and never learned to stop treating all human beings as potential friends." By the end of his life, Tory had been tortured by neighborhood boys to the point of not being able to walk well anymore. He lived to around fourteen years old, when some of the boys used him as target practice to test their Christmas rifles. Octavia chooses to focus on Tory's resistance rather than the actions of his assassins when she notes that though he could not outrun their bullets, he did make it home.[17]

Throughout her career, Octavia explored the chain of violence that begins with inherited, collective trauma and gets worked out in the family, the schoolyard, and human–animal relations. She noted in a journal entry from August 7, 2005, "Bullies facinate [sic] me."[18] Bullies held a special place in her youthful writings. In her high-school era story "Factory Reject," she opened with the observation, "Sometimes when a member of a certain species of animal is born wrong for the world it is born into, that species rejects it ... . If Leah-Ray had been a dog, her mother would have let her die." Leah-Rae Johns, the titular factory reject, practically raises herself.

Her father dies when she is four, her mother works full time, her grandmother has moved away. The teachers and other kids torture her with a combination of neglect, insults, and beatings. (Her worst bully, a boy named Richard Billings, does get his due when his drunk father drives the family into a gasoline truck.) Leah-Rae loses herself in books and dreams of having friends.[19]

Her gritty, Tory-like resilience reminds me of the poem "The Badger," by the English peasant poet John Clare. Written around 1835, it eulogizes a scrappy badger who endures being hunted and baited by dogs and men, even thrills in playing dead and egging *them* on. In his final moments, while being beaten to death, the badger bears his teeth in a triumphant grin. His spirit is uncrushed:

> The dogs are clapped and urged to join the fray;
> The badger turns and drives them all away.
> Though scarcely half as big, demure and small,
> He fights with dogs for hours and beats them all.
>   ....
> He falls as dead and kicked by boys and men,
> Then starts and grins and drives the crowd again;
> Till kicked and torn and beaten out he lies
> And leaves his hold and cackles, groans and dies.

Clare wrote of the cruelty of nineteenth-century boys who brutalized helpless creatures—nightingales, dogs, cocks, and horses. Like Octavia, he identified with the persecuted animal. *(See "B is for Bambi.")* Pictured as valiant outsiders, these protagonists are neither ingenuous, nor party to the callous ways of dog-hearted blokes.

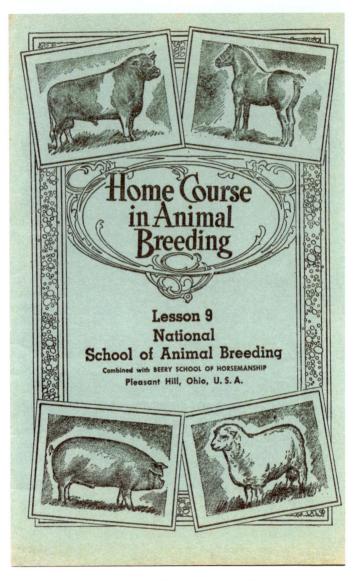

Figure 5.1 Pamphlet owned by Octavia E. Butler, *Home Course in Animal Breeding* (1944).
Author's copy.

CHAPTER 5

E

IS FOR EQUISETOPSIDA

All domestic horses fall under the subspecies *Equus ferus caballus*. The hundreds of breeds that fill up registries have been selected for over time. In horse books of all reading levels, the representative equine is pictured in profile with a signature stance. We have molded them according to our standards of color, size, shape, and behavior. We may engineer nonhuman life, but we recoil at the idea of being bred or mated, ourselves. Science fiction often probes this double standard, as Octavia certainly did in her twinned pursuits of botany and zoology.

Amidst her ephemera one item leapt out, a faded blue-green pamphlet from a ten-course educational series, *Home Course in Animal Breeding* (Fig. 5.1). Octavia owned Lesson 9, "Artificial Breeding and its Practical Application," an illustrated step-by-step guide to the impregnation of mares, cows, ewes, and sows. On the front cover, each farm animal is quaintly pictured in its respective frame. Stamped onto the back of the pamphlet, the motto: "Our Future Prosperity Lies in Our Live Stock." Across the series, anatomical diagrams of reproductive organs and the biology of cell division aid the aspiring veterinarian achieve a product "true to type." In Lesson 1, Professor C. C. Palmer, D.M.V. announces to his readers, "My aim is to help you solve your breeding problems." Clinical science is not supposed to be sexy; artificial insemination renders animal copulation obsolete. But the frank, hands-on detail might well telegraph kinkiness to a hormonal teen reader.

Unlike the other booklets in the series, this one focuses on mares. Perhaps, knowing her daughter's love of horses, Octavia Sr. brought it home, along with other cast-off books from work. Flipping to the pamphlet's black-and-white photos of a stout Percheron mare, young Octavia might have recalled that equine's popularity "in the farm and the circus." That is how it was described in the illustrated guide to different horse breeds that she had bought for herself at age ten. *(See "H is for Horse.")* Perhaps an adult Octavia picked up this text secondhand as part of her general research into biotechnology. In her Patternist novels, the breeding of mares becomes a repeated analogy for dehumanizing eugenic experiments. In the brutal world of *Clay's Ark*, infected people become ravenous for food and sex. The scientist Eli tries to hold onto his humanity by refusing to become "a stud with three mares." Horrifically, the alien organism has turned "them all into breeding animals," and the offspring are a new species of quadruped children, "kids with human minds and four legs."[1]

In *Wild Seed*, Doro uses his supernatural powers to collect and breed people with telepathic traits. Over thousands of years, he has yet to achieve the perfect species of telepathic humanoids. He

E IS FOR EQUISETOPSIDA

meets his match in a 300-year-old female Igbo healer, Anyanwu. Though she has been branded by Doro, she is a wild seed, "a breed unto herself," who only follows him to the New World to buy her children's freedom. Using a horse metaphor, she pleads with him, "Are my children to become mares and studs?"[2] And in *Mind of My Mind*, Mary Larkin resents being "just another of Doro's breeders—just another Goddamn brood mare."[3] Her horse-tinged invective echoes the others' comments. We balk at Doro's eugenics experiments. In her notes and drafts, though, Octavia saw herself in Doro. She, too, wanted success, to build a world of companions and like-minded people; not content with society as it currently existed, she made and modified new characters. She wrote, "I am Doro. Man-woman. Demon-god. Breeder of newmen. These are my stories."[4] When read as a solitary author's desire for offspring, kin, and community, literary breeding seems much less sinister. Even as she takes on the language of Doro, she inflects it with a creative rather than coercive spirit. The title phrase of the novel, "mind of my mind," appends the male-centered biblical creation myth, *This is now bone of my bones and flesh of my flesh; she shall be called "woman," for she was taken out of man* (Genesis: 2:23). In Octavia's revision, the woman's mind will overcome the man's. The Forsyth built by Mary is a kind of Star Island, the home for intelligent horse kin in a world hostile to difference. *(See "A is for Alias.")*

> In a note from January 21, 1975, Octavia jotted, "I am alone! I seek to build a society of my own kind. Psis who can cooperate, live together, be the foundation of a new race!" OEB 455.

Taking a closer look at the photo of Octavia standing next to a friend's mare amidst lush Pacific Northwest foliage (Fig. o.o), I hear the echo of a note she once wrote to herself, "What animals—or more likely plants—might hitchhike from one world to another."[5] One time-traveling evergreen in her midst would have belonged to a remarkable class of ancient flora, Equisetopsida, which combines the Latin words *equus* ("horse") + *seta* ("bristle" or "hair") + *opsida* ("appearance"). Only one genus, the Equisetum, lives on today. Octavia never wrote about these plants, but her "dictionary habit" led me to them. I was struck by the word Equisetum as I browsed a 1963 edition of the WBED (*World Book Encyclopedia and Dictionary*), a reference book Octavia often consulted for her own explorations of coevolving life forms. Its very title, combining four hefty nouns into one, inspires an equine-botanical digression....

Though named after horses, Equiseta are actually closer to minerals. Their hollow, jointed stems absorb minerals like silica, to the extent that Native Americans used them in dried form as chemically abrasive cleaners. The Blackfeet called them joint grass. A Pacific Northwest Suquamish Tribe linguist explained to me that the Lushootseed word for what we now call "horsetail" is *bubx̌ed*, which does not at all refer to horses.[6] After all, horses were only brought by Europeans to the region in the 1700s, and these plants have been around so long, relatively unchanged, they are considered living fossils.

Four hundred million years ago, gigantic, tree-like horsetails dominated prehistoric forests. They predated the dinosaurs, and existed before even grass and seed plants came along. Octavia would have appreciated the Equisetum's unusual sex life. *(See "S is for Sexy.")* In one generation, it reproduces asexually, when underground tubers branch off from their rhizomatic roots. In the next, it produces fern-like spores that unfurl into the air, germinate upon landing, and then undergo sexual, male–female fertilization. True *Equisetum giganteum* are botanical

> "I love words—their sounds, their multiple meanings and shadings, the powers we give them to teach, to wound, to build, to heal . . . ." OEB 562.

wonders that only grow in hidden wet places in the southern hemisphere. No longer hundreds of feet tall, today's thirty-two-feet giant horsetail is still impressive for a plant. If you can't journey to Bolivia or Peru to see it, a diminutive version, *Equisetum telmateia*, the northern giant horsetail, can be found in Puget Sound, where Octavia made her home for the last seven years of her life. Native to North America, the plants are nonetheless considered invasive "born colonizers," adaptable, hardy, and aggressive weeds because they outlast any herbicide. She might have seen them on one of her hikes up Mount Rainier or day trips outside Seattle. Up to six feet in height, reaching Octavia's own stature, they are one of the tallest Equiseta outside Latin America. I remember seeing them in the ditches of Washington State, near the Canadian border, where I grew up. With their striped, asparagus-like stalks, they look snaky, tropical, and slightly menacing—evergreen, yet somehow out of place and far from home.

Shortly after she returned from her Peru trip in 1985, Octavia went to Seattle to teach at the Clarion West science fiction writing workshop. She did not drive, so one of her students, Leslie, volunteered to take her around. They remained friends, and when she relocated to Seattle over a decade later, she and Leslie continued their car trips. Once or twice, they visited an Arabian horse farm in Gig Harbor, a town on the Kitsap Peninsula where Leslie kept her mare, April, and her sister-in-law's horse Morningstar, an elderly, mellow Pinto. Leslie recalls how much Octavia loved meeting the horses and feeding them carrots.[7] In the photo she took on that bright day in 1999, Octavia beams radiantly, her inner Silver Star shining through.

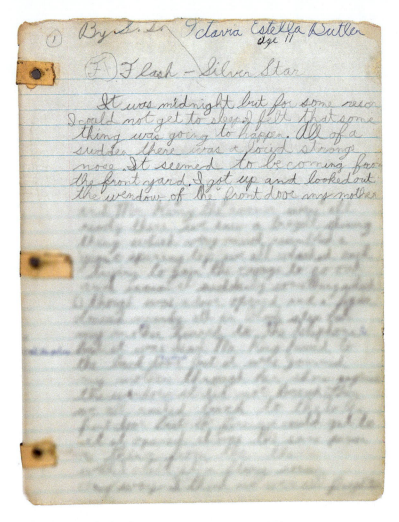

Figure 6.1 "Flash-Silver Star" story page, 1958. OEB 590.
By permission of Octavia E. Butler Enterprises.

CHAPTER 6

F

IS FOR FLASH

More than anything, Octavia's teen girl-hero longed to be loved by an exceptional male named Flash. Older, enigmatic, commanding, virile, Martian—in story after story, Flash comes to the girl narrator's bedroom in the middle of the night (Fig. 6.1). He speaks to her using telepathy and claims her for himself . . . and for the Martian cause. Her new identity will be Star, and she will join him in protecting his planet from Earth's colonizing reach. Together they intercept a missile aimed at Mars (they travel to Washington, D.C. where the fuel is being stored).[1] Another time they meet the U.S. President, and Flash engages in Cold War diplomacy with the Russians.[2] As an undercover agent, Star uses her newly acquired powers of "hypnotism" to spy on her fellow Earthlings and inform Flash of any anti-Mars developments.[3]

Estella began sharing her serial fictions with friends in junior high. One old classmate recalled in a phone conversation with me that these "page-turners" would sometimes be written up the side of a page because she would run out of notebook

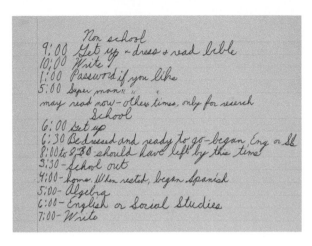

Figure 6.2 Writing schedule, c.1965. OEB Box 336.
By permission of Octavia E. Butler Enterprises.

space.[4] Another school friend sometimes sat with her at lunch and read her stories. She remembers that Octavia often looked out of place; she was gangly and sometimes she was dressed for winter on hot days. Despite her social and physical awkwardness, "Octavia wrote before her time and beyond her years."[5]

By high school, Octavia followed a schedule that built in time for TV as well as writerly pursuits. On non-school days, she got up at nine o'clock, dressed, and read the bible. Ten o'clock was designated writing time, and afternoon and evening shows included *Password* or *Superman*. A TV-announcer bravado comes through in the prologue to one story: "Contrary to the beliefs of men there is on the planet Mars a race of people.... You will also meet an earth girl who willingly becomes one of them... And now Flash."[6]

On school days, she did Spanish at 4:00, Algebra at 5:00, then English or Social Studies at 6:00. The sacred hour of 7:00 p.m.

was reserved for Writing (Fig. 6.2). She worked hard at it and learned to deal with the failures. On April 21, 1963 she wrote in her diary she had decided she would scrap a story about a deformed witch.[7] At night, after her mother had gone to sleep, she dreamed of escaping with Flash to other planets.

Sometimes Star resists Flash's advances, but never for long. Their intimacy is described in soapy detail. Sexual union with Flash is akin to cosmic travel. In one instance Star describes "a oneness that can never be experienced by prisoners of clumsy bodies."[8] She surrenders to him her mind and body and steps

> "This was sky union, and as the stars looked on unwinkingly, Flash claims me as his own in a way no Earth man would ever dream possible." OEB 921.

into a new sense of self. The details of the Flash/Star fantasies become more carnal over time, as in a racy seventeen-year-old version that involves a "thin night gown."[9] As much as these supernatural dalliances would appear to be about teen romance, they are never simply about sex. The mental communication with Flash gives her "freedom in the truest sense of the word."[10] She writes of being without a body, of no longer having to feel pain.[11] In a typewritten story called "Shephards," the narrator's mother teaches her that she was born of "black airlessness" in outer space. As shepherds of the human race, the family keeps Earth from destroying itself. Essentially, she *is* black matter—her body exists only for appearance's sake. Her true state is a form of Black freedom passed down from her mother. (The neighbors do not realize this and declare her mother unfit.)[12] Though she might have felt trapped in a socially unaccepted body, Octavia knew her Blackness was special, even otherworldly. At age fifteen, she was an Afrofuturist before anyone knew it.

In her daily life, Octavia pursued extrasensory mind travel with the zeal of an amateur researcher. She read up on clairvoyance, ESP, and telekinesis.[13] At school she devised a survey on lined notebook paper that asked classmates to write in: would they allow themselves to be hypnotized, and if not, why? The answers were divided along the lines of those afraid of losing control, and those willing to put their trust in a professional or someone they knew. My favorite response, by Sally Warren: "No, I might not come back to my normal self."[14]

It was precisely normalcy that Octavia wrote against in her Martian chronicles. On the surface, Flash was a dashing male superhero who swept Star off her feet and answered her desires for sex and love. It would be inaccurate, though, to say that he simply rescues or dominates Star. More like a hypnotist, he helps her access her inner strengths. The summer after high school graduation Octavia attended a group hypnosis session at the Melvin Powers Institute in Hollywood. Known for his line of how-to books, Powers taught Octavia ways to control her allergy sneezing. She even plotted out some of her stories under hypnosis.[15] This was the Cold War era. The word brainwashing was coined in 1950 by journalist and presumed CIA operative Edward Hunter, and soon after, hypnosis entered mainstream self-help culture. Anti-Communist paranoia was popularized through villainous, mind-controlling Asian characters on screen and in comics. In 1962, the same year that Octavia entered high school, the POW-espionage film *The Manchurian Candidate* and the first James Bond movie, *Dr. No*, hit the theaters. Their Asian anti-heroes joined an earlier era of brainwashers like Fu Manchu and Ming the Merciless, who used a Dehumanizer hypnosis machine to ensnare Flash Gordon's paramour, Dale Arden.[16]

Octavia continued her study of hypnotism at Pasadena City College. For a Health Education class she wrote an essay on its range of benefits. It could remedy skin problems, heart disease, surgery, terminal illness, anxiety disorder. She noted, "Although hypnosis is not a cure-all, it is a large, only partially explored field with great potential."[17] Since her friends and relatives were reluctant to work with her on group hypnosis, Octavia devised her own exercises. In the archive, unfolding one of her gingerly, taped-together sheets of paper felt a little like intruding upon a private, sacred ritual. And yet I was immediately drawn into the sequence of second-person mantras that seemed to speak directly to my own desires for self-improvement. They demand that "you" exorcize shame from your past, ward off future shame over mistakes that you will inevitably make, eliminate self-doubt, make your dreams come true. Octavia planned to induce future trances by reading out loud the "5 S's." She instructs herself to put the paper on the ironing board, go to sleep, and awake in two hours feeling refreshed.[18]

* * *

For years, Flash was the manifestation of Octavia's secret inner life, one filled with conflicting desires of self-empowerment and self-loathing. Her alias, Star, thrilled in knowing intimately an older, mentor figure. But to be loved by Flash was also to be owned, even abused, by him.[19] One of the recurring scenes between Flash and Star is his branding of her arm. When he visits

Figure 6.3 Detail, Flash/Star insignias. OEB 590.
By permission of Octavia E. Butler Enterprises.

her for the first time, he carves "something like a percentage sign" into her flesh.[20] She describes the experience as a type of marriage ceremony: "I saw the knife in his hand but I was no longer afraid. I felt it's cold hardness slide through the flesh of my arm. There was no pain but the small mark he made that night would be with the rest of my life. It was a mark of ownership . . . . I now belong to him. I was his to do with as he please, to keep, to sell or even to kill."[21] The erotic mark of Flash—a backwards percent sign (Fig. 6.3)—often appears on Octavia's title pages next to the letter F, or sometimes on its own. Like her star doodles, it became a private code that called forth a universe of avatars. The insignia, I realized, is hard to produce on a typewriter or computer keyboard. A rotated % usually comes out facing the same direction. It's much easier to create by hand the inversion that Octavia intended. I like to think that, once again, she turned her dyslexia into a superpower. *(See "A is for Alias.")*

When you desperately love a womanizer who cannot commit to you wholly, you are in for a world of pain. Like the bands of horses on Star Island, male Martians are polygamous and territorial. Flash reenacts the exploits of Reese the stallion when he fights his half-brother to add Star to his clan of 24–25 women.

> One of Flash's many women is a pretty "Chinees [Chinese] girl" named Perrie (Perrico). This could be an echo of Felix Salten's *Perri: The Youth of a Squirrel*, a follow-up novel to *Bambi* that features a Eurasian squirrel. Even in outer space, Octavia's beloved forest and animal worlds persist. OEB 590.

Other female characters—Iray, Mayseco, Lea, and Perrico—appear in the plots to varying extents. More than once, a girl narrator is slapped or beaten by an alien man.[22] In "Adaptability," a young girl tells of a world where men have multiples wives due to a shortage of women. Her father is on his third wife. In store for her is the fate of many young women, who at age fifteen are assigned to serve nine-foot-tall Masters with "six strong blue Tentacles."[23]

In one of the most explicit scenes of abuse, Flash appears on Earth as a man named John Compton. He reveals himself in handsome, caped Martian form to the Earth girl Penny, who falls head over heels for him. She is jealous of Star and the other "Marten" girls in his entourage. Flash hits her multiple times, and though she defiantly slaps him back, she admits that she had to take the blows silently, stoically.[24] An aside, written in Flash's voice, interrupts the story and justifies his violence to the reader directly, saying, "as you know by now I am not an earthling, I was treating her marten fashion."[25] Even her earliest science fiction addressed the bind of misogyny and intergalactic patriarchy.

From her outer space travels, Star learned firsthand that: a. world domination goes hand in hand with sexual domination, b. domination is never complete, c. masculinity needs femininity.

The fate of Mars often turns on the rivalry between Flash and his half-brother, Coranse. Their duels over the throne—and over

---

The "Patternist" novels

1976—*Patternmaster*
1977—*Mind of My Mind*
1978—*Survivor*
1980—*Wild Seed*
1984—*Clay's Ark*

Star—anticipate Octavia's first novel, *Patternmaster*, by over a decade. As early as 1961, Octavia was writing about the nearly extinct "Cla-arks" who had lost their planet, and ravaged Mars with their rabies-like disease. The world of *Patternmaster* is made up of patriarchal houses and guilds. Ultimately, every man needs a strong woman by his side. Just as the horse Silver Star joined forces with Rocket, and the girl Star with Flash, Teray finds a soulmate and fellow resistance fighter in Amber. She is a healer of injured horses, and openly bisexual. Such is the queer, fictional universe that Octavia began building through her early horse and Martian adventures.

* * *

Though nowhere near Octavia's height, I was big for my age. The other kids caught up with me by middle school, but for a time I towered over all the boys and girls alike. A sharp, quiet listener, I was given secrets to hold and adult responsibilities I never asked for. I kept a diary from first grade all the way through college. I recorded in fledgling cursive the small highlights of school and home life, and the comings and goings of relatives and family friends. I have pored over my childhood diaries for evidence of the trauma done to me by an older male cousin. But diaries do not tell all. They encode as much as they divulge.

Flash might have been an alien, but he was likely based on men Octavia knew or observed. He was more than a fictional character. She conjured him in moments of heightened desire, anxiety, or ambivalence, as though he were a special friend, or an aspect of her inner self. In her diary entry from Monday, April 8, 1963, she appealed to Flash when her mother's boyfriend King was threatening to leave. In a mix of Spanish and English, she wrote, "No sé que hacer Flash por favor viene Vd pronto [I don't know what to do Flash, please come soon]." Without skipping a beat, she goes on to talk about her fictional character, Doro, and then King's outsized ego. She then fantasizes that Flash might materialize and kiss her in the garage when she's taking out the dogs. He calls her "Star," and Estella wishes that she were ready for him.[26]

A diarist with literary aspirations and things to hide, Octavia consistently blurred the lines between fiction and real life. On Sunday, May 17, 1964 she admits she still has a crush on her Social Studies teacher Mr. Sariego: "I know how dumb it is. I have finally admitted [sic] it about Flash Its hard and it doesn't leave me anything but I had to do it. Hate to go back tomorrow." What did she admit about Flash? Who was he, exactly? We might never know, but he does tend to appear when she grapples with her feelings for authoritative father figures.

No matter how strong her female protagonists, the mistreatment of women by powerful men recurs in all of Octavia's adult novels. The sadomasochistic dynamic between the sexes is never easy to digest, regardless of the rules of the particular world she asks us to inhabit. Is this internalized misogyny? Sexual repression? Or contrarian perversity that radically defies social norms? I change my mind each time I read one of these passages. What we can say for sure is that Octavia refused to sugarcoat the power differentials at work in any kind of intimacy under patriarchy. Matters of bodily desire are rarely simple. In her mature fiction, Octavia explored sexual taboos as much as she did the freedoms of being bodiless or atypically embodied. She was an experimentalist who tried on different voices and narrative forms. In college in the 1970s, she wrote pornographic stories of sexually liberated females of all ages. A precocious six-year-old has sex with her teen male babysitter and doesn't mind being sold to men.[27] A woman enjoys a romp with multiple guys in the back of a car.[28] These could easily be scenes of rape, but Octavia makes them small acts of female empowerment.

*　*　*

When she was in seventh grade and fixated on Flash, Octavia defined love as "a four letter word meaning a feeling of closeness between two or more Individuals each has complete trust in the other."[29] Fast forward to her adult description of an author's intimacy with their audience, and she invokes the other F-word, "A good novel is a very long sweet exquisite fuck. It is the joy and the duty of every writer to give readers the best and the most intense lovemaking that they have ever experienced."[30] Octavia gave herself to this relationship perhaps more than to any other.

I used to think of Star as Octavia's alter-ego and Flash as her sex-love obsession. But later I realized that she also saw herself as Flash. He might have branded Star, but she took on the power of that backward percent sign. In real life, Octavia personalized her senior yearbook photo by penning in blue a Flash symbol on her

F IS FOR FLASH

right shoulder and a star on the left. (Fig. 1.6.) Her hand-inked insignias suggest the parallel presence of masculine and feminine in one person. I see them as virtual tattoos that together acknowledge the nonbinary posture of a Black girl with a masculine body, voice, and stature, and the flashes of courage that she would inspire in others.

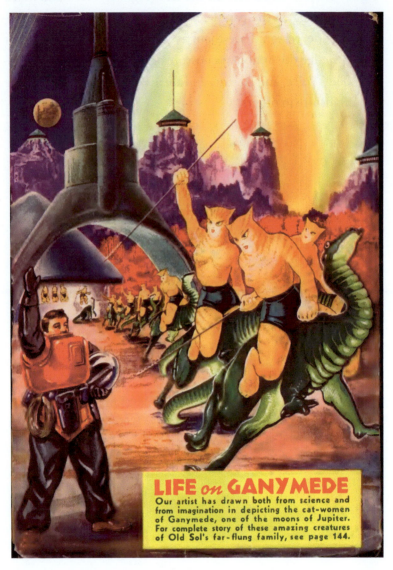

Figure 7.1 "Life on Ganymede," back cover illustration by Frank R. Paul. *Amazing Stories* vol. 14, no. 10 (1940).

© Amazing Stories, the Experimenter Publishing Company.

CHAPTER 7

G

IS FOR GANYMEDE

If planets were people, Jupiter would be the arch polygamist of the solar system. It has the most moon companions in its orbit (seventy-nine and counting). By comparison, Earth has only one naturally revolving satellite companion. We howl at it, keep time by it, make romance by its light. Unlike the other space rocks, we have given it no name. It is ours, so we simply call it "the" moon. By contrast, the four largest and most famous moons of Jupiter were named after virginal youths loved by the god Zeus (Jupiter/Jove to the Romans.) Galileo claimed to have seen them first, in 1610, but rival astronomer Simon Marius begged to differ. In his book, *Mundus Iovialis* [The World of Jupiter], Marius called them Jupiter's "irregular loves" and composed a couplet for the occasion of their appellation:

> Io, Europa, Ganymede, Callisto—all of Jove
> Preferred on Earth, around his orb in Jovian radiance move.[1]

Among the four loves, Ganymede is the only male. Born a mortal, he was snatched away by Zeus, who, in the form of a lustful eagle, flew him to Mount Olympus to be a cup-bearer and wine-pourer to the gods. As the beautiful boy-slave, Ganymede has been hailed the god of homosexuality. The Greeks further immortalized him as the constellation Aquarius, who appears in the night sky with an eagle and his water vessel, which poured out the rivers of the planet. Animal exchanges and metamorphoses have always been entwined with the rapes and romantic intrigues of the gods. Ganymede's father, the King of Troy, received compensation from Zeus for his son in the form of fine horses. They would sire an equine lineage to last through the Roman Empire.

Two of Octavia's ready reference books were Thomas Bulfinch's *The Age of the Fable* (1855) and H.J. Rose's *Gods and Heroes of the Greeks* (1957). Her research index card on "Eridani" noted that this southern constellation is named after a celestial river associated with another horse story. When the inexperienced Phaethon drove his father Helios' sun chariot across the sky and lost control of the divine horses, endangering Earth, Zeus was forced to strike him down with a thunderbolt; Octavia typed, paraphrasing Rose, "Helios recontrolled the team. Paethon fell into the imaginary river Eridanus (Eridanos) of Europe (based on the Po and other actual rivers)."[2] By some ancient Greek accounts, Phaethon was another name for the planet Jupiter, another twist of cosmic horsiness.

*   *   *

Along with Mars, the moons of Jupiter were popular sites of imagined extraterrestrial life. Science fictions about Ganymede have been penned by Isaac Asimov, Robert Heinlein, and Philip K. Dick. Today, we can see that Ganymede, covered in ice and rock, is the biggest moon in the entire solar system, topping even the planet Mercury. It has its own magnetic field. NASA's Jet Propulsion Laboratory (JPL), located just north of where Octavia grew

G IS FOR GANYMEDE

up in Pasadena, is currently making plans to explore Ganymede and other icy moons with frozen oceans for potential, future human habitats. In a separate instance of science honoring fiction, on March 5, 2021, NASA-JPL announced that it named its Mars rover touchdown site after Octavia. The scientists describe their mission on the Red Planet as astrobiological, that is, to "search for signs of ancient microbial life."[3] Their rover, which took its first drive from "Octavia E. Butler Landing" on March 4, is aptly named Perseverance. Octavia wrote about Mars from childhood on. In *Parable of the Talents*, which takes place in 2032, slime molds, multicellular organisms, have been discovered on Mars. *(See "O is for Ooloi.")* And though Lauren Oya Olamina does not make it to outer space, her Earthseed prophecy comes true by the end of the novel: the first ships transport humans to Mars to "take root among the stars."[4]

* * *

The first book ten-year-old Octavia bought for herself was about horses. The second was a book of star maps and information about the planets.[5] The character of Silver Star started out as a horse, named for the birthmark on her mother's shoulder. Star, the girl-Martian, like Ganymede, was transported to the heavens

> "Going at the speed of light, 186000 miles per second, or 5825696000000 miles per year it would take about three minutes to reach Mars at its closest point." OEB 593.

to serve at the pleasure of a powerful male. The "Into Infinity" adventures of Flash and Star spanned multiple planets and moons. Octavia wrote most of them in the early 1960s, when newly elected President John F. Kennedy declared that the U.S. would catch up to the Soviet Union and put a man on the moon by the end of the decade. Octavia, following the politicians, scientists, and writers of the era, charted her own versions of life in space. In her notes, whereas Jupiter's inhabitants breathed in carbon dioxide, the people of Pluto, Uranus, and Neptune either "vaporized" or "hibernated" through the winter.[6] The orientalized Venusians had eyes "slanted for their own protection" given the wetness of the planet and the poisonous, smoke-emitting creatures that lived amidst its huge tree swamps.[7]

In one diagram of "Races and Planets" from 1960, Octavia includes Shepherds and Protectors, who inhabit Deep Space, and the "Scattered-originals," or Cla-arks, who are the refugees of the universe. She lists Ganymede as home of "The People."[8] The People do not appear often in her writings, but when they do, they seem to be the keepers of civilization. They are able to identify the mystery man Adam Lynn by the name Doro, or God.[9] Their ruler Cartera invites Earthlings to space, declaring, "Space is open to you. We welcome your trade and your colonies."[10] He assigns his son, Cotera, to protect Earthlings from Martian aggression.

> "Ganymede is a planet of citys. . . . The few trees that do grow there have leaves like leather, and short thin tough trunks that can withstand anything from fire to flood, although Ganymede is not likely to have eather since the only water they get is in the form of snow and hell, and that is so scarce that they are forced to import more. . . .

> The population of the small sattelite is about three billion, stadic. it must be large because of the army, but birth control is inforced . . . . " OEB 1628, c.1960.

Octavia's description of Ganymede as a "planet of citys" with metallic buildings might have been inspired by illustrated pulp science fiction of the 1940s and 1950s.[11] The *Amazing Stories* magazine series published "Magnetic City on Ganymede" in 1942, and "Life on Ganymede" in 1940. Frank R. Paul's blazing cover art (Fig. 7.1) accompanied a short story by Henry Gade, in which Ganymede is populated with dome-shaped, clay dwellings and giant golden feline women who ride lizards. Females are the dominant species, and their enchanting, slanted green eyes, red lips, pointy teeth, and fur make them "as dangerous as a creature both cat and woman should be."[12] These were the kind of alien femmes fatales young Octavia disdained. *(See A is for Alias.)* In the vein of *Devil Girl from Mars* (1954), *Cat-Women of the Moon* (1953) was a black-and-white film that she referenced and mocked. It featured telepathic cat ladies who live in a cave on the moon and plot to colonize Earth. When a human spaceship lands on the moon, the femmes felines realize they can control the mind of the sole woman astronaut to infiltrate the team. It seems that Octavia borrowed the telepathy component for her stories and ditched the rest. *(See "F is for Flash.")*

Octavia loved popular culture, but she also cast a critical eye upon it. Her irreverence is on full display in a mash-up, fan fiction satire where TV and comic book worlds collide with gritty, Los Angeles street life. The sketch begins with President Kennedy walking with Superman and a professor down 77 Sunset Strip

> Scout rockets were made to launch satellites into space. The first launch of the Scout XRM-91 rocket took place on September 21, 1960.

(a reference to a detective show that aired on Friday nights.) They encounter one animal after another: Bugs Bunny pops out from the set of the Gale Storm sitcom to say, "What's up doc?" King Kong and Mighty Joe Young are also taking a stroll. Everyone is repulsed by a drunk woman named Tina whose stench and ugliness drives them away, all the way to outer space. The entire world escapes aboard "Rocket Ship XRM" to go "live with the Cat-Women of the Moon." On the surface Tina is a racist caricature—people think she has escaped from a zoo in Africa or is a long-lost sister of the apes. The final line of the story reads, "They left Tina in a wine house poring it down."[3] She is the abject side of Ganymede the wine-pourer. And yet the disgust shown her by the ambassadors of Americana also signals their callous remove from the poverty and alcoholism that plague the streets of Earth.

No matter how much she daydreamed of escaping to cities in outer space, Octavia was always conscious that our mythologies refract the realities of the most loved and most hated elements of society. Even in assignments submitted for English class, she turned the romance of family tradition on its head. One of her poems, "The Night Before Christmas Gone Beat," rewrites Santa as a holiday gangster-dealer. It makes Run-D.M.C.'s rap classic, "Christmas in Hollis," seem altogether cheery. In Octavia's version, Santa visits a "pad" where the kids are alone because "Ma was out huntin', Pa was doin' time." Santa's chimney entrance announces his lifestyle: "A bundle of beer cans he flung on his back,/ He looked like a tramp just opening his sack." He fills the family's old socks with ashes and dirt and drives off in his eight-cylinder jalopy. Octavia's teacher praised it and wrote the formal, red-lettered note: "The poem has much merit in that it manages hipster language well in a four rhythmic pattern."[14]

Octavia assigned to Ganymede the race of "The People" and envisioned it as a "Planet of cities" at a moment in the early 1960s when sit-ins, boycotts, marches, freedom rides, and the space race were changing the outlook of the people *and* the cities of the country. In 1964, on the eve of the Watts Rebellion and the founding of the Black Panther Party for Self Defense, Pasadena high schoolers joined the cause of civil rights. Sylvia, one of Octavia's schoolmates since junior high, recalled reading in the paper that Martin Luther King, Jr. was coming to Los Angeles. He had last visited Pasadena in 1960, and two years before that, spent a three-day residency with students at Caltech. This time, Sylvia and her friends met him at the airport with a sign that read, "WE LOVE YOU DR. KING." She would see him every time he came to town, and went door-to-door in Pasadena raising money for his cause. "I was a King groupie," she mused.[15]

The occasion of King's trip was his May 31, 1964 address to a crowd of 15,000 people at the L.A. Coliseum. Introduced by his friend Marvin T. Robinson, pastor of Pasadena's Friendship Baptist Church and president of the Western Christian Leadership Conference, Dr. King spoke of his trip to India, belief in non-violent protest, and the caste system in the U.S. that rendered Black people "untouchables." He called for the passage of the Civil Rights bill being debated in Congress and invoked President John Fitzgerald Kennedy and the late NAACP field secretary Medgar Evers, both slain in 1963 amidst their fights to end segregation.

Octavia was in U.S. History class at John Muir High on November 22, 1963, the day JFK was killed. Her story, "La Muerte del Presidente Kennedy," narrates her sense of disbelief as a teacher brings a TV into the classroom and rumors become reality. She scribbled furiously in her big pink notebook, writing partly in Spanish, as she did in her diary when giving voice to her most private experiences.[16] "The girl across from me was crying Kenito was dead—but he couldn't have been. Kenito? Kenny? Yes Kenny was dead."[17] It must have seemed like a parallel universe—the end of one era and the stirrings of new social and environmental movements that would rally around "Power to the People" and "Save the Planet."

Figure 8.1 Detail, horse drawing. OEB 461.
By permission of Octavia E. Butler Enterprises.

CHAPTER 8

H

IS FOR HORSE

Even in the most specialized archive, you never know what you will find. By chance, they lay before me: a set of ten large, colorful plates of horses in varying poses, one per page, marvelously pristine. *(See Horse Appendix.)* The penned outlines of each body were deliberate, as if traced, but not altogether steady; and while the lovingly colored-in browns, reds, blacks, gold, or gray defined each breed by its coat, her attempts to stay in the lines and create shade and texture were utterly aspirational. At age thirteen or so, she was definitely a writer and horse-lover, but not a visual artist. And yet, I was mesmerized. These were the best child's drawings that I'd ever seen (I am not a parent.)

Any crudeness in the artistry dissolves into their overall charm and meticulous composition. Each creature is suspended in blank space. Octavia reserves a place at the top left or right of each plate to inscribe her own captions in neatly scrawled cursive. With a frankness that is California casual and British prim all at once, she tells us which horse breed reminds her of which human character from Charles Dickens' *David Copperfield.* Some of her horse–human assignments are made on gut instinct, as in, "I don't know why this horse, the Tenn[esee] Walking horse, should remind me of Steerfourth but it does." Others embed multiple, concatenated perspectives: "I imagin if David were a horse he would want Dora to look like this."

The adult Octavia E. Butler famously described herself as having a "radio imagination," or "the kind of imagination that hears."[1] The voice that emanates from her handwriting is the most haptic and frolicking of sounds. It delights in colliding worlds across space, time, culture, genre, species. All the drawings bespeak a zany conjectural dialogue between the books of Octavia's background reading, and her irrepressible drive to adapt and recombine the words and images of others into a universe altogether original and distinctly her own. Once I realized she was interpreting Dickens in her drawing captions, I had to re-read *David Copperfield* with an eye for: 1) character development and 2) horses.

* * *

The much beloved *David Copperfield* (1850)—published in installments between May 1849 and November 1850—is not the horsiest of Dickens' novels. For that, one might look at the extended descriptions of horses in *Hard Times* or *The Pickwick Papers*. Of course, as an orphan struggling to fit into boarding school, David is nicknamed "he bites" for his feral ways; and his Aunt Betsey does give him the horse-like name, Trotwood. A solitary only child with a draconian stepfather, David finds solace in reading picaresque novels of male adventure. His library includes *Robinson Crusoe, Tom Jones*, and *The Adventures of Roderick Random*. Like a child-Octavia reading *Fun With Dick and Jane*, he lines up fictional

H IS FOR HORSE

characters with the people he encounters in real life. *(See "D is for Dog.")* He "impersonates" the villains, projecting them onto his merciless stepfather Mr. Murdstone and the man's equally terrifying spinster sister, Miss Murdstone. David survives through making something *else* of his unbearable home life. Bookishly, he makes do by "reading as if for life."[2]

David Copperfield is a story about the writing of one's life as much as it is the story of a boy's growing up. It is an act of remembering and crafting one's trajectory from nothing to something. No wonder that the budding teen writer Octavia E. Butler could relate to a storyteller who raises himself on books. In a 1982 speech titled, "Self-Construction" she wrote about finding "substitute fathers" in the male-authored self-help books she discovered once she was allowed to enter the adult stacks area of the Pasadena Public Library at age fourteen.[3] In junior high, she had been told she was a bad student, backward, unambitious, always daydreaming. But these library book advice men,

> "There was construction to be done—that whatever I became, I would be my own creation." OEB 2456.

J. Lowell Henderson, David Schwartz, or even right-wingers like Napoleon Hill, led with promising titles like: *Think and Grow Rich, Learn—And Like It, The Magic of Thinking Big.* Octavia wasn't bothered by their chauvinism, she simply changed "man" to "human" in the quotes she scotch-taped onto her wall. She said, "These men collectively taught me the value of . . . 'going the extra mile.'"[4] Through her "reading as if for life," Octavia developed herself. She started doing better in school and received encouragement about her writing from high school classmates and teachers. As one person wrote in her senior yearbook, "Estella, good luck with your writing, maybe you'll be great."[5]

* * *

At the time that ten-year-old Estella bought her first horse book she was writing "a long soap opera about a marvelous, magical wild horse."[6] In interviews she mentioned that the purchase was a book about horse breeds. After months of searching for this source and being told I would never find it, it finally materialized: Anna Pistorius' *What Horse Is It?* (1952).[7] A color-illustrated children's book and part of the entertaining *What Is It?* series, it describes the traits of twenty-five different breeds with an identifying key at the back of the book. With a playful didacticism, Pistorius heads each chapter according to a question about the horse to be described, as in, "What horse is famous for his running walk?" or "What horse was Sitting Bull's favorite?."

Of the ten horses Octavia chose to copy, two of them, the upright white Arab and the downward looking brown-and-white Pinto, became the models for Rocket and Star in her earlier "Silver Star" story illustrations. *(See "A is for Alias.")* The Pistorius book confirmed my hunch that Octavia's drawings had been traced. She had been careful to position her paper atop each horizontal page to recreate the book's spatial composition. This sometimes creates the odd effect of a horse positioned way off to one side, or floating high up on the page. It is as if she is making visible her act of excerpting the images and filling in the space with her own captions. She often couldn't make out the details of the legs, so those lines become wobbly or stiff, and we can see her erasure marks as she attempts to draw them freehand. She takes liberty with their tails, but stays mostly faithful to their coat color, making the most of the limited palette of her colored pencils. The bodies are outlined in pencil, sometimes traced over with black pen, and she uses pen to add finishing touches to the manes, tails, eyes, and nostrils.

In each case, she omits the original human riders and any sign of reins or harnesses. She essentially frees the horses from their pictured captivity, even though they retain their trained postures or action poses. They look as though caught between an original children's book scene and this Pasadena girl's reimagined Dickens universe.

To trace, from the Italian and Latin, is "to follow by foot" or "to make out and follow with the eye or mind the course or line of something."[8] There is a journey implied, as one treads a path, traces the steps, superimposes one sheet over another. Though it is always an approximation of an original, the trace aspires to be an exact replica. Especially if you do not trust your own hand to get the size and proportion right, you follow someone else's lead. Or, perhaps, you follow the line to imbibe something of the original. It can be an act of apprenticeship, fandom, or haptic transference. As I overlaid her pages atop the original book, I felt the horses come alive through the contact between her outlines and the contours of creatures she dreamed of knowing (Fig. 8.1). The drawings invite us to follow the course of Octavia's imagination as it spanned the 1850s and the 1950s. Perhaps tracing is also a form of time travel, and in this case, genre travel.

In captioning her beloved Pistorius horses with her impressions of *David Copperfield*, Octavia drew further connections between horses and humans based on their shared appearances and behaviors. We see the swagger of Tom Steerforth in the diagonal prance of a black show horse, the good-natured loopiness of Mr. Micawber in a motley, piebald pony. The robust draft horses, the Belgian and the Shire, capture the hardworking, generous spirits of David's childhood nurse Clara Peggotty and her kinsmen Ham and Mr. Peggotty. She assigned two contemptible characters of the novel, Uriah Heep and Miss Jane Murdstone, to small-sized pseudo-horses.

In Dickens' novel, neither David's childhood sweetheart Emily nor his hapless friend Mr. Micawber can survive the harsh world of British society, and both end up emigrating to the wilds of Australia to chart new lives free of shame. Octavia assigns to them Spanish horses of the American West, a far cry from the prim Southern show horses. The Palomino becomes Emily, a lost soul in search of home. Her motives and voice are largely unrepresented, but her secret affair with Tom Steerforth and decision to run away with him and abandon her family, fiancé, and reputation is the novel's driving undercurrent. Equally distinctive for its golden color, Pistorius' Palomino stands on its hind legs, head raised and mane back, with a smiling golden cowgirl astride (Fig. 8.2). In Dickens' novel, at the lowest point of her life, while living as an outcast in London squalor, Emily begs for compassion from the cruel Rosa Dartle: "on her knees, with her head thrown back, her pale face looking upward, her hands wildly clasped and held out, and her hair streaming about her."[9] Her posture as described by Dickens may be suppliant, but her emotion is pure yellow Palomino (Fig. 8.3).

Under Victorian social codes, the only option for a girl like Emily is to become horse-like, that is, to gain legitimacy by being the married property of Steerforth and take his name. *To come*

H IS FOR HORSE

Figure 8.2 "Palomino," Anna Pistorius, *What Horse Is It?* (Wilcox & Follett, 1952).

Figure 8.3 "And could this not be Emily as she vows not to come back unless she is brought back, a lady." OEB 461.

By permission of Octavia E. Butler Enterprises.

back a lady. Through all her tribulations, including abandonment by Steerforth, she keeps to this resolve even if it means staying away from her beloved family. Though she reunites with her dear uncle Mr. Peggotty, who finds and rescues her, then whisks her off to Australia, she never sees her childhood friend David again. Yet Octavia's golden Palomino stands tall. No doubt the gender of the rider in the Pistorius book, a blonde cowgirl, informed Octavia's choice to assign the horse to a girl-character. Likewise, the rider of the American Saddlebred is a girl clad in blue pantsuit and bowtie; Octavia assigns that horse to Dickens' Dora. The Pistorius riders recall the "horsey heroine" that emerged in Victorian culture, when women were appraised as masterful riders but also the property of men. To be "horsey" was to defy feminine ideals and refuse to be tamed and controlled in mind or body. Just as corsets disciplined the female body, the harnesses and the bearing-reins that held up a horse's head and damaged its windpipes forced it to take a "perpetually lively posture."[10] Octavia's mixed-species characters deserve their own taxonomy, like an "Equus sapien Emily" or a "Homo caballus Micawber." *Equus Emily*, like the other horse renderings, is pictured unharnessed. She embodies a feminine heroism born of Octavia's admiration for a girl who bucks expectations and chases her dreams, propriety be damned.

Octavia's drawing of the Palomino could be mistaken for a yellow Mustang rearing up, which happened to be her high school's mascot. *(See "Y is for Yearbook.")* Like Palominos and wild Paint horses, these equines of the West emblematized Indigenous freedom and resistance to conquest. In 1951, Marguerite Henry wrote of the Mustang's imminent extinction: "A symbol of wildness right out of the past. A symbol of liberty. Of America itself!." When she notes the horse's craving for freedom above all else—above even grass, water, or life—I hear echoes of Sitting Bull's 1882 reported speech on the difference between white people and Native Americans, "The life of white men is slavery. They are prisoners in their towns or farms. The life my people want is freedom."[11] The situation of white working-class heroines is hardly equivalent to Indigenous dispossession, and yet their displacements and despairs attest to the oppressive, patriarchal reach of British and American empires. *Equus Emily's* defiance comes through like a bright yellow clarion call.

Unlike today, in the 1950s and 60s Dickens' novels were shelved in the Children's Department of the public library (Fig. 8.4). I don't know if Octavia read *David Copperfield* in the library or in school, but she clearly knew it backwards and forwards. Some of her high school classmates remember it being assigned reading. In any case, Octavia was not a fan of *A Tale of Two Cities*. As she wrote in a diary entry from April 16, 1963: "Started to read A tale

Figure 8.4 Checkout card pocket, Charles Dickens, *David Copperfield*, c.1960s.

Boys' & Girls' Department, Pasadena Public Library.

of 2 Cities, and fell asleep on it. Good Grief. I hope no one ever looks at my work with the attitude I look at Charles Dickens'. So extrimely detailed and boring."[12]

I never actually read Dickens as a child. My first experience was with *Great Expectations* my first year of college. I remember being more taken with Miss Havisham's dilapidated mansion than with any human character. Her name still comes to mind anytime I see a boarded-up house and yard in disrepair. That house was her signature *thing*, much like Emma Bovary's provincialism. Having spent my teenage years mostly at home, not allowed to have a job, make money, or go to parties, I clearly felt for (fell for?) strong-willed women—married or not—stuck indoors. This took a gothic twist when, around that time, I also discovered the weird, glorious Bette Davis and watched in succession *Hush Hush Sweet Charlotte*, *All About Eve*, and that classic Miss Havisham remake, *What Ever Happened to Baby Jane?*.

My college years long behind me, I still do not have much sympathy for any of the adult men or women of *David Copperfield*. I cringe at the colonial implications of Emily and Micawber's self-banishment to Australia, feel impatient with Emily's shame and Agnes' martyrdom, wait for Dora to die. I root for David even as I cannot stand his post-adolescent scramble up the social ladder of respectability and paternal benevolence. I prefer his tortured scrappy childhood, homoerotic schoolboy attachments, precocious survival skills, and small triumphs over cruel grownups.

So, I also prefer Octavia's pared down captioning of Emily's farewell note to her family as she runs off with Steerforth. *And could this not be Emily as she vows not to come back unless she is brought back, a lady.* In Dickens, Emily's compulsion to leave is buried under mountains of guilt; Octavia deliberately leaves this out and affirms Emily's independence. Turning Emily's words into a horse caption is the closest Octavia comes to quoting directly from the novel (the Dickens' text reads, "When I leave my dear home—my dear home—oh, my dear home!—in the morning—it will be never to come back, unless he brings me back a lady").[13] *Equus Emily* does not exactly talk, but Octavia, as interpreter, tries on the voice of the fallen woman, adopts its cadence, and distills into one line her clear and present audacity. Like the yellow-colored horse placed mid-air on a blank page, these words first appeared to me as an enigmatic fragment. When viewing the drawings, her captions, divorced from their novelistic context, seem to be part of a private dialogue. Nowhere is Dickens or any of his characters cited. Instead, the horse–human comparisons speak directly to us, just as the Victorian novel and mid-twentieth-century horse book spoke to Octavia. (She took two things she loved and decided they belonged together.)

For everything she omits, Octavia fills in just enough to spark our wonder. *What horse is it?* These captions do more than explain or denote the image. They are what Roland Barthes would call "relay-texts" with diegetic value. They complement an image and forward its action, such that text and image are mutually dependent. An 1850s novel about growing up in London meets a 1950s picture book about North American horse breeds. To borrow from Barthes, "the relationship between the two messages is that between two cultures."[14] True to the work of a relay-text, Octavia's captions do not make the horse drawing more natural, they augment its constructedness. As drawings, they have, as Barthes would say, "projective power." Unlike a photograph, a drawing is a coded message; it can never be an exact reproduction or mirror of nature. Where a photograph records, a drawing transforms. The photo says, *this was so*, and a drawing says, *it's me*.[15] These horse drawings say, "it's me, Octavia E. Butler, and I contain multitudes."

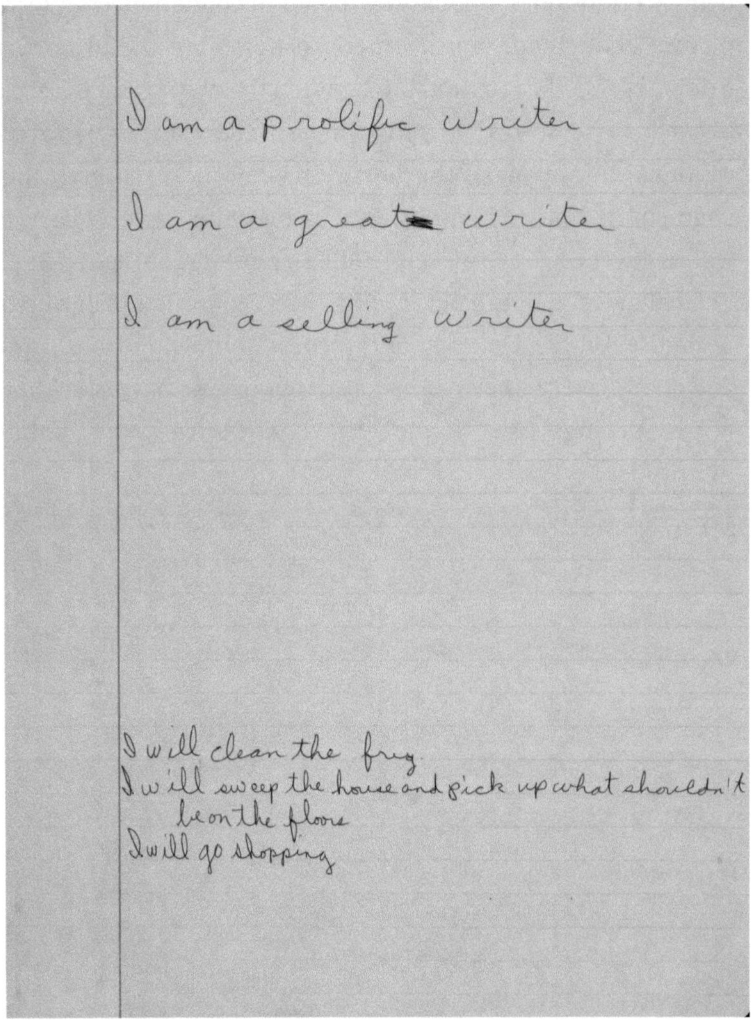

Figure 9.1 Writing mantra, *c.*1980. OEB 1517.
By permission of Octavia E. Butler Enterprises.

CHAPTER 9

I

IS FOR "I AM"

Octavia's adult "I am" mantras are small, declarative list poems that connect being with doing. Each iteration of "I am" offers an existential reassurance of her life's calling. She *is* a writer. On one lined sheet of notebook paper (Fig. 9.1), the earnest, left-tilting I's and coltish cursive together set a spell of self-determination. The effect is not unlike her teenage hypnosis exercises. I read this as a love-letter to herself. She affirms her writing dreams but inserts a physical distance between those aspirations (above) and the material obstacles that must be faced along the way. The three mundane "I will" tasks (below) seem far removed from the lofty goals of being prolific, great, bestselling. Yet everyday actions sustain a life. Sometimes housework enables mind work. For Octavia, cleaning the fridge, sweeping the floors, and doing the shopping might have felt insurmountable some days, and kept her grounded on others.[1] Her mother was a maid who cleaned up after others. She must do this for herself.

OCTAVIA E. BUTLER

Writing was Octavia's life and her love, but above all she thought of herself as a storyteller for the people. In a different "I am" list poem she wrote:

> I am
> the best possible Storyteller
> to the greatest possible
> number of people.[2]

Yet another poem-affirmation that begins, "I am a Bestselling Writer," outlines her aims for writing success: owning a home of her own (in Santa Monica), providing her mother excellent healthcare, establishing a $20 million scholarship fund "for Striving Black people."[3] For Octavia, self-help was tied to helping the community. Like her character Lauren Olamina, a spiritual leader who preaches the principles of Earthseed, she enacts "the political potential of New Age literature."[4] Her contemporary Audre Lorde even more directly invoked this spirit of self-care as survival of the collective. As a Black lesbian battling cancer in a white man's world, Lorde found herself fighting not only for her own life but also for the physical and political health of others around the world: "*Caring for myself is not self-indulgence, it is self-preservation, and that is an act of political warfare.*"[5]

As Octavia was fond of concluding, "So Be It! See To It!"[6]

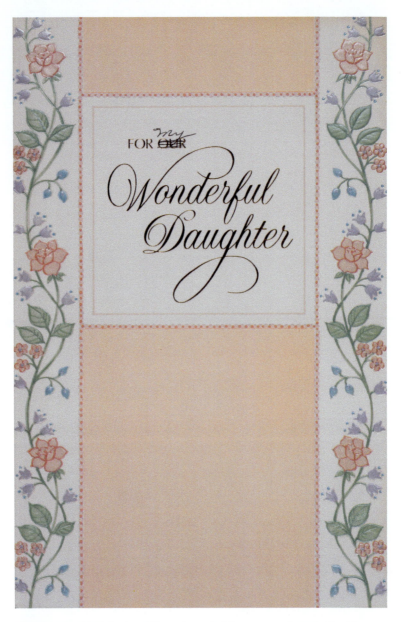

Figure 10.1 Birthday card from Octavia Margaret to Octavia Estelle. OEB 4594.
By permission of Octavia E. Butler Enterprises.

CHAPTER 10

J

IS FOR JUNIE

June is the bloomiest month, bestowing the birthdays of both Octavia and her mother, whose name she shared. Octavia Margaret was born on June 5, 1910, and Octavia Estelle, on June 22, 1947. Being someone's namesake is a mixed blessing. You have a lifelong bond, which comes with suffering the perpetual unease of coming *after*. At school, Octavia often went by Estella. At home, with her mother, she was nicknamed "Junie," short for junior. "Love, Junie," she signed the birthday cards she exchanged with her mother every year, come June. Her mother loved flowers, and luckily flowers were trademark Hallmark. Over the decades, she sent her mother cards and letters from the writing-related travels that took her away from home: Pittsburgh, where she attended her first Clarion workshop, and Washington, D.C. while researching her novel, *Kindred*. In preparation for her trip to Peru in 1985, Octavia Jr. made a packet of papers and wrote a letter to her mother. Dated June 21, it explained her living will, power of attorney, and insurance policies in case anything were to happen to her. She signed off, "See you when I get home, Love, Junie."[1]

Mother and daughter regularly enclosed money in their correspondences and wished that it could be more. "Dear Mama, Here's the money I promised you. Put this into your Home Savings account so that you will be able to cash your Social Security checks without trouble," Octavia wrote. In anticipation of being paid for her new book trilogy, *Xenogenesis*, she hoped she could send more funds next time so that her mother could treat herself to an outing. "Times are getting better! Love, Junie."[2]

I used to consider greeting cards generic and impersonal, but I now see them as artifacts of all that cannot be put into words. When Mrs. Butler crosses out the "our" of "For Our Wonderful Daughter" and writes in "My," we can glimpse in those two letters the many sacrifices she made as a working, single parent with a fifth-grade education (Fig. 10.1).[3] She had raised a daughter who made it through the storm of adolescence to become a renowned writer. From the start she saw that Junie loved to read and write. When cleaning houses, she would bring home discarded books from her employers. She bought Octavia Jr. her first typewriter at age twelve. *(See "Q is for QWERTY.")* Her namesake could enjoy so much that she never had.

All this reminds me of my own mother, who still sends me cards with pre-printed, commercialized messages that might make up for her imperfect English. She spent her life wishing she could have gone to college. Her cards convey the sentiments of an immigrant mother who lives vicariously through her girl-child's successes. Like Mrs. Butler, my mother is a pious churchgoer. Full of worries, love, pride, respectability, and regrets, the religious mother always sends her prayers, believing that faith is the most she can hope for, the most she can give.

J IS FOR JUNIE

Octavia's wish to provide for her mother was second only to her desire to be a successful writer, and as a teenager, this kept her going when life felt most unbearable. Senior year of high school, she confessed in her journal, "I'm 17 now. I have an overpowering need to be just like everybody else—and a driving need to be as different as possible. Most of the time. I enjoy living, but I wouldn't really mind death. I may never get the chance to do all the things I want to do—to sit my mother down in her own house before she is too old and tired to enjoy it."[4] Growing up together, she and her mother understood something of each other's loneliness. *(See "M is for Mother.")* Still, it was Octavia Sr.'s overbearing presence that teenage Octavia needed to escape to find her voice. She even used the idea of the communication gulf between parent and child to frame her early fiction about intelligent girls who lacked the power of speech.

* * *

The character of a mute girl named June appears in at least two "Silver Star" stories. In "Parts Unknown" June is called by her mother to do the dishes. She daydreams, looking out the window and wishes she could speak:

> I wish I were someone else, I thought, or maby
> even something else. A horse maby I always liked horses ....
> Silver yes that was a good name. Silver Star[5]

By imagining the animal, the girl envisions an alternate existence for herself, free of her disability, indeed of men and romance altogether. In this world she chooses a horse body and name for herself. *(See "A is for Alias.")* The mental drafting of the story is an act of survival by the mute daydreamer. Only she has access to this private place.

Octavia's early equus-science fiction usually featured the death of the mother. In one of her "Silver Star" tales, written around 1958, the foal loses her mother to drowning. The entire "herd" flees from men with "fire sticks" and is forced to jump across a cliff. Star's mother "was dashed to peaces on the rocks. At that time I did not know she was dead. If I had known I would not have understood."[6] Like the Stag from *Bambi*, the lead horse comforts Star and urges her to "learn to walk alone." *(See "B is for Bambi.")* After his demise, the new leader, a young stallion named Reese, rescues Star and the others from an evil ranch horse named Gray Demon. The villain vanquished, Reese joins Star, and she realizes his companionship can make up for the loss of her mother: "I was with Reese and I was happy."[7]

Just when you think it's over, skip a line and another voice begins to narrate: "Oh, if I only could be happy. If only I could talk." We learn that the entire horse episode has been concocted by a lonely "deaf-mute" girl named June, whose brother interrupts her daydreaming and calls her to do the dishes. In

> "Shyness is shit . . . It's torment, and it's shit." OEB 1278.

her daily life, June suffers ridicule and beatings by her schoolmates: "being the only mute in school. (We lived in a small town where there were no special schools)." Hope arrives in the form of Rosemary, a new girl who befriends her and happens to know sign language. Rosemary's dead sister, uncannily also named

June, was a "deaf-mute" as well. This June died after being bullied and hit to death by their brother. The story trails off just as Rosemary invites June (the narrator) over to her house.

This is no typical play date. Even Octavia's strictly human realm is a Hitchcockian one of doppelgänger Junes (three, if we count Octavia/Junie.) June #1 has invented the fairytale ending of Reese and Silver Star to escape the misery of her everyday life. The violence, like the story of June #2's murder, has a way of popping up mid-story and catching us unawares. Able-bodied horses (who long for love and companionship) are avatars for disabled humans (who long for love and companionship) in a society unforgiving of difference.

Some things can't be spoken aloud. One unsent letter Octavia wrote her mother from the Clarion workshop in 1970 echoes mute June's battle for daily survival in its longing for a confidante. She talks about being the only Black person in residence, her loneliness, and her writer's block and fear of failure, especially knowing that her mother and two other friends paid her way.[8]

> "It would be nice to win once in awhile instead of just surviving. Ants survive . . . . Love, Junnie." 1970, OEB 3825.

Between the ages of ten and twelve Octavia fantasized about traveling to the locales of the used *National Geographic* magazines her mother brought home. She describes "living impossible, but interesting lives—magical lives in which I could fly like Superman, communicate with animals, control people's minds. I became a magical horse on an island of horses. My horse friends and I made fools of the men who came to catch us."[9] We usually take animals to be mute. They only talk in fables or animated form. *(See "D is for Dog.")* Yet Octavia also repeatedly depicted *human* muteness, as if to overturn our assumptions about species distinctions. The "Mutes" of her Patternist series are meant to be "neither animals nor slaves."[10] They are intelligent beings, primitive humans, and the evolutionary predecessors of the telepathic Psi people. They can speak out loud, but not with their minds. A society determines what counts as disability and hierarchizes its world accordingly.

What does it mean to speak for the voiceless? At age seventeen Octavia wrote a short six-line poem of dialogue fragments from the perspective of a "Deaf-Mute." On the same page is another poem written in biting, William Blake fashion, called "Kloetry": "I hate you because you are a Negro,/ But please don't take it so personally./ If there were no Negroes,/ I'd just have to find/ Someone else to hate."[11] The contrast between the hesitant mute and this ranting Klansman is striking. These are experiments in perspective that dare to occupy wildly divergent mindsets. In proximity to hate, muteness becomes an embodied state of trauma and a form of silent protest.

I am reminded of Maya Angelou's description of the two times in her life when she stopped speaking: what she calls her "mutism" first occurred after she was raped as a child. She felt responsible for the death of her rapist, and she only started speaking years afterward, when she was told by an encouraging teacher that poetry can only be fully appreciated if said out loud. The second time she went mute was when Martin Luther King, Jr. was murdered. In 1968, April was the cruelest month, silencing the voice of a movement. On April 5, 1968, the day after MLK was

J IS FOR JUNIE

killed, Octavia wrote to herself, "As with Kenito [Kennedy], it is now Martin Luther King—Marty .... The man of peace is dead. Again. In this world what chance does such a man have."[12]

Octavia wrote about alternate universes where the downtrodden could find kinships beyond their human family ties. Motherless, mute children were symptoms of a world off-kilter.

> "Writing or reading science fiction can make you think not only of the far-off stars, but of problems and solutions right here on Earth." OEB 2711.

They also generated feminine visions of freedom from the shackles of tradition. Octavia claims to have put away her horse stories at age twelve. Yet it is clear that the speech-defying, telepathic worlds of her science fiction drew on the imaginings of liberated horses and girls named June and Junie.

Figure 11.1 "The Cotton Tree, Freetown, Sierra Leone, 12/22/2011."
Courtesy of artist: Daniel Tucker. daniel@pippinhedge.com

CHAPTER 11

K

IS FOR KAPOK

The Kapok was one of many Amazon trees that Octavia indexed. She was interested in how it grew and what it provided for people looking to survive. On her handwritten index card, Octavia cited the *WBED* and *Science News Letter* on the use of kapok bark for twine manufacture, and seeds for oil and the production of silken, woolly fiber. Like the aliens she invented, the tree seems to combine the properties of plant and animal. Sheep-like, it has produced for millennia one of the world's lightest natural fibers, a silky cotton often called "vegetable wool." Buoyant and immune to vermin, kapok, she noted, is perfect stuffing for mattresses and pillows, as well as upholstery and life jackets.[1] It keeps things afloat.

Every part of the kapok has a medicinal use. The tree is an antibiotic, just as it is an aphrodisiac. It tends to our bodies. In the era of climate change, Octavia was interested in bio-power of the sort that could feed, fuel, and heal the planet. One of her index cards cited the article, "Where Would We Be Without Algae?"[2] Historically, the trees of the Americas were considered marvels to the Europeans who looked abroad for the wood to build their slave ships and the dyes to color their uniforms. The Guaiac tree's *lignum vitae*, or "wood of life," was used to treat syphilis and yaws. Along with the magnetic compass and printing press (and the entire continent of America!) the Guaiac was included as one of the top nine "inventions" of modern times in Jan van der Straet's *Nova Reperta*, published around 1600. Of course, Europeans brought things as well as found them. Goats destroyed island ecosystems; plants colonized native flora. "Portmanteau biota" is what the historian Alfred Crosby called the organisms that white men brought with them to the New World. The European human could only survive and conquer Indigenous lands and peoples due to a "team effort by organisms that had evolved in conflict and cooperation over a long time."[3]

As a kid I learned the word "portmanteau" from Lewis Carroll. Humpty Dumpty explained to Alice, "You see it's like a portmanteau, there are two meanings packed up into one word." Slithy combines lithe and slimy. *Equus sapien merges horse with human. (See "H is for Horse.")* I only later learned that, in French, portmanteau refers to a large suitcase with two compartments. Language is like luggage. Octavia appreciated the stories that words carry, across all their travels.

As she noted on her index card, the kapok has two names. The most common one, kapok, is a Malay word for the cotton of the tree's seed. Indonesia is famous for producing the fiber. And yet the tree originated in the South American tropics, where it is known as the ceiba, from the Arawak for canoe. (Its scientific classification is *Ceiba pentandra*.) Caribs carved dugout canoes from its trunk, but they would not have been the ones to spread it to other continents. Some say its buoyant seed pods could have floated—like tiny, masterless ships—across the Atlantic to bring the tree to Africa. Until May 2023, a massive ceiba "Cotton Tree" (*Ceiba pentandra*) stood in the heart of Freetown, Sierra Leone (Fig. 11.1). It had been there since at least 1787. Around that time, freed African Americans, former slaves, rested and prayed under it upon their arrival to this new, promised land. The tree survived the violence of twentieth-century civil war; bystanders protected it when someone tried to chop its buttresses to use for firewood. "At times the tree [was] filled with huge flocks of thousands of bats."[4]

Trees are sacred to the Earthseed community of Acorn in Butler's *Parable* novels. As Lauren explains, they "commemorated our dead and provided us with much protein, but also they helped hold the hillside near our cabins in place."[5] In *Dawn*, the Oankali ship structure is tree-like, and Lilith plants herself in the Amazon simulation room amidst the buttressed roots of the giant kapok. *(See Introduction.)* Depending on how you see it, the kapok is:

1.

a Pharmacy, of renewable medicines.

2.

a Monster, that can grow well over 200 feet tall and tower above the forest canopy. It has spikes up and down its trunk and huge, gothic buttresses at its base.

3.

a Bridge, that connected the underworld to the human world and the heavens above, according to the ancient Mayas.

4.

a House, for in its grooves and branches reside frogs, birds, other species.

5.

a Monument, to hard-won freedom.

Figure 12.1 Mowgli and wolf, "The Law of the Jungle" Letter J, flipped. Illustration by John Lockwood Kipling, from Rudyard Kipling, *The Two Jungle Books* (1895), 113.

Courtesy of the David Alan Richards Collection of Rudyard Kipling, Beinecke Rare Book and Manuscript Library, Yale University.

CHAPTER 12

L

IS FOR LION GIRL

"Ar-r-r The hunting call of the great lion Alka," the story begins. This is not, however, a story about a lion king. When the great Alka kidnaps a human baby girl for his cubs to kill, his mate, Nocke, refuses to take the life of an infant. She banishes him from their home instead and chooses to raise her three cubs and this girl child on her own. Like Octavia Sr., Nocke is a single parent. She names the "Lion girl" Aricka, a deliberately misspelled, lion-y version of Erica that begins with a roar. Aricka's life follows the classic tales of feral children raised as animals in the wilderness. Many are wolf kids turned heroes. The twins Romulus and Remus go on to found an empire. Across the ages, others like Mowgli or Princess Mononoke defend the forest worlds of their upbringing against Men. It is likely that Estella adapted and lion-ized the colonialist Rudyard Kipling's *Jungle Book* stories about the Indian boy Mowgli, a "man-cub" raised by wolves (Fig. 12.1). The opening pages of "Mowgli's Brothers," for instance, features Akela the Lone Wolf and the rival tiger Shere Khan, who roars, "Aaarh!."[1]

To blend in and protect herself, Estella's girl-cub Aricka wears a leopardess skin and carries a knife. When she talks to the other

> "Aricka lived like a lion she was sure she was a lion . . ." OEB 3172.

animals, including a python, they address each other as "brother" and "sister." In this forest, the animals are comrades, and man is the common enemy. *(See "B is for Bambi.")* The narrator refers to a "man pride (village)" and does us the courtesy of translating village into English. Estella experiments with animal perspective. At eight years old, Aricka is asked to leave the lion den and strike out on her own. She belongs to no tribe. When she encounters men on a "sarfi" (safari) she notes they make "funny nosies with there [sic] mouths." Aricka speaks in the language she knows, "with a perfict imation of a lion's roar." The off-spelling and general lack of punctuation gives the effect of a young writer's imagination on the loose. The story ends mid-sentence with the Lion Girl's capture by two Englishmen and a safari guide. It might be unfinished; just as likely, it is designed as a cliff hanger.

Growing up mixed species, a lion girl becomes extra sensitive to her environment. More than physical dexterity, she gains perspective on the ways of men. A lion girl's state of bewilderment can be empowering. From the place of captivity, the animal, or the mute, deaf, or Martian girl sees what is wrong with the world.

Composed years before teenaged Estella began sending out her stories to literary agencies (Figs. 1.2 and 1.3), "Lion Girl" is written in the same notebook as "Torey" *(See "D is for Dog")* and is sandwiched between two pages on "Horses." First comes a horse vocabulary page (mare, filly, stallion, colt, yearling, nippers,

L IS FOR LION GIRL

mane, muzzle.) The page after "Lion Girl" lists in fledgling cursive barnyard animals (horses, cows, chickens, turkeys, rabbit, guinea pig, pigeons, birds, ducks, dogs, cats, hay barn, brood mare barn). It is as though the practice of taxonomy unleashes a category crisis, and gives birth to a hybrid, wild thing. Duck, duck, duck, *lion*. Ar-r-r-r-r-.

Figure 13.1 Gravestone of Octavia Margaret Butler.
Photo credit: Wanda Poston.

Figure 13.2 Gravestone of Octavia Estelle Butler.
Photo credit: Author.

CHAPTER 13

M

IS FOR MOTHER

Octavia Margaret Guy Butler sat down to write about growing up in rural Louisiana. She titled her hand-scrawled autobiography, "A Letter to My daughter." Her bookish California child should know something of the family's southern roots. How could she explain what her life was like before she came to Los Angeles? Her arrival on February 1, 1930 was itself a lifetime ago.[1] Perhaps the slim half-sheets of office stationery she had at her disposal made it easier to truncate the history of hardships.

She began, "When I was a little girl—My parents was very poor. My mom worked night and day Ther was no school for Blacks." With no electricity at home, they kept warm by the fireplace and used oil lamps for light. They had no TV or radio, and without a horse or buggy, walked for miles to get to church. Often she and her siblings went without shoes. She was the oldest girl. Unlike her older brother George, she had only a few, precious years of schooling before she was pulled from school to work, and she had been working ever since.[2] Still, she praised the Lord that she had a healthy and happy childhood, even without any toys or "all the other things."[3]

Her mother, Edna Estelle Hayward Guy, went first to California, and gradually brought all the children over. In L.A. in the 1930s it was a feat to find a landlord willing to rent to "colored folks," especially a family with seven children in tow. Mrs. Guy was part of a Depression-era exodus from the intolerably racist conditions in the South. By the early 1940s, 20 percent of the African American population of New Orleans had left seeking a better life in the West.[4] Like Mrs. Guy, Octavia Margaret worked cleaning houses, was a devout Baptist, and raised her child the best she could.[5] Mrs. Guy died on October 21, 1957, and she was missed every day since.[6] Octavia Margaret had come so far since Louisiana. And yet she sometimes couldn't afford to buy school shoes for her "Junnie" or dress shoes for herself. In those moments, they had to skip Sunday church service. Mrs. Butler's diary entries from 1962 are filled with the tallies of unpaid bills and her prayers for help from God.[7]

Octavia Junior, or Junie, remembers being four years old when she tore one of the soles of her only pair of shoes. Unable to play outside, she sat on the porch with bare feet, bored and feeling sorry for herself until her imagination came to her rescue.

> It occurred to me that if I could fly, I wouldn't have to worry about shoes. I began sprouting a pair of imaginary wings, began seeing myself soaring and driving and driving my well-shod cousins crazy with envy. . . . As years passed, I traded my wings in for a black Stallion, a tribe of Martians, other things. And eventually, I began to write down the products of my dazes.[8]

Later, fifteen-year-old Junie wished she could help pay off her mother's debts, especially since Octavia Margaret took out loans to help her with literary publishing fees. She wrote on

> "I never repaided her. I will though, and several times over, my word!" OEB 3111.

April 20, 1963, "Dear Diary. We went to L.A. today. Mama wants to borrow some money. I want her to wait, because I think I can start bringing home the bacon, but the debt she's in is ruining her peace of mind. She'll do it anyway."[9] Throughout their lives, both Octavias dreamed of providing a house for the other. Their closeness was tender, fierce, and undeniable.

And yet young Octavia Estelle decided early on that she could not abide by her mother's religiosity. She saw the dangers of blind belief in God's word. She grew ever more critical of her mother's unthinking adherence to authority for tradition's sake. Her realization that "Men need gods" would become the basis for her *Parable* novels.[10] At age sixteen she determined she had a faith of her own. While watching the TV evangelist George Vandeman on his hit show, *It Is Written*, she took offense at the biblical idea that animals should be killed as symbols of Christ.[11]

Despite her disagreements with orthodox Christianity, teen Octavia still enjoyed the communal feeling of church services. In her diary entry of April 14, 1963, she wrote about the fullness of the congregation on Easter Sunday. Her heart lifted with the choir's singing, and she approved of Reverend Byrd's sermon. Luckily, her view was unobstructed, since "The woman in front of me had a small hat."[12] An adolescent diarist prides herself in the details she learns to notice from the seat of a pew while keeping the fidgeting at bay.

I grew up Catholic. My atheist father refused to attend mass, but that didn't stop my mother from dragging my brothers and me to church while we were young enough to comply. Because we inevitably arrived late, we usually sat near the back of the church with all the other single-parent families. While she recited all the prayers in Chinese, I faked my way through the Apostle's Creed and patted myself on the back when I correctly anticipated when it was time to kneel, stand, or sit. It baffled me that some of the most rebellious kids from school showed up every Sunday and sat meekly up front with their respectable mothers and fathers. I also marveled at the daring of all the white people who drank directly from the shared wine goblet; my mother was more concerned about germs than missing out on the blood of Christ, even if it was just grape juice. Church did not provide us with community, it only reminded me how little we fit in, no matter how hard my mother tried.

Even for the devout, churchgoing can often be a vexed experience of belonging and alienation. In the 1950s era of racial segregation, Octavia and her peers drew comfort from their Black church communities despite many of the prohibitions on teenage behavior. Baptists were not the only strict ones. Octavia's schoolmate Sylvia grew up in the Black Seventh-day Adventist Church of Pasadena on Sunset and Pepper.[13] When her mother arrived from Canada around 1943, she was ousted from the church for wearing jewelry, namely her wedding ring. It took a new minister to allow her back in. Sylvia recalls "being in a community that loved me," even though that same church forbade dancing, drinking, smoking, card playing, wearing jewelry or makeup, and going to movies. Homosexuality was way out of the question. Back then, the world was full of "closeted folk pretending they were heterosexual and living lives of quiet desperation," and "men telling us how to live, what to think,

M IS FOR MOTHER

what to wear, what to eat."[14] The disciplining was such that her minister would assign a deacon to monitor each of Pasadena's four movie theaters on Saturday nights, and "if they dare[d] to attend a movie it would be reported."[15]

In writing *Parable of the Sower*, Octavia channeled into the character of the young female preacher Lauren Olamina all the liberatory unorthodoxy that had no place in 1950s Pasadena. The book Olamina is composing in 2024(!), *Earthseed: The Books of the Living*, will become a bestseller one day. Spread throughout the novel in the form of *Earthseed* quotations are theological tenets like, "We do not worship God. We perceive and attend God," or "We shape God . . . . And God is Change."[16] As Jayna Brown so beautifully puts it, "In Olamina we can trace the history of black women itinerant preachers and of Harriet Tubman; in the movement of Olamina and her people north and, ultimately, to the stars, we can see the history of escape from slavery and migration and the tropes of flight and fugitivity."[17] Unfortunately, sometimes the most extraordinary women leaders are the least available mothers to their own children. In *Parable of the Talents*, Olamina's long-lost daughter Larkin comes to know her mother more through her writings and service to the rest of the world than from their direct relationship. Octavia dedicated this novel, published in 1998, to her aunts Irma Harris and Hazel Ruth Walker and to the memory of her own mother, Octavia Margaret Butler. In an interview included at the back of the 2000 edition, Octavia describes the impact of Mrs. Butler's death on the writing of the novel. Unlike the fraught dynamic between Olamina and Larkin, she and her mother "had had quite a good relationship." That her passing breathed life into a story of mother–daughter estrangement only underscores Mrs. Butler's undying support of

Octavia's writerly pursuits. As she put it, "it [her death] was my mother's last gift to me."[18]

* * *

A mother's sacrifices can be the hardest gift for a daughter to bear. When she lives for your success and you are meant to live out all her unfulfilled dreams, maternal love can feel life-inhibiting. At age thirty-one, Octavia Estelle contemplated having children, but she concluded that even parenthood was no guarantee of

> "I long to love someone. I fear to be completely alone. My mother will die and I will be completely alone." OEB 3216.

feeling less alone. She accepted that no one would ever love her like her mother. She also resented the "emotional ammunition" that came with such devotion.[19] She wrote these words on January 2, 1978. Two months later, on March 3, she revisited the question of her relationship to her mother. She could trace her own anxieties to her mother's fear-based mentality and inability to commit to any single path. Octavia Margaret would flit from one get-rich scheme to another but never see a project through. It was "fear and intellectual laziness," stemming from her reliance on God's grace, Octavia thought, that prevented her mother from helping herself. She refused to inherit this self-victimization. *(See "I is for I am.")* "I am not my mother. I need not repeat the style of her life. She is of a different era, a different world. I divorce her. I reject her way."[20]

Divorcing one's mother takes time. The wounds of patriarchy are not so easily healed. For Octavia the process began when she was an adolescent. She wrote "Evolution" when she was fifteen

M IS FOR MOTHER

and had five friends read it over.[21] In a war-ravaged world, starving people turn to cannibalism to survive. A mother hides her mutant child, Adam, from the intolerant masses, as he grows wings and a unicorn horn. At age five he has the maturity of an adult. Flying home one day he witnesses his mother being beaten to death by five ravenous men. He cannot save her in time. He wonders at his indifference toward her death, even as he appreciates her efforts to usher in the new, posthuman race that he will lead.[22]

In another story titled "Negroid," an eighteen-year-old Octavia tells of superhuman children who experience only one year of childhood before they become advanced intelligent beings with telepathic powers. When a mother leaves her three kids alone at home, they experiment with their powers, and two siblings inadvertently conjure a blizzard in Los Angeles. Their mother is back home within two minutes of the blizzard. She knows exactly what her children are capable of. "It was then that Mother stopped being our mother and became our teacher. The simply carefree life of a child was over for us then."[23] In these stories of precocious alien children who outgrow their mothers, Octavia embraced her difference and individuality. She owed everything to her mother, the woman who scolded her for being "hardheaded and stubborn," and also assured her she would one day discover her own unique gifts.[24] Octavia took care of her mother up to her death in 1996, just as her mother had done for her grandmother. Along the way Junie continually carved out the space to be her own person.

* * *

On a scorching hot summer day, I drove onto the grounds of Mountain View Cemetery in Altadena, California. I had come to pay homage to Octavia E. Butler. With the help of Denny, the affable groundskeeper, I found her grave, a clean gray stone with a palm tree, beach, and sunset template. Etched into the sky were a few lines from her novel, *Parable of the Sower:* "*Octavia Estelle Butler, 1947–2006. All that you touch, you change. All that you change, Changes you. The only lasting truth is Change. God is Change.*" (Fig. 13.2). Fresh sunflowers had been left recently. It felt crass, even sacrilegious, to have my picture taken next to the tombstone. But when the groundskeeper offered, I knelt down and posed. I stared at the stone slab, hoping to hear something. I didn't know what to do next. I remembered that her mother was also buried in this place, and Denny and I set out to find her.

We left the car and walked across the drought-yellowed grass. The San Gabriel Mountains jutted up into the skyline just beyond. Octavia Senior was hard to find, and nowhere nearby. The online locator app told us the section, lot, and grave number, but we still had to hunt, head down, grave by grave. We were joined by Wanda, the resident expert and unofficial archivist of the cemetery. She knew most everyone's whereabouts. When we three found her, it was Octavia's voice that echoed forth from the overgrown weeds and the letters barely readable due to the dust and glare of the afternoon sun: "Beloved Mother, Octavia Margaret Butler, 1914–1996, God is Love" (Fig. 13.1). Wanda whipped out her broom and pumice stone. She swept and polished. With her

> Octavia chose *God Is Love* for her mother's gravestone, whereas her own stone reads, *God is Change.*

spray bottle she wetted the mottled, red-and-black granite to make it glisten and readable. Together we pulled back the weeds and tended to the gravesite. Here lay Octavia Senior, all the way across the cemetery, lovingly interred but surrounded by strangers—and at a good enough distance from her daughter. Wanda gave me a bottle of water and drove me over to her family's plots. She shared stories of her dear deceased father and explained how she first started coming to visit him and their relatives and then kept coming back to take care of other, neglected gravesites. She knew how the cemetery was divided into different enclaves by class, race, and ethnicity. The African Americans, Armenians, Jews, Japanese, and Chinese each had their own historic areas. We spent the afternoon together chatting and wandering about in silence, stumbling upon the plots of strangers with familiar sounding names—a community of husbands and wives, children, grandparents, daughters and mothers.

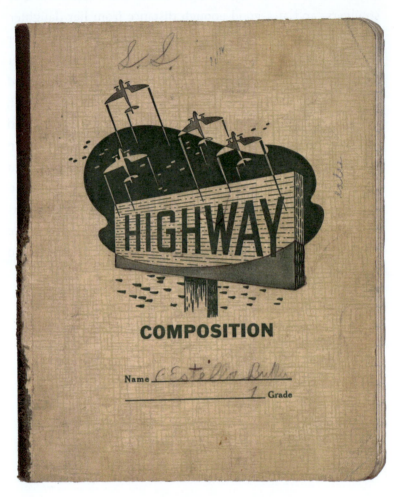

Figure 14.1 Seventh-grade notebook, 1960. OEB 323.
By permission of Octavia E. Butler Enterprises.

CHAPTER 14

N

IS FOR NOTEBOOK

"I carry a notebook everywhere. . . . I especially collect people—those who stand out in some way, the kind I'm likely to remember with or without notes because of the strong impression they make on me." (1981) OEB 322.

"I hid out in a shabby hand me-down brown three-ring binder. I made myself a universe in it. There I was a magic horse, a Martian, a telepath. There I was anywhere but here, any time but now, with any people but these . . ." (c.1995) OEB 1278.

"People tended to expect me to act my size rather than my age. I reacted by hiding in my room with Felix Salten, Robert A. Heinlein, Edgar Rice Burroughs, Superman, and my notebook."
(c. 1970-1990) OEB 2717.

The archive is vast and her notebooks, legion. Organized by size or date, they contain too many subjects to catalogue. One can't possibly read them all, but you see her mind at work through even a partial viewing. In her notebooks (Fig. 14.1) she made word lists, jotted call numbers, transcribed song lyrics, practiced spelling, developed characters, scribbled stories, tried out names, conducted surveys, doodled stars, pondered facts, confessed her fears, drew conclusions, lost herself, found herself.

"Yes Kenny and the Governor had been shot in Dallas Texas . . . . I swore to myself and grabbed my big pink notebook . . . ."
(Nov. 22, 1963) OEB 1241.

[At age ten] "She was pressing my hair. I was sitting bent over someone's cast-off note-book, writing a story." [Mother said] "everybody has something they can do better than they can do anything else. All they have to do is find out what it is." (c. 1995) OEB 1278.

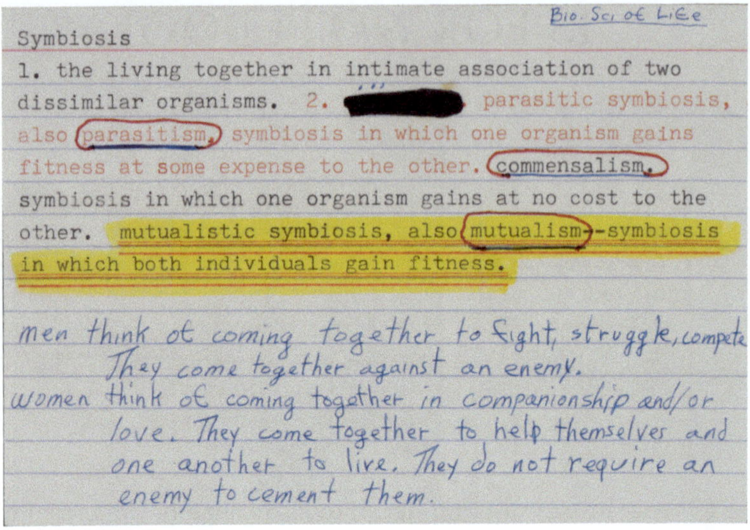

> Bio. Sci of Life
>
> Symbiosis
> 1. the living together in intimate association of two dissimilar organisms. 2. ▮▮▮▮ parasitic symbiosis, also *parasitism,* symbiosis in which one organism gains fitness at some expense to the other. *commensalism,* symbiosis in which one organism gains at no cost to the other. mutualistic symbiosis, also *mutualism*-symbiosis in which both individuals gain fitness.
>
> men think of coming together to fight, struggle, compete. They come together against an enemy.
> women think of coming together in companionship and/or love. They come together to help themselves and one another to live. They do not require an enemy to cement them.

Figure 15.1 Index card on symbiosis, OEB Box 161.

By permission of Octavia E. Butler Enterprises.

CHAPTER 15

O

IS FOR OOLOI

Even the word ooloi oozes sex. There are three O's. They sandwich an "l" and slide into an "i". In the alien Oankali universe, it takes three parties to procreate: male, female, and ooloi. Usually the third-sex partner mates with its brother and sister. It forges the reproductive bond. With its tentacled sensory arms it can plug into a body and make chemical changes—switch on pleasure, switch off pain, heal wounds, activate new sensations and abilities. *(See "S is for Sexy.")*

In *Dawn*, the first book of Octavia's Xenogenesis trilogy, humans enter the scene. The Oankali need them to diversify the gene pool and evolve their species. Each male–female human pair is assigned an ooloi to mate with. Against her will, Lilith grows to love her ooloi, Nikanj, even as she resents her chemical

"Ooloi is another word for catalyst." OEB 3227.

dependency on it. It has "fixed" her so that she cannot be sexually intimate with anyone else on her own. The ooloi connect *and* divide people. They render the couple form obsolete. In her notes, Octavia described them as the ultimate arbitrators, "neither male nor female, but something in between."[1]

Octavia was fascinated by group dynamics. Having been bullied as a child, she knew firsthand the human predilections for cruelty, hierarchy, fixity. The Oankali, instead, would be ever-evolving, genetic nomads with superior intelligence. They would challenge the sanctity of individualism. She would make her readers uncomfortable when the humans are stripped of control over their own minds and bodies. A genetically modified Lilith has no choice but to merge with an Oankali family and take on a compound identity. Her new name, impossibly long, still contains a trace of her old self: *Dhokaaltediinjdahyalilith eka Kahguyaht aj Dinso*. The name is an accumulation of one's parents, kin, and habitat. As I rifled through folders of notes on *Dawn* I came upon pages of Hindi and Arabic words. She phonetically spelled out the Hindi for "Yes: jee haan," "No: jee na-heen." She noted "Kha-joor" for Dates, "me-her-baa-nee kar-ke" for Please, and "ba-hut dhan-ya-vaad" for Thanks very much.[2] I realized that Oankali names sound like a mix of the Hindi, Sanskrit, Gaelic, Greek, Arabic, and Hawaiian names Octavia spent years collecting for her grand "Thesaurus of Names" project. *(See Introduction.)*

Her own name, Octavia Estelle Butler, bundled together the names of her mother, grandmother, and father. As she jotted in red atop one page of notes, Octavia connotes the number eight and the musical octave.[3] Octavia pursued unusual pairings, triads, composites, and mixtures in her characters' names and desires. Mixed-race couples are a staple of Octavia E. Butler stories, even when aliens are involved. *(See "Y is for Yearbook.")*

O IS FOR OOLOI

Lilith Iyapo is attracted to Joseph Li-Chin Shing. On Earth they would have made an odd couple. Postapocalypse, they still stand out amongst the group of human survivors. Lilith is labeled a traitor when she joins forces with the Oankali. Joseph, too, is suspect for his acceptance of Lilith. He half-willingly enters into a threesome with her and Nikanj, to the horror of the phobic, macho white men who cannot handle the thought of being penetrated. Octavia wrote in her notes: "Big woman, small man; black, oriental: demonstrative, reserved; soft, hard; both strong, utterly trustworthy, responsible, hard working. And utterly loyal to one another."[4] Her opposites do more than attract, they evolve together.

*   *   *

On her index card on "symbiosis" (Fig. 15.1), she typed out the biological definitions of mutualism but added handwritten notes that extended the consideration of living organisms to gendered social dynamics:

> men think of coming together to fight, struggle, compete
>   They come together against an enemy.
> women think of coming together in companionship and/or
>   love. They come together to help themselves and
>   one another to live. They do not require an
>   enemy to cement them.

Given the masculinist barriers to human mutualism, Octavia looked to the natural world for models of non-hierarchical ways of being. Take the slime mold. *(See "G is for Ganymede.")* On December 31, 1988, Octavia wrote in green pen that slime molds defy a basic distinction between individual and group when they merge into a multicellular entity. Angler fish and insects, she noted, are other examples of colony organisms that act as collectives. The Portuguese man-of-war, a tentacled marine organism that resembles a jellyfish, is in essence "a single animal." Various polyps that attach to one another work together in order to survive.[5]

At the bottom of the page of notes on slime molds appears my favorite OEB neologism, maybe second only to ooloi: *multi-dividual*. Octavia writes: "Consider: Agragate multi-dividuals are intelligent or can develop intelligence as units. Never as individuals." Multi-dividual does not roll off the tongue. But I like the extra syllables and consonants that make it awkward and hard to pronounce. It seems right that something ungainly would be coined to break the mold of individualism.

In her twenties, Octavia wrote a short story about an introverted, multi-dividual girl that drew on her adolescent school days. Written from the "we" perspective, it is titled, fittingly, "The Individual We." A schoolgirl has a lively conversation with herself during arithmetic class. She is bad at math. She wonders about the fate of the horse characters Silver Cloud and Rocket that she has been developing in her precious notebook. *(See "A is for Alias.")* Back and forth, the two inner voices discuss the plot of their horse adventure, which involves a canyon landslide, or maybe two. They argue with one another. One part of her asks the other if Rocket reminds them of their crush, Ted Sutton, who is impressively good at math.

Octavia banishes the "I" pronoun from the narrative, as in, "Our fingers touch the battered old three ring binder that Silver Cloud is confined to during class hours." The girl tries to hide her inattention from her teacher, but "Suddenly we, the numerous creatures that enhabit my body notice that Mrs Ballard is frowning at us severly."[6] The teacher is concerned that the girl is too attached to her notebook and insists that she leave it in the classroom during recess and go play with the other children. *(See "N is for Notebook.")*

Of the three drafts of the story, two are typed, and one has red-penned writing instructor's notes on it. A befuddled "Who is speaking?" comment appears in the margin next to one line of dialogue. (The instructor didn't quite grasp the story, but still gave it an A-.) The teacher's confusion is somewhat understandable. The story does not identify clear-cut characters. Girlhood even merges with horsehood when the narrator(s) write(s): "Then we are thinking of the Silver Cloud silvery maned wild horse *we become* during recess."[7] The more identities, the better.

I admit I was disappointed to see that the final typed version cleans up some of the delicious ambiguity of the earlier drafts. The internal speakers are identified—as Tina (T) and Elane (E)—and many of the "we" pronouns are changed to the third-person "they." All versions, though, retain the triumphant escape of the multi-dividual and their notebook: "We quickly pick up the cloud notebook and lose ourself in the kids crowding through the door."[8] The story is as much about a solitary girl who keeps herself company, as it is about surviving arithmetic class and crushing out on a smart boy. In the end, she tells herself to shut up, get better in Arithmetic, and be whatever she wants to be."[9]

Octavia's original title for the story was "The Royal We," but she found in "The Individual We" less a message of unimpeachable authority, and more, one of beauty in multiplicity. Walt Whitman once wrote, "I am large, I contain multitudes." Octavia never lost sight of that singularity, but her experiments with the plural first-person, or the ungendered "it" of the ooloi, absorbed the personal into the collective, and human into the multicellular.

Figure 16.1 Peter Pan Frieze, Pasadena Public Library Children's Room.
Photo credit: Author.

CHAPTER 16

P

IS FOR PUBLIC LIBRARY

At age six Estella got her first library card, and this changed everything. She dreamed of owning a horse, she talked about them incessantly to uninterested ears; in lieu of having one she read horse books borrowed from the Pasadena Public Library's Children's Room (also known as the Boys' and Girls' Department), where she spent most of her time. During these years, concocting her own equine tales helped young Octavia escape the idea that she was an undisciplined daydreamer and a "backward," "colored" girl with a bleak future.[1]

Looking back from the vantage point of 1981, Octavia recalls being ten and depressed at the thought of having to choose any one of the four vocations that seemed available to her: maid, nurse, secretary, teacher.[2] These were the roles of the 1950s that made sense to her mother and aunt. Octavia Sr. had started working at age ten, and did not get to high school, so more than anyone she understood the power of books.[3] *(See "M is for Mother.")* She brought home to her daughter any publications her white employers threw out, no matter what shape they were in—tattered, torn, marked up, coverless, even partially burnt.

Young Octavia stacked them in corners like canned treats.[4] Most of her reading material, though, came from the Pasadena Public Library, which she called her "second home" and the place where she had "half lived" since the age of six.[5]

In her time, the Children's Department was housed in the Peter Pan Room, named for the gigantic brick and concrete fireplace that had been installed by local Pasadena sculptor Maude Daggett in 1927. No longer in use, the fireplace still stands, having become, as the artist intended it, a lasting homage to childhood imagination and the land of make-believe (Fig. 16.1). Its mantelpiece frieze of J.M. Barrie's *Peter Pan* inspires awe even in adult-sized viewers. I gazed up at the lithe, androgynous ensemble of four Lost Boys in relief, lounging freely at the center while next to them, Peter Pan crows. On one side the Darlings cluster together in an embrace with a bunny at Wendy's feet, and their dog-nurse Nana sits on the other side, safely within sight. Children rule the scene. The pirate ships and crocodiles that ornament either end of the mantel suggest adventure but pose no threat. Even Captain Hook and Mr. Smee are rendered harmless gargoyle-esque heads on the plinths below.

You catch the hint of seagulls, wind, and beach. The impasto strokes built up from the sculptor's scraper and the grain of the once-wet concrete gives the entire work the feel of a perfectly preserved sandcastle. It celebrates the daydreaming that Octavia was normally chastised for. It was hearth and altar of the sanctuary she shared with other child readers, in which every detail, down to the dark oak wainscoting, walls of shelves, and ¾-sized tables and chairs, was meant to echo the gravitas of the rest of the building.

Among Octavia's ephemera at the Huntington is a pamphlet, "Where To Find a Book," printed by the Pasadena Public Library

P IS FOR PUBLIC LIBRARY

as a guide to the areas of the building and its stacks and call number locations.[6] Octavia no doubt knew the place by heart. To get to the Children's corner of the library, you enter through the Main Hall, with its Italian marble floors, ornate doorways, pendant lights, and majestic, forty-five-foot tall, coffered ceilings. It enthralls, and the public shuffle of papers, books, and steps reverberates with the activity of individuals together seeking shelter in knowledge. Such hushed vibrancy is conducive to concentration—here you can't help but take yourself seriously. Like other great public libraries built in the nineteenth century, it is something in-between a train station and a cathedral.

On April 29, 1986, Octavia stood on the corner of Fifth and Grand in downtown Los Angeles and watched the public library burn. Quick-fix budget cuts had led to a neglect of the building that mirrored the national crisis in privatization. Jobs shipped overseas and university tuitions skyrocketed to unaffordable rates: the damages, she noted, were everywhere felt. In her published 1993 essay about the impending extinction of the library as a social good, she wrote, "Public libraries in particular are the open universities of America. They're free; they're accessible to everyone; they may offer special services to shut-ins, to children, even to nonreaders. They offer worlds of possibilities to people who might otherwise be confined by their ignorance and poverty to continued ignorance and worsening poverty."[7] Above all, they were places for kids to come to after school and be safe. As a child, she made the library her chosen home. As an adult writer, she had a regular seat in the History room of the L.A. Public Library. When she had writer's block she would flip through books on anthropology, medicine, religion, politics, and biography until the words came to her. She wrote in 1981, "Worlds are born out of the chaos of my reading and living. World creating is synthesis, inspiration, serendipity."[8]

In 2006 Octavia was invited back to Pasadena as the honoree for the library's "One City, One Story" book of the year, *Kindred*, but sadly, she passed before she could make the trip. She did, in 1992, give a lecture on "The Importance of Free Libraries," which paid homage to the Pasadena Central Library:

> I'm a writer at least partly because I had access to public libraries. I'm black, female, the child of a shoeshine man who died young and a maid who was uneducated, but who knew her way to the library. I'm also a product of librarians who read stories to groups of avid little kids and taught them to look for books about mythology and horses, dinosaurs and stars. At the library, I read books my mother could never have afforded on topics that would never have occurred to her. I escaped from text books that seemed intent on teaching me how dry and dull reading can be. At school I learned that reading was work. At the library, I learned that it was fun.[9]

As Octavia recalled in some of her notes on childhood school days, "I used to talk around with my head always down. I whispered . . . . I thought I was ugly and stupid and clumsy and hopeless. I also thought everyone would notice these things if I drew attention to myself. I wanted to disappear. Instead, I grew taller. Boys in particular began to resent me out loud."[10] Books, however, did not care how tall or shy she was (Fig. 16.2). Growing up in the Pasadena Public Library she began to write and develop her tastes. At twelve she "escaped" from the Peter Pan Room into the science fiction magazine area. When she was allowed to enter the adult stacks at fourteen, she started checking out mainstream self-help books on success and achievement. *(See "H*

P IS FOR PUBLIC LIBRARY

Figure 16.2 Fourth-grade class photo, Lincoln School, 1957. Octavia at the center of the back row. She stood above the rest.
Courtesy of Bebe Martin-Smith.

is for Horse.") Because her high school didn't offer creative writing classes, she also learned the craft and business of writing from these books.[11] They helped her correspond with New York editors like the Mead Company, to which she sent her writing in 1961 and 1962.[12] (Figs. 1.2 and 1.3). Even though she received her first rejection in 1960, when she was thirteen, the self-help books were much more helpful than the agent that her mother had paid to try to get her published.[13] In the 1960s, public libraries were spaces for professional development, community, and activism, especially for Black artists and people of color searching for histories of non-Western civilization and their ancestral diasporas.[14] All across the city and country, these libraries provided for what wasn't being taught in schools.

* * *

Like Octavia, I loved being surrounded by books. At the school library, I devoured all the biographies I could find, lives upon lives. It was thrilling to sign out the little hardback biographies in the Bobbs-Merrill "Childhood of Famous Americans" series and learn how legends got their start. Checking out a book was a physical act, which entailed slipping the card out of the pocket, signing your name in newly learned cursive, getting it stamped, and seeing who else had read it and when. It was the mark of an individual amidst a village of readers.

School library cards from the 1950s certainly offer a glimpse of all the girls reading horse books: Pamela, Miriam, La Nette, Margie, Terry, Dorothea, Marian, Judy, Mary Lou, Ethel, Marsha, Susan, Joan, Shirlyn, (twice), Suzanne, Elinor, Carol, and the occasional Bruce H. or James, as the case might be (Fig. 16.3). There are only a handful of original books from Octavia's childhood still in circulation in the Peter Pan Room, now called the Children's Room. The ones with checkout cards intact only occasionally register a patron's name, and sometimes the odd home address, next to their five-digit library card number and the date stamp. Of these, Octavia no doubt borrowed the Will James' 1920s and 30s

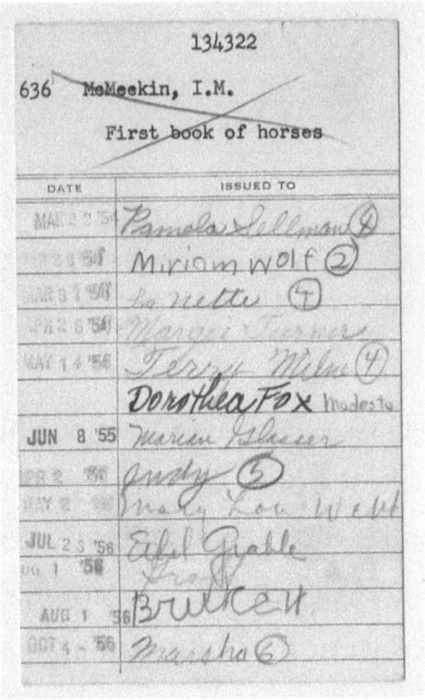

Figure 16.3 1950s school library checkout card, I.M. McMeekin, *First book of horses*, with girls' and boy's signatures. San Diego State University.

Photo credit: Author.

Westerns, *Sun Up* and *In the Saddle with Uncle Bill*, given how much she loved his *Smoky, the Cow Horse*, and perhaps Frederic Remington's 1895 cavalry frontier chronicle, *Pony Tracks*, for its horse illustrations. *(See "C is for Character.")* She might have perused the much-beloved *Dog of Flanders* by Marie Louise de la Ramée (aka Ouida) and the copies of the early twentieth-century animal fictions by Holling Clancy Holling, Berta and Elmer Hader, and Meindert De Jong. These books track baby dogs, cows, mountain goats, and horses, as they develop into mature animals and learn to survive their environment, be it the Rocky Mountains or the streets of Antwerp. We can imagine all the other, non-extant horse books Octavia would have checked out, and where her card number and perhaps signature would be penciled in amidst numerous other 1950s girls and boys.

Octavia's eclectic reading habits and penchant for research were undoubtedly shaped by the art of browsing the stacks. When she could eventually afford her own house, she filled it with books.[15] One of her brilliant late-teen stories, "Factory Reject," features an outcast girl named Leah-Rae Johns *(See "D is*

> "I like being surrounded by books. I've made an effort to be for most of my life. When I was little I used to go to the library to do a lot of my reading and later my writing. Now I have a house filled with books." OEB 276.

for Dog") who is told from age five that something is wrong with her.[16] First, she compares herself to an unwanted dog, and then, to a manuscript no one wants to publish—it is as though she carries around with her "an invisible rejection slip." Whether animal or paper, she does not belong to the human race. From day care through junior high and high school, she is bullied and she finds friends only in her books and dreams. *(See "J is for Junie.")* "Sometimes she daydreamed about what it would be like if the people in the books could really be alive and talk to her." After her mother dies, she spends all her savings on the cemetery plot, sells their house, and is all alone until the day a man and his wife appear in her room and ask her to go away with them. Together, they "simply oozed into a book that lay open on Leah's desk. A diary." Bodies transmogrify into the ether of the pages, and all that was cumbersome about this world vanishes. She has finally become one with her life's fiction.

Figure 17.1 Remington Rand typewriter advertisement, c. 1957.

CHAPTER 17

Q

IS FOR QWERTY

At age ten, young Octavia got her first typewriter, a portable Remington (Fig. 17.1). She had begged for one until her mother gave in, against the advice of friends who thought it would be a passing dalliance. Little did they know. Estella wasn't allowed to take typing in school until the second semester of eighth grade, so, as she put it, she "two-fingered" it for three years. She knew her typing, like her spelling and grammar, was pretty awful. When it came time to send out her first stories, she enlisted her science teacher Mr. Pfaff to type them up in a presentable fashion.[1]

By ninth grade, her final year of junior high, Estella was putting her newly acquired QWERTY keyboard skills to work for school assignments and potential job applications. She listed her type-writing teacher Mr. Mika along with the Rev. John F. Smith of the Pasadena Baptist Church as references on a hypothetical January 22, 1962 cover letter for Junior Office Clerk trainee at the upscale Huntington-Sheraton Hotel over on South Oak Knoll. She also fabricated an experience working part-time for her "father who operates a dry-cleaning business."[2] The newspaper classifieds of the day were filled with calls for typist-clerks, or "Girl Fridays," and secretary trainee positions. It's understandable that Estella envisioned working at the Huntington over Allstate Insurance or one of the many small business offices that were advertising. The hotel was designed by Myron Hunt, the same architect of the Pasadena Public Library *(See P is for Public Library.)* Today, under the aegis of the Langham Huntington Pasadena, it continues to be a landmark of luxury, located behind an exclusive, leafy bend in the road just two miles from the Huntington Library archives.

With her thirty words per minute, Estella would have been underqualified for most office jobs. Her desire to be a better typist might account for the premise of a cautionary tale she typed for a tenth-grade school Physiology class, "Those 'Wonderful' Pills." To deal with her workplace anxiety, a government typist named Betty begins taking prescription pills that turn her into a model worker. They "freed her of all her nervousness and worry" and allowed her to "type like a typist with years of experience." Soon all her co-workers are buying pills off the black market. They find themselves chattering less and working in a daze. The loss of sleep and appetite start to take a toll, and the girls become increasingly ill, until one day Hannah hallucinates that their supervisor is turning into a wolf. At which point the doctor is brought back in and finds that the pills contain the amphetamine Benzedrine, the infamous bennies of the era. With matter-of-fact concision, Estella points out that the drug is often misused by dieters and truck drivers and can result in "permanent psychosis."[3]

Through high school, Estella's typewriter was one of her prized possessions, along with her accordion.[4] Years before, her mother had also taken lessons for a time but found the instrument too hard to master.[5] I wonder how young Octavia took to it. Among her manuscript papers are diagrams from the "Stancato School of Accordion" that assign each of the five fingers to corresponding, lettered treble keys and bass buttons.[6] Having spent countless years of my youth practicing the piano and violin, the accordion's combination of keyboard, buttons, *and* bellows always struck me as impossibly unwieldy, no matter how cheerily handled by the old white men of *The Lawrence Welk Show*. Estella put to work her hand–eye coordination when doggedly typing or playing music on the accordion or the piano, on which she sometimes "banged out some hymns" to accompany her mother's singing. Her piano skills were "pretty Bad," she admitted in an April 21, 1963 diary entry.[7]

She did love music, though. In the archive are reams of lyrics that she typed out, over the decades, with loving exactitude. They range from the TV show theme songs of *Zorro* and *Mr. Ed (See "T is for TV Westerns")* to Mahalia Jackson's spiritual, "Somebody Bigger Than You and I," and the Righteous Brothers' "Unchained Melody." She listened to the latter on the radio while away from home for the first time and feeling out of place at the Clarion writers' workshop in Pennsylvania.[8] In high school she and her peers loved early Motown and crooners like Brook Benton, Marvin Gaye, and Nat King Cole. Her schoolmate Sylvia remembers getting a memo from her Seventh-Day Adventist Church that forbade listening to music "that causeth the foot to tap." She checked with her brother, "they mean Black music don't they? He said yes."[9] Characteristic of her cataloguing habit, Octavia at one point wrote out in cursive twenty-three "Top Songs" of 1964; they ranged from R&B to folk, surf rock, and garage rock.

The Beatles appear twice, and two of the bands, The Premiers and The Blendells, were Mexican American groups from the vicinity of East Los Angeles and San Gabriel. Seven of the artists on her list are Black performers. She made sure to write out all six ums of Major Lance's hit, "Um, Um, Um, Um, Um, Um" (minus the commas) and added a parenthetical "(ugh!)" next to the title "Baby Love" by The Supremes.[10]

In predigital times, it took vigilance to learn TV song lyrics. No rewinding or pausing: you'd have to watch and rewatch a show in real time to catch all the words and organize them into lines of verse. What made songs catchy, and how could one capture their transportive power? Estella's typing transferred horse-riding rhythms into word units on a page. Looking at them now, they resemble nonsensical versions of the inspirational self-help mantras of her adult commonplace books . . . *Ride on Ride on Ride on. Rolling rolling rolling/ Movin' Movin' movin'.* If you are a fan, you can hear the music in your head. The TV Western songs carry the cadence of a genre and an era. As incantatory, commanding, and terrifically compact storytelling, they were ritualistic initiations into the thirty or sixty minutes of sanctioned escapism within Estella's strict Baptist household. These were internalized soundtracks that kept her company at school, while doing her homework, and writing horse and Martian stories.

* * *

I always found something mesmerizing and empowering about typing. The rote finger work, the comfort of the carriage-return lever and ding of the margin bell at the end of each line. I remember mastering the keyboard as a child. In my household, elementary school summers were designated times for self-study.

My father, always the aspiring businessman, was convinced that I could get ahead in life by checking out two types of workbooks from the library: math and typing. With one you could make money, with the other you could telegraph your success to the world. As an eight-year-old, I punched out pangram sentences and got to know the machine keys as I did the piano keyboard, committing the QWERTY to finger muscle memory, learning not to look down. By the time typing class was required in high school, I was a wiz. While my ninety words per minute helped in getting me temp work after college, it was a strange skill to acquire as a child. Fingers flying, you copy letter combinations you don't have to interpret or invent. No writers' block here. Yet something of the prescribed exercises must seep in. Repeat "Every good boy does fine" enough times during violin lessons or retype "Now is the time for all good men to come to the aid of their party" (Fig. 17.2), and might we become just a bit more complicit in reinforcing the naturalness of male virtue? I wonder what other messages might be embedded in our small everyday gestures.

* * *

Remington had been the first to adopt the QWERTY keyboard back in 1874 when it came out with the Remington No. 1. In the 1950s, Remingtons still sold well, and held up against competitors like Royal and Smith-Corona. Like a cowboy and his horse, a twentieth-century writer was nothing without their trusted typewriter. Octavia's first real writing mentor, the SF writer Harlan Ellison, had also gotten his start on a Remington portable in the 1930s. He had been the one to help get her into her first Clarion Workshop in 1970. On July 25, 1970, Octavia wrote to her mother about being the only "Negro" in the workshop at Clarion

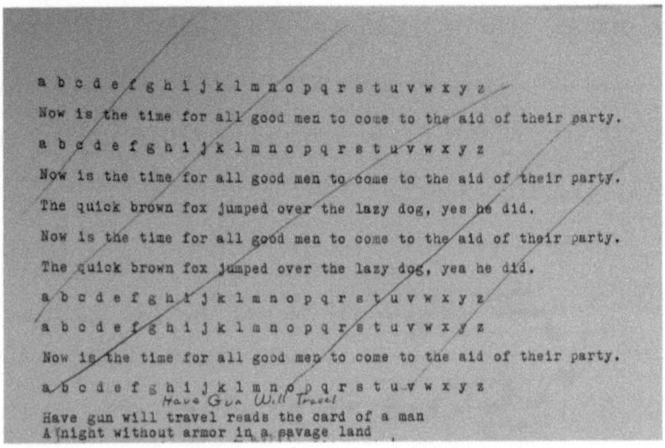

Figure 17.2 Estella reused a page of her typewriting practice to transcribe the lyrics to TV shows *(See "T is for TV Western.)* OEB Box 325. By permission of Octavia E. Butler Enterprises.

State College. She described the insufferable humidity of upstate Pennsylvania, and the novelty of summer storms and lightning bugs. The only other nonwhite student in the group was Russell Bates, an American Indian one of the white girls had a serious crush on. And then there was the teacher Harlan Ellison, who had not only paid $50 for her entrance fee but also gifted her a new typewriter.[11] While at Clarion he bought her story, "Childfinder," which he planned to publish in a collection in 1971 (though that book never came out). Octavia sold another story, "Crossover," to the workshop leader Robin Wilson, who published it in an anthology. *(See "A is for Alias.")* She wrote to her mother that, no matter what the future had in store, at least she had already sold two stories.[12] She was on her way.

There were three portable Remington typewriters on the market in 1957. The Quiet-Riter was marketed to students, and at around $130, it was the top of the line, followed by the Letter-Riter at $110, and the Travel-Riter, $87. I don't know which one Octavia

Sr. bought for Estella, but she must have used credit. Even if she took advantage of the $1/week payment plan, it would still have taken a large bite out of the family budget.[13] After poring over so many of Estella's stories and typing exercises, I needed to see for myself the machine that had launched her writing career. My 1957 vintage Quiet-Riter arrived on the doorstep in a large, recycled drum snare box shipped from Bakersfield, California. At over fifteen pounds, it was much heavier than I'd expected, and neither portable nor quiet by today's standards. I had chosen this one for its shiny, forest-green keys. Unboxed, it looks like a desert sage, cartoon army vehicle. There was still enough ink on the ribbon for me to type out Estella's words, "I hope someday I will be the owner of a ranch for girls." *(See "V is for Victorville.")* No wonder Estella used two fingers for so long. Each stroke is a small feat of punching down about two inches of air to form a letter on the page. I can picture her ten-year-old self perched over it, ready to make her mark.

Figure 18.1 *Tom Bass and Rex McDonald* (2011).
Courtesy of artist: Jeanne Newton Schoborg.

CHAPTER 18

R

IS FOR REX MCDONALD

At the turn of the twentieth century, Rex McDonald was a household name. When he died in Mexico, Missouri, the entire town took part in his funeral. The editor of the local paper wrote a full-page tribute to the black stallion that began, "The King is no more. Death has claimed the greatest saddle horse the world has ever known."[1] He was born in 1890 and died in 1913. People who saw Rex perform described him as the "poetry of motion."[2] Even as a colt, they said, he had the greatness of a champion stallion. He would go on to master all five gaits American Saddlebreds are taught to perform, but he especially excelled in the rack. Like the running walk of the Tennessee Walking Horse, the rack is a highly virtuosic, manmade movement. Each hoof strikes the ground separately, in four extremely fast beats that turn front and back legs into spinning pinwheels. Hence the Saddlebred's reputation as a "Peacock of the show ring," and young Octavia's decision to assign this breed to Charles Dickens' vainglorious femme, Dora. (See "H is for Horse.")

Over his twenty-three-year life, Rex was owned and ridden by multiple horsemen of Missouri and Kentucky. But most famously, he was bitted and trained by the legendary African American equestrian Tom Bass (Fig. 18.1). A formerly enslaved man from Missouri, Bass gained world fame for his work with horses, including those of Buffalo Bill Cody, Theodore Roosevelt, and William McKinley. In fact, one of the few horses to beat Rex McDonald was Tom Bass' prodigy mare, Miss Rex (they shared the same sire, Rex Denmark.)[3]

Tom Bass was the original horse whisperer. He had an uncanny ability to communicate with horses without the use of whips or clubs. He dazzled audiences when he waltzed with one of his superstars, the black mare, Belle Beach. He would save injured horses and nurse them back to health. One-eyed or neck-scarred cast-offs could become champions under his care. He designed a special mouth bit, the Bass Bit, to alleviate the pain caused by the metallic devices. Over the course of his career, which ended in 1934, he won countless competitions in the show ring, including at the Columbia World's Fair in Chicago, and New York's Madison Square Garden. In a postbellum, segregated era, he was often the only Black man allowed entry.

Estella would have read about Rex McDonald in the horse books she checked out from the Pasadena Public Library. In *Album of Horses*, the popular children's book author Marguerite Henry described an old man at a state fair who sees a blue-black horse that transports him back in time: "He was a young man, watching a young horse. No! He *was* that horse. That blue-black bullet, prancing around the rings, all over Kentucky, all over Missouri. Walking, trotting, cantering, stepping, racking. He was grand champion of the world. He was Rex McDonald!"[4]

R IS FOR REX MCDONALD

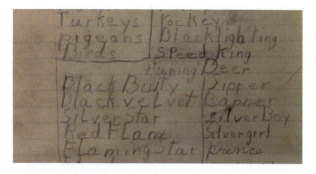

Figure 18.2 Detail, Animal–character list, *c.*1957. OEB 1620.
By permission of Octavia E. Butler Enterprises.

Rex sired hundreds of sons, so chances are that a black stallion or mare on screen in the 1950s and 60s would be one of his descendants. If he was the real-life "Black Beauty," his great-great-grandson Highland Dale became a horse celebrity in his own right. Dale's impressive IMDB page is filled with guest appearances on TV shows like *Lassie*, *The Monkees*, *The Munsters*, and *Bonanza*. He was the star of the series *Fury* (1955–60) and was paid $1500 per episode, plus five percent of the show's profits. He made more than the human actors, and he was the second highest paid animal actor in show business, after Lassie. *(See "D is for Dog.")* In 1946, Highland Dale also starred in one of the most famous children's books ever made into film, *Black Beauty*. It might have been an unfaithful adaptation of the novel and a low-budget Hollywood production, but it made an impression thanks to Dale's celebrity.

A decade or so after *Black Beauty's* release, ten-year-old Estella sat down with her notebook and pencil. She carefully compiled a list of barnyard animals alongside dozens of human and nonhuman names, inspired by the animals celebrated on the page and onscreen (Fig. 18.2). She listed Fury and "Black Buity," her own character, Silver Star, and a host of other cosmically inflected inventions such as Flaming Star, Red Thunder, Silver Girl, Sky Boy, and Red Rocket.[5] *(See "Z is for Zorro.")* Her taxonomy mixes and matches common and proper nouns, in upper and lower-case letters (i.e., "Black veLvet"; "SPeed King"; "pigeons"; "Dogs"). Still learning the rules of writing, she experiments with gender parity ("Silver Boy" and "Silver girl") and the power of adjectives like "black" to elevate elemental objects to legendary status (i.e., velvet, lightning, cloud). Spelling out these word combinations transformed the everyday animals she loved into personae with stories to tell. As she later reflected, "I loved dogs and later cats, found pigs, goats, and cattle interesting when I encountered them, eventually fell in love with horses."[6]

For some years, the Muir High School football mascot was a black Mustang pony named Sky-rocket, who resided at the Rancho Elastico animal farm in Altadena. In 1962, it kept company with Bozo the rival bulldog mascot of Pasadena High, a mare named Sun Bonnet, her filly Princess, eight baby lambs, a talking raven, monkeys, chickens, ducks, goats, rabbits, and other pets.[7] Florence McKay ran the 4H club from this 5.5-acre headquarters at 533 E. Calaveras Street for nearly thirty years. At one point it had five horses and ran pony rides for the visiting children.[8] There were other ways to encounter a horse around Pasadena in the 1950s and 1960s. At least one of Highland Dale's fellow Hollywood horse actors was stabled locally, for instance, at the Arroyo Seco Stables.[9] Others resided at Altadena Stables, the family-owned Williams Ranch, or more elite spaces such as the Flintridge Riding Club. Groups like the Rose Bowl Riders were active around town and on view at the annual Tournament of

Roses Parade. Even in mostly private, white spaces, Black stable hands and riders would have been present.

Locals knew Altadena to be a locus of Black equestrianism between the late 1940s up through the 1990s.[10] Some were semi-professional cowboys who occasionally competed for cash prizes at Griffith Park in Los Angeles, maintained the neighborhood trails, and went on planned horse outings with their friends. Young people would ride around Devil's Gate Dam in the Arroyo Seco.[11] One Muir alumnus, Peaches Jones, who graduated five years or so after Octavia, even became one of the first Black stuntwomen in the movies and trained in her Altadena backyard with her father.[12] An older generation of Muir student, Mr. Michael Mims, Class of '56, remembers encountering all kinds of animals around town, including a llama at the north end of Fair Oaks, which may have wandered onto the streets from Zorthian Ranch. On Sundays his older brother got dressed up in his riding habit and went riding with friends in Griffith Park. If you could not afford to own and stable a horse in Altadena, you could go elsewhere to rent one. When Mr. Mims was older, he drove out to Hansen Dam in the San Fernando Valley to ride, and even ventured as far south as Ensenada, Mexico.

Horse cultures are histories in the making. Some who came to L.A. fleeing Jim Crow would have been used to living with farm animals, which fit right in with Altadena's ongoing "country town" feel.[13] August Simien, a Civil War reenactor and military historian with the New Buffalo Soldiers, teaches all manner of kids and adults about the history of the Black cavalry. In 2018, former Altadena Town Councilmember Judy Matthews helped erect an interpretive plaque commemorating the original 9th and 10th Buffalo Soldier Cavalry regiments at the Loma Alta Equestrian

Park. Like many, Judy and her family moved to Altadena over forty years ago for the diversity of the community and her love of the outdoors. She doesn't ride, but she looks out for horses daily on her walks near the Altadena Crest Trail, and her daughter-in-law, a surgeon by profession, has been riding since age six and still loves it. She is a horsewoman who hails from Colombia, land of cattle ranching and *llanero* cowboys. We all come from somewhere else; when we move, we bring old habits to new homes.

In the 1960s, artsy types came to Altadena for Black community and for space, peace, and quiet. The renowned painter and portraitist Charles White, for example, had been introduced to the area by his movie star friends, turned neighbors, Sidney Poitier and Ivan Dixon. White and his mixed-race family lived for a time in Altadena Meadows just down the road from the grave of abolitionist Owen Brown, son of the antislavery Kansas insurrectionist John Brown, whose descendants had settled above El Prieto Canyon back in the 1880s.[14] Hills draw maroons of all sorts. In her memoir, Mrs. Frances Barrett White noted the significance of "living in the shadow of John Brown's Mountain" given that Brown was the first white person her husband Charles ever drew. Though segregation was alive and well, the Whites felt relatively "at home in Altadena [where we] found people friendly and apparently uninterested in our color differences."[15]

Today Altadena is still a place where people mix amongst animals. When I spoke with L.A.-area equestrians, they weren't surprised to learn that Octavia loved horses. Altadena rider Meredith McKenzie pointed out, "The kind of people who are horse people live close to the earth, are intuitive, and the pleasure of riding a horse is not to have a machine [a car]. You live in a slow world, meeting people on the street, having conversations."[16] Octavia certainly was intuitive (and she didn't drive.) "If she was into horses, she had to be decent," August Simien added. Today

> "Horses reach deep into people's core."
> "If you're cruel toward animals, you'll be cruel to people."
> August "A.J." Simien.

he still has six horses, and two mules. His favorite, Baby Doll, is a Tennessee Walker, the breed young Octavia assigned to Dickens' Tom Steerforth in her adolescent equi-sapien drawings that used horses as a judge of human character. *(See "H is for Horse.")* As someone who also grew up poor and came to L.A. from Louisiana, August recalls reading horse books at the public library and looking to *The Black Stallion*, in print and on screen, to develop his understanding of horse–human relations. Today, in the tradition of Tom Bass, August favors the gentle, talking method of training a horse, rather than disciplining with a bar that pulls on the horse's face.

* * *

When fictional horses open their mouths, they seem to know it all. This goes for the sassy advice-giving Mr. Ed or the haughty, superior Houyhnhnms of *Gulliver's Travels*, and especially for the beloved horse didact Black Beauty created by Anna Sewell in her 1878 novel, *Black Beauty*. It was first made into a movie in 1946, but audiences would have to wait until the 1994 remake to experience the horse talking on screen, as voiced by the Scottish, always fabulous, Alan Cumming.

OCTAVIA E. BUTLER

The original Black Beauty was British, and he was a talker. The novel is notable for its subtitle, "The Autobiography of a horse / Translated from the original equine." Black Beauty, like Estella's Silver Star, holds forth. She no doubt took note of the white star on his forehead. Sewell published her novel shortly before

> Estella listed *Black Beauty* as the eleventh "Most Popular Book" for "Boys" on a typewritten school assignment. (Number one was *Treasure Island* by Robert Louis Stevenson.) OEB 336.

she died in 1879. Like Octavia, she lived to age fifty-eight. Her legs disabled from a childhood accident, Anna relied all her life on horses for her mobility. She had a religious mother, a Quaker evangelist, and *Black Beauty* is as much a manual for social reform as it is a horse story. The first-person horse perspective narrates episodic accounts of equine mistreatment by cruel men. Beauty schools the boys and men on the evils of horse abuse, which range from the use of whips and the fashionable bearing-reins that damaged the mouth, to the poor sanitation of stalls, which could cause thrush. As with Felix Salten's *Bambi*, the novel shaped public conversation about cruelty toward animals. *(See "B is for Bambi.")*

Black Beauty is a horse journalist. He recounts his time spent with masters of different social classes, and interviews other horses about their experiences and traumas. His only friend, Ginger, describes the bloody tongue and chafing which results from the improper use of bits and rein: "You who never had a bearing-rein on, don't know what it is, but I can tell you it is dreadful.[17] Maybe Estella identified with Black Beauty's yearning for a friend, and his compulsion for storytelling amidst adversity. He loses Ginger and one good master after another as he is sold and increasingly ruined through abuse and bodily degradation. He describes wanting "liberty" but being made to stand still for hours in the stable. He then recounts with anatomical exactitude the discomfort of the bit in his mouth. Horses talk to each other and to the reader, but they remain silent when it matters the most. To the people who govern them, they cannot "make known [their] wants."[18]

Anna and Octavia would have admired Tom Bass, the gentle trainer known for saying, "horses are like humans." Bass was grateful for the coming of the automobile, because it would mean less animal abuse: "I'm glad that automobiles came in when they did. They were the emancipation of the horse."[19] Sewell too promoted the ideal of good communication between horses and their drivers. When "partners who understood each other" fulfilled their God-given obligations, everything would be right in the world. But the world was not right in late-1800s industrial England. The changing role of the horse was a sign of the times. Her novel contrasts Black Beauty with the train, a "black frightful thing" that lurks in the background, transects the countryside, and contributes to a culture of human desensitization.[20] *Black Beauty* dissects the violence that permeates the brutal system of wage earning in a machine age. Cab drivers, butchers, and the working poor suffered from a seven-day work week, and, under constant duress to respond faster to consumer demands, they became the worst horse abusers. Drunken riders were thrown to death, and horses suffered due to the alcohol-induced neglect. Horse and human health are interlinked.

Still, Sewell's aim was reform, not revolution. Her fellow Victorian, Karl Marx, also saw that horse power was becoming obsolete because of steam-powered machine engines. In his 1867 book *Capital*, he wrote that for a horse to stay healthy, it could not possibly work over eight hours a day; given the demands of a capitalist economy, the horse becomes useful only where obstructions like crooked fences "prevent uniform action" of a machine.[21] As Marx pointed out, when we talk about horsepower, we transfer collective animal strength into a unit of efficient machine energy. He and Sewell were writing at a time when the English countryside and the American frontier were both being transformed by the fossil capital of rail and steam technologies. These were the settings for both the Victorian novels and the frontier romances that would develop into the Westerns of the mid-twentieth century. *(See "T is for TV Western.")* In an era of plane and car mobility, Octavia was glued to the TV performances of handsome horses and their dashing riders. Like much of the country, she bought into the cultural nostalgia for a bygone era of horse-powered heroism.

Young Octavia had no explicitly political or historical intention in captioning her horse drawings with glosses on Charles Dickens' *David Copperfield*. Yet in her drawings the horses hold their poses as if on their own, without the apparatus of bit, harness, reins, or trainer. *(See "H is for Horse.")* The noticeable absence of white riders intimates other unpictured humans, like the Black trainers, stable-tenders, and jockeys who made occasional appearances in illustrated children's horse books. The stories of Tom Bass and Rex McDonald, *Black Beauty*, and *The Black Stallion* contribute to a genealogy of Black horsemanship and varied migrations of Southern communities into southern

California. Whether domesticated like the American Saddlebred or feral like the Mustang, horses are often icons of wildness. People train them to perform, name cars after them. They test the limits of human control, and even the idea of untrammeled animal freedom. Legendary or not, the horses of the past and present move us, and move with us, while technologies change and the countryside vanishes. They persist in taking up space and slowing down time as together we make our place in the world.

Figure 19.1 "I ran as I had never run BeFore," Rocket and Silver Star (with star birthmark on shoulder). OEB 2472.
By permission of Octavia E. Butler Enterprises.

CHAPTER 19

S

IS FOR SEXY

A litmus test for any story Octavia wrote (or read): is it <u>sexy</u>? She had a broad definition of sexiness. Courage could be sexy, as could silence. On one ruled notebook page, she highlighted in pink fourteen categories followed by the phrase "is sexy": Partnerships, Power, Touching, Knowing, Silence, Intelligence, Mystery, Sex, Loving, Courage, Self-control, Struggle, Arrogance, Strength. Some warrant extra emphasis: "Power is sexy. Boy, is it ever!" Or, "Struggle is sexy especially person against person [Doro & Anyanwu]." (For that matter, Rocket against Silver Star, Fig. 19 1.) Most of them come with qualifiers. For example, "Sex can be sexy, but isn't necessarily." Or, "Arrogance is sexy if not advertised to excess." As she added at the top of the page, "Anything not dangerously repulsive <like child abuse> can be sexy, if you, the author, feel it is sexy."

Across several pages of notes she confessed she was open to various kinds of partnership—"one sex or two, love, work, or survival." She found Anne Rice's writing of vampires "remarkably sexy." She considered the megalomaniacal Doro her sexiest character. Sometimes "S.O.B.'s" like Coransee [*Patternmaster*] or Rufus [*Kindred*] were infuriatingly sexy.

In high school Octavia wrote about kinky alien sex in stories like "Adaptability." (A nine-foot-tall alien with six strong blue tentacles plans to take the human girl protagonist for himself when she turns fifteen.)[1] But the ultimate icon of sexy "knowingness" was her teen crush, Paul Bryan, the lead character on the 1960s TV show *Run for Your Life* (a close second were the cowboys of Louis L'Amour.) When composing her novel *Clay's Ark*, she asked herself, "Who will be sexy in Clay's Ark?" Ever mindful of her calling as a writer, she noted, "Lesson: Sex, sexiness is power. Readers want it."

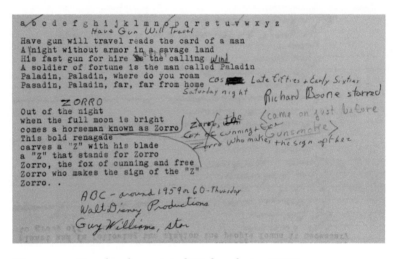

Figure 20.1 Typed and annotated TV show lyrics. OEB Box 325.
By permission of Octavia E. Butler Enterprises.

CHAPTER 20

T

IS FOR TV WESTERN

Octavia was a kid in the mid-1950s, whereas I grew up in the early '80s. And yet we religiously watched some of the same TV shows. Long-running Westerns like *Gunsmoke* (1955–75) and *Bonanza* (1959–73) spanned our childhoods. In a predigital era of finite channels and limited programming, frontiers-y black-and-white reruns aired concurrently with the latest family fare. Some of them transitioned to color mid-series. *Bonanza* helped pioneer the bright yellow title font, a look that reappeared in another personal favorite, *The Littlest Hobo*, starring an itinerant German shepherd. *(See "D is for Dog.")*

Who doesn't remember the catchy openings to the TV shows we watched as children, especially ones with live action animals? *Zorro* and *Lone Ranger* featured a horse rearing up, striking a pose like Equus Emily. *(See H is for Horse.)* I can still hear the galloping instrumentals of *Bonanza*: Dun dada dun, dada dun, dada dun, dada dun, DUN! Lorne Greene starred as the father of three sons by different women (English, Swedish, French Creole), a blended family if ever there was one. Tie-ins and crossovers have always been the stuff of entertainment media, especially in the era of newly networked television. I followed Michael Landon from playing a son in *Bonanza* to kind-hearted Pa in *Little House on the Prairie*. The *Bonanza* songwriters also wrote for *Mr. Ed*, and *The Lone Ranger* (1949–57) and *Lassie* (1954–73) were owned by the same company. The white stallion (named Silver) and the Rough Collie (Lassie) could not hail from more different fictional universes. Imagine the kid viewers' excitement when the Lone Ranger made a guest appearance in Episode #179 of *Lassie* in 1959. I don't know if Estella tuned in that Sunday afternoon in Pasadena. Clearly, she had already been reimagining both the Man + Horse and Boy + Dog formulae in her own adventure stories. Her Silver (Star) was a heroic, white girl-horse. She also wrote about Queen, the brown collie, and her beloved cocker spaniel, Tory. (She dispensed with the Man and the Boy.)

Though her mother disapproved of watching movies in the theater, Estella was allowed television at home. She documented her viewing by transcribing by hand and then typing out the lyrics to the opening theme songs of all the shows she loved: *The Rebel. Wyatt Earp. Gunsmoke. Jim Bowie. Zorro. Tombstone Territory. Have Gun—Will Travel. Shotgun Slade. Rawhide. Gunslinger. Maverick. Wagon Train. Cheyenne. Bat Masterson. Lawman. 26 Men. The Rifleman. Death Valley Days. Boots and Saddles. Pony Express. Pioneers. The Deputy. Branded.* Westerns dominated the networks, but she also liked cop shows like *77 Sunset Strip*, and *Car 54, Where Are You?*. She watched *Robin Hood, The Buccaneers, Mr. Ed*, and sitcoms like *The Patty Duke Show*. Local to Los Angeles was the children's evening show, *Sheriff John's Lunch Brigade*. Estella saw it for the first time in 1953, along with the local news and two programs featuring puppets, *Time for Beany* and *Thunderbolt the Wondercolt*.[1]

T IS FOR TV WESTERN

The fifteen-minute episodes of *Thunderbolt* had a limited run. But for a while, at 6:00 p.m. every night a hick, buck-toothed horse puppet would transform into "defender of the animal kingdom" by donning a "supersuit," helmet, and goggles. One of its powers was flying to the moon and back in a blink. Estella likely found inspiration for her Silver Star stories from these various horses of the small screen.

At home with her trusty Remington, Estella practiced her typing by copying out TV song lyrics. *(See "Q is for QWERTY.")* They taught her the power of a dramatic, narrative lead-in. Unlike the abstract tunes of today's hit shows, TV Western openers contained entire plots and character portraits. Some of their key features:

   i. The protagonist/hero is introduced as one of a kind. (*Mr. Ed*)
   ii. He is an enigma to the audience. (*Gunslinger*)
  iii. The landscape makes him legendary. (*Zorro*)
  iv. His words matter as much as his actions. (*Lone Ranger*)
     (Note: Rossini, an Italian composer, wrote a French opera about the Swiss independence fighter William Tell. The opera was originally based on a German play. The American West—as we dreamt it—was never homogenous.)

As an adult, Octavia studied and even annotated her childhood TV transcriptions. She noted the nights they aired, and who starred in them. *Have Gun—Will Travel*, with Richard Boone, came on just before *Gunsmoke* on Saturday nights. Walt Disney Productions' *Zorro* showed on Thursdays, on ABC, and starred Guy Williams. (Fig. 20.1). She watched Scott Brady in *Shotgun Slade* in late afternoon reruns. She never forgot *Rawhide*'s Eric Fleming as Gil Favor and Clint Eastwood in the role of Rowdy

Yates.[2] Westerns traffic in loner heroes and outlaws on the run. In her novel *Parable of the Talents*, the name of the pimp who enslaves and collars Olamina's younger brother Marc is named Zorro. Marc bitterly recounts, "All these guys seem to have stupid names."[3] Ever a student of genre, Octavia mined popular culture for plots that could be exported to outer space or speculative African American history.

At thirteen, Estella tried her hand at writing a screenplay called "The Whip." The cast of the "Outlawed" included three "Richards" brothers, two "Marshel" brothers, plus the Richards' father and a sheriff, both good men. She typed out the descriptions for the characters and the sets. In pen she added one woman, Ruth Marshel, a smart, pretty girl with a temper and plenty of sex appeal. Her choice for the lead character was Nick Andrews, a nice but "tuchy" young man in his early twenties who would wear a "spotless white suite" and specialize in whip fighting.[4] His name echoed Nick Adams, Estella's number one actor. On her handwritten list of "Favorite Movie Stars" she circled his name and gave him five stars. She loved him as Johnny Yuma in *The Rebel*. Close behind, though, were Richard Greene as Robin Hood and Gardner McKay as Adam Troy in A.I.P., her shorthand for *Adventures in Paradise*.[5] *(See "A is for Alias.")* Her love for Gardner did have limits. In a diary entry from April 3, 1963 Estella remarked that she had written a note to her friend Connie saying "I had given up Gardner McKay . . . . I really still like him, I'm just tired of his rerun on A.I.P."[6]

My favorite of Estella's TV Western stories is untitled. It features a seven-foot-tall fugitive gunslinger who goes by the name Rex, short for "Tyrannosaurus" Rex. Estella liked her heroes larger than life, and noticeably taller than her. Rex, the dinosaur vigilante on a horse, wins the heart of a runaway Native American girl named

> "Our lips met with hard crushing force. At first I struggled a little. But Rex using only one arm was to [sic] much for me." OEB 2893.

Sun. After he saves her from committing suicide with her father's hunting knife, Sun finds him hard to resist. He is the first white man she has known, and she kind of likes taking orders from him. *(See "F is for Flash.")* Sun admires how Rex piercingly stares down the town marshal of the "white man's village." Later, she saves Rex's life by removing a bullet from his shoulder. Their kiss is steamy. The story contains all Estella's obsessions: mixed-race romance, a tall handsome male heartthrob, and unending adventure. As she put it, "What difficulties lay ahead for a cross marriage [sic] and half breed children."[7]

Octavia's early Western heartthrobs stayed with her. They became the prototypes for the sexy aliens of her later novels. *(See "S is for Sexy.")* In *Survivor*, Diut is the hirsute, virile, green Tekohn who brutalizes and then becomes the devoted lover of the human girl, Alanna. Octavia based him on Michael Ansara, the Syrian actor who played the Apache chief Cochise in the 1950s show, *Broken Arrow*. In her notes on *Survivor* she wrote, "Diut was wonderfully sexy <Michael Ansara doing a romantic Cochese>."[8]

A young Octavia saw, early on, that Westerns *were* a kind of science fiction, set in desolate, alternate universes of settler colonialism where only the fittest survive. In one of her Silver Star stories, Flash asks a human named Ed if he knows what Martians do to Earthlings: "yes he said I - - - - saw it on the ~~western~~ marten movie."[9] She crossed out "western" and wrote Martian instead. Octavia came of age as Westerns were on their way out. The 1960s ushered in new blends of genre fiction. The two-year series *Shotgun Slade* combined Western and private eye drama. Gene Roddenberry, a writer for another show Octavia watched, *Have Gun—Will Travel* (1957–63), went on to create *Star Trek*. A decade later, talking apes rode horses, Western-style, on a future Earth in *Planet of the Apes*. Westerns were moving into outer space.

Survival amidst an unforgiving terrain, especially desertified Southern California, became one of Octavia's signature themes. *(See "V is for Victorville.")* In fact, her *Patternist* novels are essentially Westerns—more searching than Manichean moralizing—and noticeably horsey in setting. *Patternmaster* (1976) takes place so far into the future that Earth seems like a different planet. Yet people ride horses across its postindustrial, postapocalyptic landscapes. One man journeys on horseback southward to Forsyth, California. He aims to escape from bondage under his brother and find sanctuary in the house of his powerful father. In her draft notes, Octavia underscored the importance of this man's struggle for freedom.[10] An advanced race of telepaths rules the world of *Patternmaster*. In this society of masters, lords and apprentices, feudal houses, sectors, and guilds, duels are fought between formidable "Patternist" men who wield, not guns, but mind-ammo and mental shields. One of the final battles is fought between the horse-riding Patternists and the primitive Clayarks on hilly and otherwise deserted terrain. Akin to the "Indians" of the Cowboy-and-Indians genre, Clayarks are humanoid but animalistic. They are highly infectious, having mutated centuries ago from diseased humans to nomadic quadrupeds who rove between the settlements of the Patternist-dominated territory. The Patternist hero, Teray, is young and inexperienced but has the makings of a Western-Martian John Wayne. Octavia wrote of his loner sensibility, "The most prominant fact about the Young One is that he is alone. Throughout his life, he has stood somewhat apart."[11] Teray cannot accept the mental slavery of being controlled by his brother Coransee, so he strikes out on his own and eventually rises to take the place of his father Rayal, the head patriarch who controls the network of mental linkages that is the Pattern.

In this world, horses are a remnant of ancient "Mute" (human) culture. The Mutes, who do not have the power of mental "speech," exist outside the Pattern and live as servants and slaves who are overseen by a muteherd. Like mutes, the horses of this land cannot speak telepathically. One Housemaster, Joachim, has bred and trained show horses for his own pleasure. He allows his stallion to exist free of the mental controls placed on his other subjects: "Gingerly, Teray felt the stallion out. Gingerly because animals, like mutes, were easily injured, easily killed. And too, uncontrolled animals unconsciously hit intruding Patternist minds with any emotions they felt. Especially violent emotions." The stallion has been programmed to maintain composure under fire, so that, as Joachim goes on to explain, "This horse doesn't need to be controlled any more than the average mute."[12] We are meant to sympathize with the plight of Mutes and horses even though they exist on the sidelines. Like the horses of Octavia's drawings, they do not speak, but they have stories that we are not privy to.

The classic Western is not my preferred genre. I never fell in love with John Wayne the way Joan Didion described ("when John

Wayne rode through my childhood, and perhaps through yours he determined forever the shape of certain of our dreams."[13]) On television and in the movies, Westerns still perform amnesia about the genocide of American Indians and the bison that roamed the plains. These TV Western men always struck me as too white, too womanizing in their policing of very dusty places. Of course, lone ranger types were never truly alone. Sassy women talked back to them. Their sidekicks or cooks, usually smaller, darker, or more effeminate in stature, hid unspoken stories behind their helpful, comical demeanors. I did, however, enjoy the cowboys' masks and alter-egos, and their ability to talk while riding and ride while sleuthing. Even if from a white vantage point, they pronounced the plight of the downtrodden. As captured in the lyrics to *Branded* that Octavia typed out, the innocent man, wrongly accused, must withstand the shame and still, fight for his name.

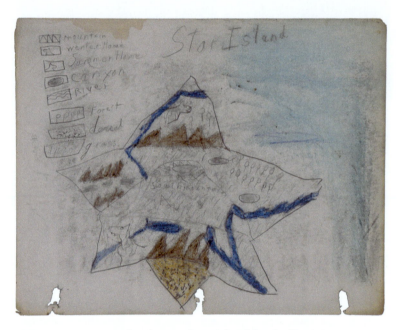

Figure 21.1 Topographical map of Star Island, land of horses, c.1958. OEB 2472.
By permission of Octavia E. Butler Enterprises.

CHAPTER 21

U

IS FOR UTOPIA

In her blue, five-star notebook from 2001, Octavia griped, "Utopia irritates me because it's nonsense! It doesn't exist, cannot exist simply because to be worthy of the name, it would have to please everyone."[1] Her quarrel with utopic thinking had been long in formation. As a high schooler in the early 1960s, she had some reservations about the promises of Communism and "socialistic democracy." When the topic came up in her eleventh-grade Social Studies class, she grudgingly approved of her classmate Steve Blustine's "Pro Communist" position, even if he was a mansplainer.[2] She elaborated on this in another one of her diary entries.

> Wed April 17 (1963)
>
> "I [think] the nearest to a Utopia human nature will ever let us reach is a Communistic or socialistic democracy.... The people own their own homes but the government owns the huge tenements and hotels. This is only part of the idea. There is no possible perfect government

> because people are not perfect. . . . . They will not stop considering themselves better because their skin is light." OEB 3111.

Despite her desire for state-owned factories, farms, and public housing, young Octavia stops short of endorsing an end to private home ownership. Growing up poor, she saw that people need a place to call their own. Her pragmatism also told her racism would persist no matter what; humans were simply too selfish to embrace colorblindness. *There is no perfect government because people are not perfect.*

In the months leading up to the August 28, 1963 March on Washington for Jobs and Freedom, Black Communists from differing vantages called attention to the entanglements of race and class and debated the most promising way forward. The night before Martin Luther King, Jr. made his "I Have a Dream" speech, W.E.B. Du Bois passed away. Only two years before, he had become a Communist at the age of ninety-three. In a letter to Gus Hall, Chairman of the Communist Party of the U.S.A dated October 1, 1961, Du Bois explained his decision to abandon Socialism and apply for Party membership so late in life. He had helped found the NAACP in 1909, but after many decades of work and protest, he now found the organization damningly "capitalist orientated." After his studies of Karl Marx and his travels to the Soviet Union and China, he concluded, with renewed vigor: "Capitalism cannot reform itself; it is doomed to self-destruction. No universal selfishness can bring social good to all."[3]

Meanwhile, even more critical of the NAACP, the Detroit autoworker, labor organizer, and radical intellectual James

Boggs was distancing himself from Marxism and his colleague C.L.R. James in his calls for Black Power. His 1963 book, *The American Revolution: Pages from a Negro Worker's Notebook*, would become an instant hit amongst left circles.[4] Four years later, he elaborated upon his contention that African Americans were "the chief social force for revolt against American capitalism."[5]

The Black radical tradition might not have been what Octavia considered utopic; but she certainly spent time pondering the visionary politics of Black leaders and their freedom dreams. Since her adolescence she had faulted institutionalized religion for the false promise of utopia. *(See "M is for Mother.")* Fire and brimstone were no doubt part of the Baptist upbringings of her mother and grandmother. Octavia culled plenty of fiction material from the Bible (apocalypse, incest, patriarchal punishments and sacrifices, primordial duels, up-and-coming prophets.) But

> "The true benefit of Negro Christianity is in fact gained by whites as their religion controls and molds Negros to docilely accept, endure, wait, and pray. It is interesting to note that Both Richard Wright and James Baldwin found it necessary to remove themselves from the influence of the church . . . . to begin to work effectively." OEB 501.

for guidance on how to be an autonomous thinker lovingly committed to the African American community, she looked to other writers' relationships to the church and state. In the handwritten "Essay on Blacks and Christianity," she speculated that Richard Wright and James Baldwin had to end their reliance on religion to be successful writers.[6] (Like Octavia, they died too young, at ages fifty-two and sixty-three.)

How does one "work effectively" and feel secure in the world when the traumas of past generations live on? Around 1968, Octavia wrote in her green Hytone Spiral notebook, "God is a frame of mind, a wish for perfection a wish for security a need to be cared for."[7] By the time she was finishing community college in 1968, and the war raged on in Vietnam, the Black Panthers had formed their Ten-Point Program of basic "wants" and "beliefs." In the long history of radical manifestoes, their tenth demand seems so basic and yet still universally unrealized: "We want land, bread, housing, education, clothing, justice and peace."[8] In Octavia's final year at PCC, seventeen-year-old Bobby Hutton was the first Panther to be shot dead by Oakland police. Soon Angela Davis would be fired from UCLA for her membership in the Communist Party. As Octavia developed her speculative fictions throughout this period and beyond, she imagined communities—from Forsyth to Acorn—that contended with the disasters of authoritarian rule and modern-day slavery. They are multiracial, sometimes interspecies and pansexual, and far from perfect: they are spaces of "unrelenting tension between consent and coercion, compulsion, and repulsion."[9] Again, utopias take work.

* * *

As a teenager she found ways to defy the beatific vision of heavenly paradise. Her high school stories dwelt in human imperfection and the miseries of earthly existence. She experimented with the impossibility of happy endings. More than once Octavia had contemplated taking her own life. *(See "J is for Junie.")*

U IS FOR UTOPIA

Could she make a story about interminable suffering? "The End?" begins inauspiciously, "It was a lousy world . . . ."[10] A man commits suicide by taking pills, only to wake up surrounded by slimy wetness. We realize, along with him, that he has been reborn as a fetus. In a corrected draft of the typed story, Octavia penned in extra statements about the impossible finality of death. The man would find no reprieve, only endless dying.[11]

Octavia wrote those words when she was sixteen. Toward the end of her life, she revisited this scenario of the soul's transmigrations into new bodies and fresh perspectives. On June 26, 2005, four days after her fifty-eighth birthday, she brainstormed ideas for a novel called *Spiritus*, aka "Bodhisattva," which pondered the possibility of dying, awaking in the womb, and watching yourself live through multiple rebirths.[12] Octavia had been ill and having trouble writing. Her heart medications made it hard to focus. Her friend in Seattle, Leslie Howle, remembers the toll the medicines took on her body and spirit.[13]

I wonder if Octavia would have drawn comfort from her irreverent, eighteen-year-old self who wrote about unheavenly afterlives. Her story, "The Fire," is certainly another variation on utopia, or rather, dystopia. A mother warns her two kids of the torment of hell, while extolling the blissfulness of a heaven where work did not exist.[14] After the child narrator falls terminally ill and dies, she realizes she is entering hell. Unlike all her mother's teachings, here she finds an exquisite sense of belonging: "I am one with my friends and with the fire. The isolation that my human body brought me is gone."[15]

To be free of one's human body and join with nature: this was the fantasy of her early equine hero Silver Star, named for the star birthmark on her shoulder *(See "A is for Alias.")* Estella's

203

topographical map of Star Island (Fig. 21.1) includes a key to help her reader locate the horses' wintering grounds at the southern end of the isle, near the desert. In the summers, they sought shade in the northern mountain forests. We can count six canyons on the island, and blue-crayoned rivers that run along its outer edges. Did she have in mind The Meadows of Altadena when she etched in the grasslands of "South Mountain" in the middle of the map? Or her grandmother's ranch when she colored in the tan terrain of Star Island's patch of desert? *(See "V is for Victorville.")* The island's star formation has not five, but six arms, like the branching appendages of some deep sea Ophiuroids (basket or brittle stars). Star Island conjures earth, sea, and sky.

* * *

When Englishman Sir Thomas More wrote *Utopia* in 1516, he set a precedent for the island locale as a laboratory for an ideal society. The doubled Greek etymology of utopia, *ou-topos* and *eu-topos*, refers to both "no place," and "good place." Only in the nineteenth century, with the advent of industrial capitalism, did the word assume more derogatory meanings, as in "to utopiaize" or to be a "utopia-monger." Utopias are by definition ideal, imaginary, impractical. Most adults today are hard-pressed to describe what utopia looks like; it can be more easily imagined through the ephemerality of sights and sounds. When artists were invited into the Butler archives in 2016 to make a series of commissioned works inspired by her manuscripts, some picked up on Octavia's attention to far-out settings and natural environments.[16] At the exhibition in Pasadena, I was mesmerized by Lauren Halsey's sculpted white landscape, a polar diorama built with foam, plaster, cardboard, and wood that brought to life Octavia's notes

U IS FOR UTOPIA

about an "ice desert." It spread out from a corner of the gallery floor like a glacier on the move.[17] When you walked around it, the silver foil surfaces of the terraced foam sheets caught the light.

On the other walls of the space hung exquisite color photographs by Connie Samaras that superimposed Octavia's Amazon photos onto a manicured Huntington lawn, or bits of her manuscript text amidst the alien-looking succulents of the cactus gardens that Octavia used to visit.[18] Samaras' analog method of photographing mylar text placed up against the cacti captured, by chance, the 8 a.m. light glowing off the plants. She described the ghostly effect as "not a séance, but a presence."[19] Amidst the plant and tree life of the gardens she could feel Octavia's presence. In the gallery I stood before Connie's beautiful diptych of Octavia in a red-flowered shirt with the garden's red roses shimmering through her body and eyeglasses. It filled me with reverence, and in a flash, I recalled my childhood reading of Madeleine L'Engle's *Wrinkle in Time*, in which the interplanetary Mrs. Whatsit "shimmers" into the shape of a flying white horse.

Different as they are, these artworks gleam, not with large-scale "epiphanic shimmer,"[20] but rather with unfinished, palimpsestic glimmerings that collapse time and space. They invite speculation. The archival materials of Octavia's life and work shine through. *Speculation derives from speculum, a reflective surface or mirror that assists with vision.* When handling the physical Star Island map, the glint of the waxy blue crayon gloss leaps off the page. The pencil lines of the horse figures and captions have smudged and faded over time, but not the blue rivers that run in the direction of the star's arms. These are the water sources that sustain the horses, if not cowboys, in the north and the south of this utopia *(See "C is for Character.")* Shine also encases teenaged

Octavia's messages on utopia and Communism, contained as they are within her "One Year Diary": its white faux-leather cover is ornamented with glinty gridlines and fleur-de-lis ornaments that imitate gold-leaf. At the top of the diary, she has penned a small backward percent sign, her own secret ornament *(See "F is for Flash.")* It is impossible to photograph the cover without capturing the glare off the gold. The sheen signals that there are precious words contained within.

For Octavia, utopias were homages to imperfection, and experiments in problem solving. She wrote, "SF gives me the chance to create worlds that do not exist—worlds in which problems are handled in different ways—or in which there are different problems."[21] As much as she worked to be a bestselling author, she never set out to please everyone. She refused utopias because they were at once too abstract and too subjective.[22] Yet, she wanted her invented worlds to be free of bigotry and offer alternatives to current reality. In 1982, she wrote in her journal that she preferred to imagine "not utopias, but sexually egalitarian societies in which women do as they please. No such place exists."[23] *No place is a good place.*

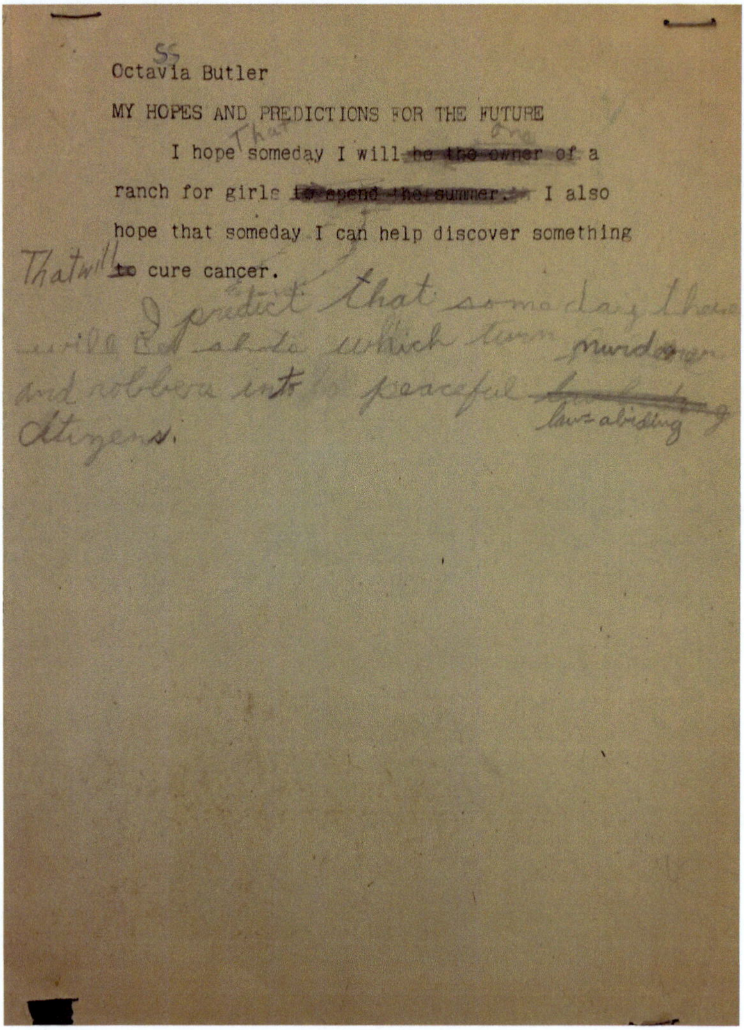

Figure 22.1 "My Hopes and Predictions for the Future," *c.*1957. OEB 1519.
By permission of Octavia E. Butler Enterprises.

CHAPTER 22

V

IS FOR VICTORVILLE

If you head east on the I-10 highway from Los Angeles, it takes you straight out to the desert. On an early October morning I borrowed my mother's car, stocked with plenty of water and gas, and drove toward San Bernardino. Sometimes you must exit the archives to understand the past. This was the route Octavia likely took with her family when she would, as a young girl, visit her grandmother's Victorville chicken ranch in the early 1950s. I wanted to see for myself that remote place where she first gazed up at the Milky Way, far from the city lights, and pondered the extraterrestrial universe.

My first stop was the County Historic Archives, a small, one-room affair at the end of a confusing, commercial cul-de-sac. They had already mailed me copies of the deeds of Edna Estella Hayward Guy, so I knew she had built her ranch on a parcel of land in the vicinity of Bell Mountain in 1947, the same year

> "The desert gave me the kind of perspective I would need later for writing SF, for my stories—when I was 3,4,5,6, I [visited] lived there, off and on, with my grandmother.

> The open spaces <no human sign>
> The stars <the milky way—no smog, no lights>...." OEB 1584, c.1985.

Octavia was born. I was hoping to handle the original documents Mrs. Guy had signed, but they no longer exist, as all the records are on microfilm. The archivist must have noticed my disappointment. She offered to bring out the massive ledger book that indexed grantors and grantees. About halfway down the machine-printed gridlines appeared in faint type the deed record of "Edna Estella" Guy, dated March 13, 1947. I saw that ten days later, a couple rows down, Octavia Guy had also bought land from the same seller, Wendell P. Gladden. This was the official record of the family's once-held claim to a bit of the desert.

The locals in the archive room warned me to get onto I-15 north before traffic would become gnarly at Cajon Pass. En route to the Apple Valley, the road first climbs to the 4000-foot summit. Truck exhaust mixes with the surrounding dust, wind, and overhead haze. Descending into Hesperia, the landscape seemed even more arid. At one point a snake of beige train cars wound its way through the sandy slopes as though they were packaged blocks of desert on the move. From

Figure 22.2 View of Bell Mountain, looking south from where ranches used to stand.
Photo credit: Author.

the deed, I had an exact location: "The East half of the Southeast quarter of the Southwest quarter of Section 9, Township 6 North, Range 3 West, San Bernardino Base and Meridian, San Bernardino County, State of California, containing 20 acres more or less." Using Google Earth, a local historian and former surveyor had kindly drawn for me his estimation of the spot. I knew the house would no longer be there, but this also meant I would be seeing the land the way the African American homesteaders from Los Angeles would have as far back as one hundred years ago.

I parked on the side of the road and ventured on foot into the expanse. No one was around. It was eerily quiet, and yet the thoroughfares of Quarry Road, Stoddard Wells Road, Dale Evans Parkway, and the highway beyond were close enough that the distant whooshing of the trucks blended with the warm, enveloping caress of the Mojave wind. To my south rose Bell Mountain, at a distance appearing to be a pointy molehill (Fig. 22.2). Octavia would have known it by sight. I tried to imagine Mrs. Guy's ranch. There were no signs of habitation left here except for the scattered rusty, half-buried cans, stray tires, and occasional detritus hanging out under the pencilly sage brush. I walked across dried stream beds and the tracks of off-roading escapades, taking note of the yucca and greasewood and tamarisk shrubs, and the creaturely holes that led to cool, underground hideouts. Treading the spongy, crunchy soil crust, I was suddenly aware of the ecosystem beneath my feet.

It is hard to imagine a moment when the Mojave River flowed, and fruit orchards thrived in the valley just to the south. Up through the 1920s, there were pears, grapes, cherries, apples, and alfalfa fields. Before the First World War, the government advertised irrigation projects to water the desert. That promise

> "I have to get up and go sometimes. I'm too much of a hermit normally. It's too easy for me to [get] into a rut."
> c.1980–84. OEB 3222.

and the Los Angeles promoters of Black land ownership lured people like Carrie Story, a formerly enslaved woman who came in 1910 at the age of fifty and built the ranch where she lived until her death in 1938. Her place would have been about a mile to the north of where I stood, close to the former Sidewinder Well and mine that had been erected by even earlier Black homesteaders. Like Story, Octavia's grandmother originally hailed from Louisiana. But she was part of a generation of city folk who came to the high, dry climate looking for relief from asthma or other ailments, or seeking a measure of farming utopia. Some built homes and visited only on weekends. Others made a life raising cattle or poultry. Mrs. Guy must have worked hard to make sure her chickens, and their eggs, stayed cool under the scorching sun.

Just two years after Octavia's family arrived in 1947, the African American residents of Bell Mountain pooled their resources to build a community center. It would have stood right across the way, putting the Guys at the heart of things. By then there would have been electricity, but no phone service for another two or three years. People rode horses to deliver information between the ranches. In the 1940s there were thirty-seven Black families in the area.[1] Mrs. Guy's most famous neighbors were Nolie and Lela Murray, whose racially integrated "Murray's Overall Wearing Dude Ranch" drew locals, journalists, and Hollywood celebrities.

V IS FOR VICTORVILLE

I had not realized the cinematic iconicity of the rocky, desert landscape I'd been driving through all morning. You can take local tours of the boulder formations where countless Westerns' shoot-outs and ambushes were filmed. These are the landscapes where, historically, Paiutes and Mormons faced off in the 1860s. What used to be called Bell Mountain Road is now Dale Evans Parkway, after the singing partner and wife of cowboy star Roy Rogers. At the junction of Highway 18 and Apple Valley Road, you can't miss the twenty-four-foot tall, orange statue of Rogers' other screen partner, Trigger, the beloved Palomino. He (or she?) stands on hind legs like Equus Emily. *(See "H is for Horse.")*

Although the city of Victorville had begun sponsoring show rodeos in 1934, Black celebrities started coming en masse to Murray's only after the 1937 visit by the world heavyweight champion, Joe Louis, who brought the paparazzi. He continued to train at the ranch for over a decade, joined by luminaries like architect Paul Williams and actors Nina Mae McKinney, Bill "Bojangles" Robinson, Louise Beavers, Hattie McDaniel, and Lena Horne. During World War II, USO performers stayed there while on tour. People came for the Black camaraderie, the seventy-foot-long swimming pool, famous chicken dinner meals, horseback riding, tennis, softball, and hunting. At Murray's, as featured in *Life* and *Ebony* magazines, you could get wilderness with the modern amenities of hot showers and electricity.

Did Octavia know the films of Herb Jeffries, the first Black singing cowboy, who shot *Bronze Buckaroo* at the Murray Ranch, just on the other side of Bell Mountain? Jeffries combined Blackness, city, and country, Octavia style, with movie titles like *Harlem*

213

on the Range and *Two-Gun Man from Harlem*. His screen horse was even named Stardusk, which has a Silver Star ring to it. *(See "T is for TV Western.")*

* * *

That day and the next I drove through the surrounding flats and hills, stopping frequently to walk about, encounter the remains of burnt houses, former septic tanks, and old mining railroad tracks. I surveyed Bell Mountain wash and the Bureau of Land Management site from above, noting the Walmart distribution center to the south of the former Guy ranch. In this dusty, likely toxic place, the stuff of modern-day capitalism is warehoused next to the military and mining operations that continue apace. The craggy outcroppings and Joshua trees could be the backdrop of an alien planet. As one local proudly mentioned to me, Beyoncé had recently shot a video out here. At one point, surrounded by dirt and Creosote bushes, I saw out of the corner of my eye something large and gazelle-like whiz by. Could it have been a roadrunner? a coyote? Or, uncannily, a humanoid clayark? Suddenly uneasy, I hurried back to the car.

Published in 1984, *Clay's Ark* is Octavia's most desert-y novel. She dedicated it to the memory of her dear friend Phyllis White, who had died of cancer two years before. The novel mourns her through its landscape. Set in the "future" of 2021, a father and his two daughters drive from Needles to Flagstaff along the old Route 66 through car-rattling winds and mountains that, like Bell Mountain, were formed from volcanic, igneous rock. The youngest daughter, Keira, loves the desert. As they travel toward her grandparents' home in Arizona, they are seized by predatory half-humans who have been infected by an alien organism.

V IS FOR VICTORVILLE

Figure 22.3 Highways to Victorville, Barstow building mural detail, "The Mormon Trail."
Credit: Kathy Fierro and Main Street murals, www.mainstreetmurals.com. Photo credit: Author.

Years before, the spaceship Clay's Ark had crashed in the desert and brought to Earth a parasite that needed human hosts to propagate itself. The enclave of the infected, which includes people from Victorville, lives on a rocky mountaintop homestead. They survive by raising chickens, hogs, rabbits, and cows in the manner of nineteenth-century Apple Valley ranchers. In this past-future moment highways are conduits of risk. The U.S. 95 is nearly gone, and danger lurks along the desolate stretch between State Highway 62 and Interstate 40. A trucker named Lupe is captured when her vehicle breaks down on I-15. (Fig. 22.3)

Governed by the organism inside them, the infected humans become sexually ravenous and commit incest and rape against their own will. Only the mixed-race girl Keira is unafraid of the monstrous offspring of the impregnated women, lithe, cat-like children, the future Clayarks of *Patternmaster*, who run on all fours up to one hundred kilometers an hour. As humans become animal-like, their "ethics, too, must become other."[2] Unlike the others, Keira thrives in this godforsaken place. Her cancer, formerly her weakness, is miraculously cured after she is infected with the Clayark "disease." *(See "X is for Xenogenesis.")* Her unborn child will become part of a new, cross-species race.

I realized that the novel's postapocalpytic homestead is a nightmarish version of the Murrays' utopic Victorville dude ranch. Octavia would not have known the ranch during the 1930s, when Mrs. Murray ran it as a hospice for sick children with tuberculosis, arthritis, and asthma, or when it served as a Black "Boys Town" for troubled youth.[3] Two years after Octavia was born, Lela Murray passed away, but her husband Nolie continued to run the ranch into the 1950s; he sold it in 1955 to the Broadway and TV star Pearl Bailey and her husband, who renamed it the Lazy B. Surely young Octavia would have heard of or visited it, and seen the Black youth of the area working there and riding horses. Perhaps it was the Murray Ranch that inspired her to write, around the age of ten or younger, a list of her "Hopes and Predictions for the Future":

> I hope someday I will be the owner of a ranch for girls to spend the summer. I also hope that someday I can help discover something to cure cancer. I predict that someday there will be shots which turn murderers and robbers into peaceful law-abiding citizens. (Fig. 22.1)

Octavia typed her name at the top of the now yellowed page, adding by hand her "SS" Silver Star alias. *(See "A is for Alias.")* Not only did she dream of a ranch for girls, but also of cures for cancer and criminality. Octavia would spend her adult life researching

V IS FOR VICTORVILLE

and writing about these three things: gender, social problems, and illness, cancer in particular.

On October 21, 1957, maybe the same year she typed this essay, her dear grandmother died of cancer in Pasadena, under the care of her family. Edna Estella Guy was born at the turn of the century in Louisiana, to Samuel Haywood and Margarete Veritt.[4] She had lived a remarkable life. She raised seven kids on her own, did fieldwork and housework, and bought land in several states, an

> "None of my worlds is ever created smoothly. I generally give up on them over and over again—like a smoker trying to quit. I'm told I have discipline. In me, discipline means the ability to develop an addiction to my work." OEB 3222.

enormous feat given that she had only been allowed to go to school until the third grade.[5] As an orphan, she was raised by foster parents, and escaped them at age twelve by marrying a forty-year-old man. By the Depression, she was a widow. And like so many others from the South, she came to California searching for better opportunities. Octavia's final novel, *Parable of the Talents*, was inspired, she said, by "the two most important women in my life: my mother and grandmother."[6] (See "M is for Mother.")

What did Mrs. Guy and the other elders see when they laid eyes for the first time on Bell Mountain and its environs? What were their hopes and predictions? Before I drove on toward Barstow, I took the Apple Valley exit from SR-18 east to 165, Wild Wash Road. I had been counseled by Octavia's cousin to turn right and look out onto the vista.[7] Black homesteaders had once seen promise and security in this stony terrain. I could not begin to predict what will come of all the dryness in future decades. I look to Octavia's writing for her clear-eyed mixture of hope and disaster. Later in life, she noted her three major, girlhood influences were: 1) the desert, 2) being read to sleep at night by her tired, but hopeful mother, 3) being taken to the library before and up through the first grade.[8] For the Pasadena girl who spent time on her grandmother's Victorville chicken ranch, the desert was the gateway to the universe of the mind.

Figure 23.1 Drawing of "White Sun," c.1958. The subtitle, in parentheses, reads: "(captured)," as if to make sure we know Estella would never otherwise depict a horse in a harness. OEB 2465.
By permission of Octavia E. Butler Enterprises.

CHAPTER 23

W

IS FOR WHITE CLOUD

The Holly's moved slowly across the paririe going west always west.
The old covered wagon creeked and groned as if each time the weels
turned it would fall to peaces.

One of Estella's earliest stories from the archive is an exquisite five-pager, in two parts. Part One of "White Cloud" begins on the prairie. Drama quickly ensues when the Holly family's covered wagon is blown to bits by rifle-toting Indians. Nothing is left of Father and Mother Holly or the children—Connie, David, Fredrick, and Dianel (Estella's spelling)—not even their scalps. Miraculously, baby Sara survives thanks to the thick swaddling blankets that pad her fall.

At the start of Part Two, Estella introduces a lapse in time and switch in identities, all in one punchy, carefully calculated sentence that announces a twelve-year-old Sara has been renamed White bird. Adopted by a young Indian brave named "The Wolf," White bird has been raised, not by lions *(See "L is for Lion Girl")*, nor as a half-dog *(See "D is for Dog")*, but by a human "wolf" family. The Indians mistreat her. Children throw stones at her, women work her to the bone, men spit on her and kick her "as though she was a dog." The outcast girl is a recurring character of Estella's, whether the story is set in Holocaust Germany, Cold War Pasadena, the American West, or the African jungle. As she would later note, "Take a character from one background and set him down in the middle of another, you have your conflict ready-made." *(See "C is for Character.")*

At age ten, Estella's collection of fictional names for horses and humans recombined some of her favorite nouns: Gray Fox, Gray Demon, Silver Star, Silver Cloud, White Sun (Fig. 23.1), and White Cloud. In this story, White Cloud is the great stallion that White bird (Sara) has managed to tame. Whenever she can, she sneaks away from the Indian village to visit her stallion friend in a hidden valley of wild horses. When White bird is found out, the Indians accuse her of being a horse-whispering demon, and the scene turns into a witch hunt. Tied to a post and about to be burned at the stake, she is at the last minute rescued by her animal friends, one of whom is a huge dog she rescued from starvation and managed to keep as her secret pet. She shouts that she will kill all her captors unless she is untied, and her crew set free. (Perhaps unintentionally, Estella has substituted the horse's name, White Cloud, for the girl's.) The story concludes cinematically with a band of misfits roaming the land: "many times a lone rider will report seeing on a dark moonless night the shadow of a girl on a horse with a huge dog running beside her." I find this silhouette image of the girl, horse, and running dog unit utterly zany and delightful. The outcast has found her tribe.

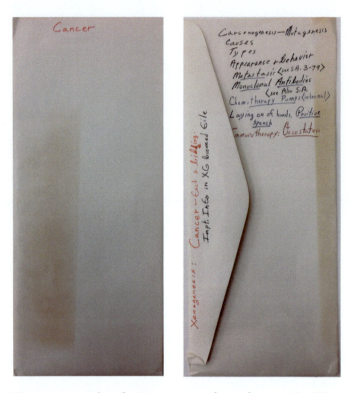

Figure 24.1a and **24.1b** Cancer research envelope, c.1985. OEB 3013. By permission of Octavia E. Butler Enterprises.

CHAPTER 24

X

IS FOR XENOGENESIS

The white envelope labeled "Cancer" has yellowed over time (Figs. 24.1a, b). The imprints of light and air remind me that even flat, ordinary things mutate on a molecular level. On the back of the envelope, Octavia has jotted down the topics of her early-1980s scientific research. *Carcinogenesis, mutagenesis, metastasis, monoclonal antibodies, chemotherapy pumps, immunotherapy, oncostatin* . . . . In bright red ink, the header running up the envelope flap reads, "Xenogenesis: Cancer—fact & bibliog. Impt. Info in XG biomed file" (Fig. 24.1b).

The index cards held by this envelope were only a small portion of the biomedical files she had amassed for her Xenogenesis project, but even this sampling reveals the range of her reading. She consulted science journals, encyclopedias and medical dictionaries, popular books on cancer from the L.A. Public Library, and local news radio. *(See "C is for Character.")* She wrote or typed out biology vocabulary as well as quotations such as, "Cancer is the by-product of civilization and industrialization."[1] Ruth Wilson Gilmore in writing about the Black Radical Tradition invokes the Xenogenesis trilogy as a diagnosis of social ills,

OCTAVIA E. BUTLER

"using the scariest life-substance—cancer—to reflect on expansive constantly changing sociality."[2]

Octavia was intensely interested in ideas of change and growth—cellular, social, political. The 1980s was the era of gene science. Experiments in cloning and mapping were spurred by hopes that cancer-producing oncogenes might be thwarted by anti-oncogenes and tumor-suppressing proteins.[3] Bone marrow transplants for blood cancers were being paired with mega-doses of chemotherapies. And yet, the federal "War on Cancer" declared in 1971 seemed far from being won. President Ronald Reagan fought increased funding of the National Institutes of Health, just as he refused to talk about HIV/AIDS, that other, new, devastating "cancer" that ravaged gay, trans, non-conforming, and straight communities in the U.S. and abroad. In this decade, cancer became a metaphor for everything insidious and toxic.

As a child, Octavia dreamed of curing cancer, the disease that took her grandmother from her. *(See "V is for Victorville.")* She might not have become a scientist, but through

> What fictions might cancer produce? An index card defining oncogenes includes, in pencil, a hypothetical character, Hedeonkos, "destroyer of tumors," based on Greek and Hebrew etymologies. OEB Box 161.

her stories and novels she enacted miracles of cell regeneration and transmutation. Her novel *Clay's Ark* (1984) featured a girl with acute myeloid leukemia (AML); an unpublished short story (*c.*1985) opens with an adolescent who has osteosarcoma, bone cancer, having already lived through acute lymphocytic leukemia (ALL) as a child.[4] The three novels of her Xenogenesis

X IS FOR XENOGENESIS

trilogy—*Dawn* (1987), *Adulthood Rites* (1988), *Imago* (1989)—were built upon a world defined by cancer and how to survive it. Her index cards make explicit the connection between xenogenesis and carcinogens.[5]

Ever the wordsmith, Octavia found that all three meanings of "xenogenesis" listed in her *World Book Encyclopedia and Dictionary* applied to the science fictional world she was envisioning. The first definition she could apply to alien sex, that is "the alteration of generations in which a parthenogenetic [asexual] generation alternates with a sexual generation." *(See "E is for Equisetopsida.")* The second related to cross-species reproduction: "the supposed generation of offspring completely and permanently different from the parent." And the third, "spontaneous generation," likewise captured the hypothetical strangeness of "producing life from non-living matter."[6]

Her interest in spontaneous generation placed Octavia in a long history of science fiction reaching back to that foundational monster text, Mary Shelley's *Frankenstein*. In 1818, Shelley took as her premise the radical, even heretical, idea that human life could be made without male–female intercourse. She was familiar with the theories of poet-scientist Erasmus Darwin (grandfather of Charles Darwin) who wrote, in a rhyming couplet, "Hence without parent by spontaneous birth/ Rise the first specks of animated earth."[7] In the character of the modern mad scientist Victor Frankenstein, Shelley sounded the question that has preoccupied generations, "Whence did the principle of life proceed?" And like Mary Shelley, who called her novel her own "hideous progeny," Octavia found comfort in contriving new forms of life that made her own life more bearable, less lonely.[8]

227

In *Dawn*, Octavia introduced the Oankali race, a nomadic species that depended on mixing with foreigners to survive. I like how Patricia Melzer puts it, "The Oankali define themselves, not through their form, but through the genetic exchange—therefore they *are* difference."[9] Each generation of Oankali is distinct because not all groups participate in the latest bioengineered

> Some of her cancer notecards connect medical definitions with their relevance to *Xenogenesis*. Anaplasia, the reversion of a cell into a non-functional embryonic state, helped her to imagine the limb regeneration of the Oankali. OEB Box 161.

gene exchange. They rely on difference to evolve and stay alive. They cannot afford the human fear of difference or resistance to change. In her notes, Octavia wrote, "The Oankali know that xenophobia is death. Solitary pointless death. It is a childhood through which some races do not live to pass."[10] Her three Xenogenesis novels follow the saga of posthumanity as childhood development writ large. I find it telling that she chose to conclude with *Imago* and not "adulthood" per se. An imago refers to an insect's final adult stage, and, in psychoanalysis, "an unconscious childhood concept of a parent or other person carried over unchanged into adulthood."[11] Whenever possible, Octavia troubled assumptions of human superiority and progress.

Adulthood, according to Octavia, was overrated. She wrote the Xenogenesis novels amidst the Cold War nuclear arms race between the United States and the Soviet Union. On one notecard she wrote, "Humanicide: What is Nuclear 'War' It is not war. It is humanicide. A killing of the human species."[12] She followed news of the mass protests against the nuclear proliferation and missile defense policies of Ronald Reagan's administration. Sometimes the nightmare of the political present can feel like time travel. In a typed letter to her friend Vonda N. McIntyre, dated January 28, 1985, she wrote:

> I'm not sure 1984 is over in spirit.... Reagan is going to leave so much that needs undoing.[13]

Then, on April 26, 1986, the Chernobyl Nuclear Power Plant exploded. What does science fiction do when precarity turns catastrophic and the surreal is the real? Octavia cited Reagan's belief in a winnable nuclear war as inspiration for her trilogy. She felt humans were "programmed to self-destruct" and world leaders were responsible for this destruction.[14] In *Dawn*, the character of Gabriel Rinaldi was, like Reagan, "an actor, who had confused the Oankali utterly for a while because he played roles for them instead of letting them see him as he was."[15] On Earth, government and military figures who had created much of the destruction were "hiding deep underground" and then rescued by the Oankali. In a turn of power, the aliens used them as human subjects to learn biology, language, and culture. From this the Oankali believe, incorrectly, that all humans are venal.[16]

The rainforest was, for Octavia, a place of rebirth. She placed her nuclear war survivors in the Amazon basin, where they would rely on oils and not fossil fuels for power. If the Xenogenesis books were motivated by cancer and by Reagan, they were also Octavia's Amazon novels. While writing the trilogy, she read as much about the Amazon, and environmental and nuclear politics, as she covered genetics and bioengineering. On one notecard she divided her reading list according to "Anthropology" (books about the Amazon and Samoa) and "Zoo." The latter included titles such as *Gorillas in the Mist, The Education of Koko, Man and Dolphin.* She also made three categories of how humans control nature: 1) national parks, 2) pets, and 3) zoos. The latter, she called "a prison, however well run. Exists for the benefit-entertainment and scientific—of those outside the cages."[17] *(See "D is for Dog.")*

The protagonist of *Dawn*'s brave new world, Lilith Iyapo, is a zoo experiment for the Oankali. They study her, just as she studied others in her previous life on Earth as an anthropology major. She becomes a leader of human–alien relations, belonging fully to neither group, in part because she has cancer in her genes. Without her consent, the Oankali opened up her body to study the disease before they cured her of it; they also enhanced her abilities to chemically heal herself and others. The Oankali refer to Lilith's predisposition to cancer as a "talent." Self-destruction switches to self-preservation. Her gene mutations and anaplasia allow her to save the life of the ooloi, Nikanj. *(See "O is for Ooloi.")* As Nikanj, the third-sex alien, reassures Lilith, "It [the cancer] isn't a problem anymore . . . . It's a gift. It has given me my life back."[18] This is perhaps the most radical and wondrous premise of the novel, that someone might thank cancer for its mutational possibilities. In an alien universe, the disease is, simply, cell growth. Even if tumorous, growth can be harnessed for evolutionary survival. Octavia saw cancer in and through many phenomena, including the history of medical experimentation and racial slavery.[19] On her notecard on "Chimera," she gives the biology textbook definition, a single organism made of two or more tissues of distinct genetic composition, but goes on to

X IS FOR XENOGENESIS

note, in red pen: "Seems to me a Chimera can be a person with a cancer."[20]

*   *   *

From a human perspective it is hard to imagine being grateful for cancer. Everyone knows it's out there, but when it touches you or someone close to you, it becomes an all-consuming nightmare. On June 9, 2017, my mother was rushed to the emergency room. Her white blood cell count was through the roof, and the doctors quickly confirmed she had acute myeloid leukemia (AML). The next day I flew out to California with a carry-on suitcase, and I stayed for a full year fighting for her life against the odds. She would need a bone marrow (stem cell) transplant of the kind Octavia had begun to read about in the 1980s. I began to scan the published research of the hematologists and oncologists and tried to absorb the science of proteins, cells, and gene mutation. I read popular non-fiction that described leukemia as "cancer in a molten, liquid form," which made me picture my mother's blood spreading inoperable malignance throughout her body.[21] My brothers and I waited as the hospital searched the world for a stem cell donor, knowing how hard it would be to find a 100 percent match. I could barely comprehend the statistic that one in three women, and one out of two men, will have cancer in the course of their life. Though that implicated me and everyone I knew, it still seemed impossible to believe that, with no family history of cancer, my mother would fall ill. She was the strong one who was supposed to care for—and outlive—my father.

When someone is in the hospital for months at a time, you learn the rhythms of the hallways, the quirks of the cafeteria and the elevators. The building itself can become a comfort. You cling to anything knowable. This includes the letters and numbers that signal the patient's inner vitality. I took a daily photo of the white

> "<Children are not little adults, but Adults are big children.>" September 30, 1981, OEB 3177.

board that monitored WBC, Hgb, Plt, K, Cr, Mg. I watched the chemotherapy take effect and wipe out her entire immune system, reducing her white blood cells to zero. She had to be protected from everything. We entered her room in mask, gloves, and gown. Every tickle in my throat or sign of a cough might endanger her. She stayed sane in her own way, by praying to God, but also by assiduously recording in her notebook every dosage of medication and minute procedure throughout the day. The nurses learned to patiently spell out medical terms for her. Over the months, she had fevers, blood transfusions, allergic reactions, neutropenia, loss of hair, loss of appetite. A Hickman tube, embedded in her chest for eight months straight, pumped medicines into her intravenously.

The hospital staff counted down the days until the transplant, and then the days afterward. Day Zero, transplant day, came with a candle on a cupcake and a Happy Birthday song. With an entirely new blood system, she was in effect a newborn in an adult body. She went from a 20 percent chance of survival to miraculously cancer free, and is now seven years out, and counting. The cancer vocabulary I grew to know so well has somewhat faded, but I know that it could be reactivated at any moment.

During a crisis, I kick into high gear. I can handle anything. After six months I began to burn out, and my own body started breaking down. The compliment I often got, "You're such a good daughter," made me oddly disconsolate. It felt like I had no choice but to be the self-sacrificing, Asian daughter. I found an emotional lifeline in the Huntington archives, just a short drive from my parents' home. When I could get there, I would open a box of Octavia's papers. One day I came upon a notecard labeled "Leukemia," in which Octavia noted the poor prognosis for AML, which ravages the body of Keira in *Clay's Ark*.[22] I found it hard to believe she was writing about the very leukemia my mother had. She had studied this cancer and used it to tell a mixed-race, mixed-species story of survival. Around the same time, I discovered Octavia's childhood horse drawings and realized she imagined each horse as a Charles Dickens character. *(See "H is for Horse.")* I began to inhabit her Silver Star world as an adult keenly aware of being a child, parenting my own parents, undertaking everyday time travel.

In the archives I immersed myself in the young Octavia's struggles to survive. In her senior year of high school, around 1965, Octavia wrote, "For a long while, I was afraid nobody would notice me. That I would live and die and no one would ever know or care or remember. I used to think about it a lot. I don't know how many times it made me move the revolver away from my head, put it down and pick up the pen again and start writing."[23] *(See "B is for Bambi.")* Later in life, as she continued to dwell on the human propensity for self-destruction, she noticed that there is no word that is the opposite of "self-destruct." And so, she coined her own verb, "self-construct," which she defined as, "to construct one's self, to create oneself."[24]

In this day and age, we all have cancer stories. Octavia's early 1980s notecards sought to turn loss and destruction into a story of creation. One of my favorite notecards lists the wildly different books she was reading at the time: *The Chemistry of Love*; *Sex and the Brain*; *Deceit and Self-Deception: In Plants, Insects, and Ourselves*; and *Right-Wing Women: The Politics of Domesticated Females*. Xenogenesis had to do with all of the above: sex, desire, science, plants, and politics. Octavia found the principle of change to be key to survival. On another card, she paired the Latin phrase "*Mutatis Mutandis*, <u>with</u> <u>the</u> <u>necessary</u> <u>changes</u>" with that of "*Sine Qua Non*, Without which, not <an essential part>." For a time, my mother's cancer was the *sine qua non* of my being. It demanded selflessness, and seemed life-destroying, but has taught me, *mutatis mutandis*, how to self-construct.

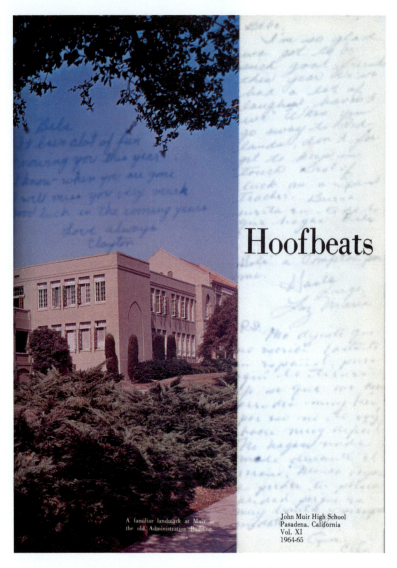

Figure 25.1 Title page of John Muir High Yearbook, 1964–65.
Courtesy: Bebe Martin-Smith and John Muir High School.

CHAPTER 25

Y

IS FOR YEARBOOK

In the 1960s, John Muir High was the only integrated high school in the city, noticeably different from the elite white campus of cross-town rival Pasadena High. Its mascot was a wild yellow Mustang, and its yearbook was titled "Hoofbeats" (Fig. 25.1, 25.3). Paging through Octavia's yearbooks, you see kids of different colors posed side by side in clubs, sports teams, and student government. They remind me of a paradigmatic moment from *Parable of the Sower*, which describes the people taken in by Olamina as "the most racially mixed that I had ever met .... [One] woman had a Japanese father, a black mother, and a Mexican husband."[1]

At school Estella might have been quiet and shy, bullied by some and ignored by many, but she was recognized as a writer. By her senior year, even Mrs. Miller, the Secretary, wished her good luck with her writing. Teachers and staff signed her yearbook, "Estella, I have deeply enjoyed your keen insight and excellent writing," and "My greatest wish is that all my students would be exactly like you." Over and again, her peers comment in loopy blue or black-inked cursive, "I sure hope you finish that novel cuz you left off at a very suspenseful place" and predict her future success.[2]

Figure 25.2 Octavia's senior yearbook photo. Far left-center: Octavia (starred.) Directly beneath her: Romay Callos, labeled "A Winner." OEB Box 337.
By permission of Octavia E. Butler Enterprises and John Muir High School.

> "I write about an integrated world because I live in one. I've never lived in an all black neighborhood or gone to an all black school.... Whites can portray themselves in their fiction as living in an all-white world. Blacks, for reasons of self preservation, can afford no such illusions." OEB 651.

Y IS FOR YEARBOOK

Yearbook signing is a peculiar American ritual, steeped in Hallmark sentiment and the bright-eyed performance of future nostalgia. For the shy and downtrodden, it is a sanctioned moment to approach people you'd never talk to otherwise and ask for their autograph. You suspect they will say generic things, yet you hope for something special. Scrutinizing the handwritten notes in Octavia's yearbook, I got an inkling of her classmates' personalities. The most revealing page is the first one. In the space above the title, "Hoofbeats," her good acquaintance Romay sweetly compliments her on all the science fiction stories she's written in the past two years. She encourages Octavia to finish her novel and wishes her a wonderful summer. "Best of luck in your writing, even though I know you'll succeed in that field." She pledges to be friends forever. (Fig. 25.2).

Beneath Romay's message appears the old-fashioned and wobbly penmanship of a proud, unlettered elder:

> Dear daughter: I am Very Proud of Octavia E. Butler She is a Wounderful daughter. she has never given me one monets truble. She is Very loving—Kind Person, I Love her Very much. She is also Very helpful. I can't ask for a Better daughter. Mother.[3]

As an afterthought, perhaps for posterity, she puts at the top of the message her own initials, O.M. Butler. Motherly testimony is usually off-limits in a high school yearbook, but Octavia Sr. knew more than anyone how far Estella had come. *(See "M is for Mother.")* She had encouraged her to write—she was the one who had brought home discarded books from her cleaning jobs and had bought Estella her first typewriter. *(See "Q is for QWERTY.")* And, she must have known how much her daughter struggled to fit in.

OCTAVIA E. BUTLER

At school, people knew Estella as an odd girl with a notebook, but most didn't really get her. Some of her classmates responded to my email inquiry that they wished they had known her better. Yet, she observed them closely, always looking for material for her stories. As an adult, she revisited her yearbooks for inspiration, underlining people she knew and annotating those with distinguishing traits. She circled in red felt pen the most notorious Muir grad, Sirhan Sirhan (Class of 1963, who was on Junior and Senior Class Council). Octavia wrote in the margin next to his name that he was the shooter of Robert Kennedy.

Yearbooks were repositories for two of Octavia's research passions: names and personalities. At the end of one of her many alphabetized, handwritten lists of names, she included several classmates: Danetta, Joetta, and Romay.[4] She even wrote a short story, "Lifesong," (c.1965) with a protagonist named Romay. In multiple drafts, Romay, the sympathetic lover of Alon, is punished violently by the nonhuman Kaeomon. (In one version, she dies when the alien rubs her face with deadly fungi.) In her marginal notes Octavia experimented with her friend's last name, scribbling "Callos" and, backwards, "Ollac."[5]

When I spoke to the actual Romay over the phone, she had no idea Octavia thought so well of her. She admitted she had only learned of Octavia's illustrious writing career after her death, although her daughter-in-law had become a fan by reading Octavia's novels in college. I asked Romay what she remembered of high school, and she described how cruel the kids could be to Octavia, who was incredibly quiet and so much taller than everyone else. She and Octavia had known each other since junior high, when they would always sit next to each other in class due to the alphabetical proximity of their last names, Butler and Callos. She became one of Octavia's most avid story readers, a practice that continued into high school. Octavia would ask her if the writing made sense or not. She found them "so fascinating and so well-written." Romay was an outgoing girl who liked everybody, but who found friendship with misfits. She said of Octavia, "I loved her."[6]

* * *

Most of the Muir alumni I spoke with think fondly of their time there and, at least at first, did not recall much racial tension. Everybody pretty much got along. Barbara, a third generation Pasadenan, felt a "sense of equality" growing up in such "liberal-minded" environs. Yet she also felt different coming from a mixed-race family. As a couple her parents were "trailblazers" for their time.[7] During the war, while her Japanese mother was sent to the internment camps, her Black father served in the military. As much as Octavia wrote interracial couplings into her novels, they were far from sanctioned in the early 1960s. Her classmate Dani attended the Turkey Tussle one year with a white boy and was yelled at in the stadium by several Black boys for betraying her kind. Dani was also part of the homecoming court the first year Muir elected a Black homecoming queen. The celebratory moment fell short when they were not featured in the yearbook, and the principal declined to conduct the crowning ceremony. (Instead, the duty was given to the inexperienced student class president, and even the actual crown "kind of fell off" her head.) When Dani published a letter in the school paper protesting the discrimination, it cost her much goodwill.

Other Muir students experienced even more direct racism. As Sylvia put it, "No white kid was guilty and no black kid was innocent." One day at school she was cornered by a white girl, who called her the N-word. She knew there was no point in reporting

Figure 25.3 Muir students with Mustangs banner, 1965.
Courtesy: Bebe Martin-Smith and John Muir High School.

it. As bleak as things could be, times were also changing; her beloved older brother Thomas (Class of 1962) had the distinction of being the first Black student body president.[8]

A decade or so after graduation, Octavia made a typology of human behavior based on the adolescents archived in her Muir yearbooks. *(See "C is for Character.")* Most of the portraits are unflattering. She extrapolated the worst traits of her classmates into a character list of bullies, complainers, whiners, turncoats, leaders, followers, queen-bee, and pairs such as "Macho Bully & Slave" or "Abused child bully." Two boys epitomized the nasty men of the world, "The controlled, Intelligent, Sociopath" and lizard-like men.[9] There is the short, no-neck, squat one. The one who was ostracized for being prettier than another. The rebel who had sex by twelve and got married right after high school. She wondered about the girl who liked organizing other people's lives but secretly feared being alone: "Kindly, good hearted, generous, gregarious and hopelessly flawed."[10]

Octavia included an entry on "Mother" in her yearbook character chart, referencing her mom and "Big Mom, Grandmother Estelle. *(See "V is for Victorville.")* "The work of her life," she writes,

Y IS FOR YEARBOOK

"was her children . . . . She was kept ignorant, much abused, abandoned, cheated, and she was the stronger for it."[11] She came through the fire intact.

* * *

Like a cemetery, a yearbook is a collection of people who didn't necessarily choose to be grouped together for posterity. Both the class photo and the gravestone place an individual within a community of other unique individuals and render them generic within the organized grid of pages or plots. In novels like *Dawn* and *Mind of My Mind*, Octavia's female protagonists build a new society by selecting members based on their profiles. Each type has a role to play in the survival of the species. They gather names and backstories as though compiling a census of the future.[12]

Octavia turned her yearbooks into a resource for her writings on human adolescence, which she considered a societal problem. Everything gangly and awkward, cliquish and cruel, had novelistic value. In her yearbook notes she wrote that a bully like Dorothy was probably abused at home, an unfashionable Linda did not receive enough love from her fundamentalist parents, that Octavia herself was socially inept and badly dressed.[13] She dwelled on the past not for the sake of holding grudges, but to learn from the power of the bullies.

Today, Muir High School proudly displays her photo in the main hallway, right above the metallic lockers numbered 179 and 181. Students probably rarely look up to notice it, much less have time to wander down the hallway to the two small rooms that house the school museum. Octavia was inducted into the Alumni Hall of Fame in 1992 along with a cartoonist, urologist, and football player. Her field is incorrectly listed on the plaque as "Journalism." Then again, she did report on the world as she saw it.

243

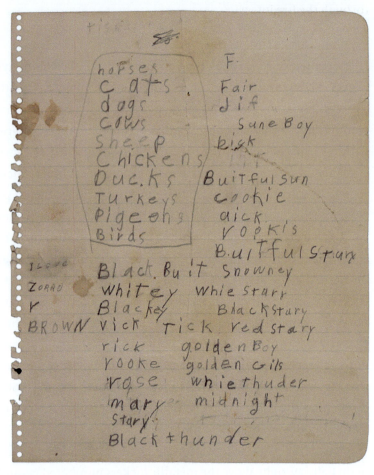

Figure 26.1 (unfolded) and **Figure 26.2** (folded) List of animal/character names, c. 1957. OEB 1620.
By permission of Octavia E. Butler Enterprises.

CHAPTER 26

Z

IS FOR ZORRO

The penciled list begins with horses and barnyard animals and then graduates to a smattering of adjectives and proper names for potential horse heroes, landing on Black Thunder at the bottom of the page (Fig. 26.1). It's not likely Estella would have known Arna Bontemps' 1936 novel *Black Thunder* as an elementary schooler, but the name rang of fiery rebellion nonetheless. Running down the list are experimental variations on the celebrity equines that galloped across the silver screen. These were magnificent beasts with cosmic monikers like Silver, Silver Bullet, Golden Cloud, White Flash, Thunder, Black Jack, Black Diamond, and Black Beauty. *(See "R is for Rex McDonald.")*

Estella had plans of her own. Intermixed are girls' names (Rose, Mary) and the sounding out of kindred words (vick, tick, rick, rooke) that might come in handy for a horse heroine such as the one she would become, Silver Star. *(See "F is for Flash.")* My eyes are drawn, though, to the margin. In all caps, a fangirl's confession: I LOVE ZORRO Y BROWN. I'm not sure about Brown, though she did later list Peter Brown as one of her favorite actors in his role as the young, lady-loving Deputy Johnny McKay on TV's *Lawman*.

There is no doubt as to Señor Zorro's appeal to a girl who trafficked in alter egos. A masked avenger with a dual identity, his name was Spanish for "fox." With intellectual cunning and expert swordplay he left his mark on the villains of 1800s California by slashing his "Z" mark onto their faces. Like Estella, aka Karen Adams, aka Silver Star, he made sure to sign his work but gave away nothing of his true self. *(See "A is for Alias.")*

El Zorro kept his black horse Tornado in a secret cave attached to his hacienda. Garbed in all black—hat, mask, silk cape, and clothes—he was not only fox-like, but bat-like. He inspired the young Bruce Wayne to take up the disguise that would turn him into Batman.

The page has been torn out from a notebook and folded up (Fig. 26.2), as if it were a talisman to be carried in a pocket for good luck or safekeeping. It might inspire confidence or remind her of the animals, nouns, aliases, and future stories that were things she could be sure of, and hold tight. However shakily spelled, each word conjures a small, other world unto itself.

BUTLER'S WORKS CITED

"Crossover" (1971)
Patternmaster (1976)
Mind of my Mind (1977)
Survivor (1978)
Kindred (1979)
Wild Seed (1980)
Clay's Ark (1984)
Dawn (1987)
Adulthood Rites (1988)
Imago (1989)
Parable of the Sower (1993)
"The Book of Martha," in *Bloodchild and Other Stories* (1995)
Parable of the Talents (1998)
Fledgling (2005)

HORSE APPENDIX /
APPENDIX OF HORSES

Attached in this Horse Appendix are all ten of the drawings Octavia traced from Anna Pistorius' *What Horse Is It?* and ingeniously captioned according to their breed traits, that is, those she felt best corresponded to the fictional characters of Charles Dickens' *David Copperfield*. I have grouped them in pairs of "character species." *(See "H is for Horse.")*

(Note: an American Appendix Horse is a mixed breed, first-generation cross between a Quarter Horse and a Thoroughbred, which combines their respective qualities of agility and strength. It tends to be excitable. It can be all colors and sizes but is generally very tall.)

HORSE APPENDIX / APPENDIX OF HORSES

Character Species #1: The Diminutive Villains

It's no coincidence that Octavia assigned two of the most despicable characters of *David Copperfield* to small-sized pseudo-horses, one a donkey and the other a shaggy feral horse named after a Russian-Polish explorer of Central Asia, and by some counts considered its own species, *Equus ferus przewalskii*. Octavia puts the cloying embezzler Uriah Heep and the dour, controlling Miss Jane Murdstone in their place.

HORSE APPENDIX / APPENDIX OF HORSES

Figure 28.1 "Preshevalski's Horse." Anna Pistorius, *What Horse Is It?* (Wilcox & Follett, 1952).
Figure 28.2 "IF [*sic*] Uria Heep were a Horse he would look like this." OEB 461.

By permission of Octavia E. Butler Enterprises.

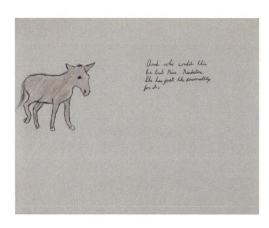

Figure 28.3 "Donkey." Anna Pistorius, *What Horse Is It?* (Wilcox & Follett, 1952).
Figure 28.4 "And who could this be but Miss Murdstone. She has just the personality for it." OEB 461.

By permission of Octavia E. Butler Enterprises.

HORSE APPENDIX / APPENDIX OF HORSES

Character Species #2: The Gentle Giants

In contrast to the pint-sized villains, we have the hefty, lovable paragons of servitude, the working-class Peggotty family. Octavia likened them to draft horses used to pull massive weights. Long before they became beasts of burden, the Belgian and the Shire were ridden by armored knights. They served nobly. So, too, David's childhood nurse (Clara) Peggotty, was the devoted servant of his late mother, also named Clara. She dedicates her life to caring for David. Her brother, the selfless Mr. Peggotty, takes in and adopts his orphaned nephew Ham and niece, Emily. Mr. Peggotty raises Ham to be like him, a working-class Yarmouth boatman. Both men pledge themselves to love Emily, no matter how far she falls from respectability. They are the beautiful, uncomplaining workhorses who persevere, giving endlessly of themselves.

HORSE APPENDIX / APPENDIX OF HORSES

 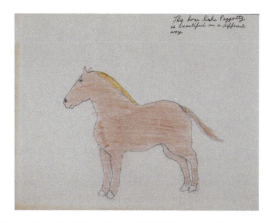

Figure 28.5 "Belgian." Anna Pistorius, *What Horse Is It?* (Wilcox & Follett, 1952).
Figure 28.6 "This horse like Peggotty is beautiful in a different way." OEB 461.
By permission of Octavia E. Butler Enterprises.

Figure 28.7 "Shire." Anna Pistorius, *What Horse Is It?* (Wilcox & Follett, 1952).
Figure 28.8 "This could stand for Ham or Mr. Peggotty. It is the largest breed of horse in the world". OEB 461.
By permission of Octavia E. Butler Enterprises.

253

Character Species #3: The Successful Parents

Agnes Wakefield and David Copperfield overcome countless obstacles to gain a stable and virtuous home life. Even as they step into the proper roles dictated by Victorian Christianity, Dickens distinguishes their kind of moral purity from the patrician, power-hungry unions of social pedigree. Beautiful, beatific Agnes is ever loyal to her infirm father, and a friend to David in his time of need. She is like a sister, that is until she becomes his second wife, mother of his children, and partner for life. Octavia achieves the whiteness of Agnes the Arabian by leaving the torso uncolored, such that it is a rather ghostly outline. She has removed the sheik on the horse's back and re-gendered Pistorius' stallion as a mare with a mane that cascades down sideways. The Arab, known for its breed purity, has a counterpart in the glistening brown Morgan, a famous American breeder. Octavia leaves this horse curiously unlabeled, but it might well be David Copperfield himself, looking intelligent and authoritative. It is the only horse to look straight out at us. It stands upright and alert with expressive, jet-black eyes and mane. A Morgan stallion founded the other famous American breeds, the American Saddlebred and the Tennessee Walking Horse. It is, like David, known for its versatility; its exact pedigree, too, is unknown.

HORSE APPENDIX / APPENDIX OF HORSES

Figure 28.9 "Arabian." Anna Pistorius, *What Horse Is It?* (Wilcox & Follett, 1952).
Figure 28.10 "The Arab is said to be the Purest breed in the world. It could represent no one but Agnes." OEB 461.

By permission of Octavia E. Butler Enterprises.

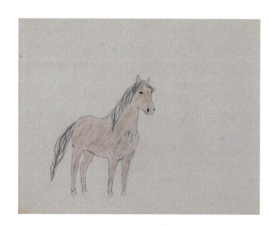

Figure 28.11 "Morgan." Anna Pistorius, *What Horse Is It?* (Wilcox & Follett, 1952).
Figure 28.12 Uncaptioned [possibly David Copperfield]. OEB 461.

By permission of Octavia E. Butler Enterprises.

255

Character Species #4: The Tragic Performers

Two charming American show horses in learned, artificial poses and curled left front legs stand in for the charismatic Tom and Dora, David's youthful obsessions. In the novel, each beguiled him with their looks, confidence, and lively rhythm. From his school days on, David reveres the gallant, action-oriented Tom, who has a way of casting a spell over adults and children alike. His horsey counterpart is Dora Spenlow, the ever-girlish daughter of David's lawyer boss, whom David falls for and then marries. Pretty Dora delights in her lap dog and fails at being a homemaker. Dora, like Tom, flashes brightly but cannot outlast the thrill of courtship. Her tragic, early death from illness marks the end of David's youthful folly and makes way for his mature life with Agnes. Even Dickens, in his time, remarked that "The American saddle-horses are the prettiest creatures imaginable out of a circus, and are as prettily harnessed."[1]

HORSE APPENDIX / APPENDIX OF HORSES

Figure 28.13 "Tennessee Walking Horse." Anna Pistorius, *What Horse Is It?* (Wilcox & Follett, 1952).
Figure 28.14 "I don't know why this horse, the Tenn. Walking Horse, should remind me of Steerfourth [sic] but it does." OEB 461.

By permission of Octavia E. Butler Enterprises.

Figure 28.15 "American Saddle Horse." Anna Pistorius, *What Horse Is It?* (Wilcox & Follett, 1952).
Figure 28.16 "The American Saddle Horse is nicknamed 'Peacock of the show ring.' I imagin [sic] if David were a horse he would want Dora to look like this." OEB 461.

By permission of Octavia E. Butler Enterprises.

HORSE APPENDIX / APPENDIX OF HORSES

Character Species #5: The Searchers

Good natured, hapless, and aspirational, Mr. Wilkins Micawber is always looking for something. He lives a life of debt and continuous woe, and his wife and children are perpetually "in difficulties." Though he cannot make it in England, he eventually finds a magistrate position in the overseas Commonwealth. Octavia's drawing of *Equus Micawber*, the Pinto, bears the least resemblance to the original, whose complicated pose has its body turned to overlook a band of wild horses in the distance; it's as though Octavia had difficulty disengaging the Native American rider, Sitting Bull, and the horse, who are pictured as one. She changes the Pinto's inter-patched white and brown into neat black splotches on a white horse. Yet I find rather brilliant her repurposing of the turned body and downward gaze to embody the comically abject Micawber. Emily, David's childhood sweetheart, also wanders through life having pursued love to her own demise and exile. Octavia makes her a figure of resistance in aligning her with the golden Palomino rising up on its hind legs.

HORSE APPENDIX / APPENDIX OF HORSES

Figure 28.17 "Pinto." Anna Pistorius, *What Horse Is It?* (Wilcox & Follett, 1952).

Figure 28.18 "If this pony appears to be looking for something, he is. Its [sic] Mr. Micabwer [sic] looking for the 'something' that will turn up some day." OEB 461.

By permission of Octavia E. Butler Enterprises.

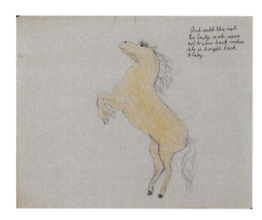

Figure 28.19 "Palomino." Anna Pistorius, *What Horse Is It?* (Wilcox & Follett, 1952).

Figure 28.20 "And could this not be Emily as she vows not to come back unless she is brought back, a lady." OEB 461.

By permission of Octavia E. Butler Enterprises.

INDEX OF NAMES

Ada Matsumoto
adrienne maree brown
Aesop
Agnes Wakefield
Aimee Meredith Cox
Alanna
Alexis Adkins
Alfred Crosby
Alison Saar
Amber
AnaLouise Keating
Angela Davis
Anna Pistorius
Anna Sewell
Anne Rice
Anyanwu
Ashraf H. Rushdy
Audre Lorde
August Simien, Jr.
Ayana A.H. Jamieson
Barbara Richardson-King
Bebe Martin-Smith
Bette Davis
Beyoncé
Bill Downey
Black Beauty
Bob Barnes
Bruce Wayne
Carl Abbott
Carrie Story
Charles Dickens
Charles H. Rowell
Charles White
Christina Sharpe
Connie Samaras

Conseula Francis
Dana Jones
Dani Black Patterson
Daniel Defoe
Daniel Tucker
Daria Topousis
David Copperfield
Dora Spenlow
Doro
Edna Estelle Hayward Guy
Emily (Little Em'ly, niece of Mr. Peggotty)
Erasmus Darwin
Ernestine Walker
Eve L. Ewing
Felix Salten
Gardner McKay
Gene Roddenberry
Gerard Manley Hopkins
Gerry Canavan
Gina M. Dorré
Grace Lee Boggs
Guy Williams
Gwendolyn L. Brooks
Harlan Ellison
Harriet Tubman
Herb Jeffries
Highland Dale
Ira Berlin
Jackie Robinson
Jacqueline Woodson
James Baldwin
James Boggs
Jan van der Straet
Jayna Brown

INDEX OF NAMES

Jean Phillips
Jeanne Newton Schoborg
Jeffrey Elliot
Joan Didion
Joan Fry
Joetta
John Berger
John Brown
John Clare
John F. Kennedy
John Wayne
Jonathan Swift
Jorge Cho
Joseph Li-Chin Shing
Josh Sides
Judy Matthews
Julia Meltzer
K-Ming Chang
Karen Adams
Karl Marx
Keira (Maslin)
Kellie Jones
Kiki Smith
Larry McCaffery
Lassie
Laura R. Barraclough
Lauren Halsey
Lauren Oya Olamina
Laurice James Butler
Leah-Rae Johns
Lena Maloney
Leslie Howle
Lewis Carroll
Lilith Ayapo
Lorne Greene
Louis L'Amour
Lynell George
Lynn Guy
Madeleine L'Engle
Madhu Dubey
Mahalia Jackson
Man Ray
Margaret Cavendish
Marguerite Henry
Marilyn Mehaffy

Marion J. McCue
Martin Luther King, Jr.
Mary Larkin
Mary Shelley
Maya Angelou
Megan Behrent
Meredith McKenzie
Michael Ansara
Michael Mims
Michele Zack
Miss (Jane) Murdstone
Mister (Wilkins) Micawber
Mowgli
Moya Bailey
Natalie Russell
Nathaniel Mackey
Nikanj
Nisi Shawl
Nolie and Lela Murray
Octavia Margaret Guy Butler
Ouida
Pablo Miralles
Patricia Laffan
Patricia Melzer
Paul Bryan
Pearl Bailey
Peggotty (Clara)
Peggotty (Ham)
Peggotty (Mr.)
Peter Pan
Priscilla Wald
Ray Bradbury
Rebecca Wanzo
Richard Wright
Robert F. Kennedy
Roland Barthes
Romay Pavlick, née Callos
Ronald Reagan
Rudyard Kipling
Ruth Wilson Gilmore
Saidiya Hartman
Sami Schalk
Samuel Delaney
Shelley Streeby
Shori

INDEX OF NAMES

Sidney Poitier
Silver Star
Simon Marius
Sitting Bull
Spot
Stephen Best
Stephen Kaneshiro
Steven Harper
Superman
Susana M. Morris
Sylvia Rhue
Tananarive Due
Teray
Thomas More
Tod Everett
Tom Bass

Tom Steerforth
Tory (the dog)
Trigger
Uriah Heep
Valerie Smith
Veronica Jones
Vonda N. McIntyre
W.E.B. Dubois
Walidah Imarisha
Walt Disney
Wanda Poston
Whittaker Chambers
Will James
Zeus
Zorro

ENDNOTES

Preface

1. Equisapiens reference the virile, mutant revolutionaries of Boots Riley's film, *Sorry To Bother You* (2019), which materializes the metaphor of "work horse" to brilliant and horrific extremes.
2. Jacqueline Woodson, "on paper," from *Brown Girl Dreaming* (New York: Puffin Books, Penguin Random House, 2014), 156.
3. Man Ray, Introduction to *Alphabet for Adults* (Beverly Hills, CA: Copley Galleries, 1948).

Introduction

1. Octavia E. Butler, *Dawn*, in *Lilith's Brood* (New York and Boston: Warner Books, 1989), 30.
2. Butler, *Dawn*, 35, 226.
3. Butler, 199.
4. Butler, 200.
5. Michael Mims, interview with author, January 25, 2021.
6. Bebe Martin-Smith, email to author, February 6, 2021.
7. Pablo Miralles, interview with author, July 26, 2018, and *Can We All Get Along?: The Segregation of John Muir High School* (Arroyo Seco Films, 2019).
8. Michael Mims, interview with author, January 25, 2021. See also Michele Zack, *Altadena: Between Wilderness and City* (Altadena, CA: Altadena Historical Society, 2004), 184.
9. *Altadena African American Historic Resources Survey* (Altadena, CA: Los Angeles County Department of Regional Planning, September 8, 2020), 4–13. Thanks to Daria Topousis and Jean Phillips of the Altadena Historical Society.
10. Bob Barnes, "The History of John Muir: The Golden Years 1954–1985." Accessed 6 April 2018.

ENDNOTES

11. Bebe Martin-Smith. See also *Altadena Resources Survey*, 4–28.

12. Charles Dickens, *David Copperfield* (New York: Modern Library, 2000), 54.

13. OEB 273. All references to manuscript materials in the Octavia E. Butler Papers held at the Huntington Library will be cited according to their Huntington "OEB" cataloguing number.

14. Susana M. Morris, "Black Girls Are from the Future: Afrofuturist Feminism in Octavia E. Butler's *Fledgling*," *WSQ: Women's Studies Quarterly* 40.3–4 (Fall/Winter 2021): 158. See also Morris, "'Everything is real. It's just not as you see it': Imagination, Utopia, and Afrofuturist Feminism in Octavia E. Butler's 'The Book of Martha,'" in *The Black Speculative Arts Movement: Black Futurity, Art+Design*, eds. Reynaldo Anderson and Clinton R. Fluker (Lanham: Lexington Books, 2019), 77–90.

15. I borrow this phrase from Rebecca Wanzo's review of recent scholarship on black speculative fiction, "The Unspeakable Speculative, Spoken," *American Literary History* 31.3 (2019): 564.

16. OEB 323. From here on, all quoted misspellings are direct transcriptions of the original.

17. OEB 2456, 2457, 2458.

18. OEB 2456.

19. OEB 446.

20. OEB 562.

21. OEB 3275.

22. OEB 3210.

23. In their study, Moya Bailey and Ayana A.H. Jamieson helpfully refer to their method of engaging with the Octavia's life and fiction via the Huntington manuscript collection as "palimpsestuous memorialization," building on M. Jacqui Alexander's work on palimpsestic time in *Pedagogies of Crossing*. See Bailey and Jamieson, "Guest Editors' Introduction: Palimpsests in the Life and Work of Octavia E. Butler," *Palimpsest: A Journal on Women, Gender and the Black International* 6.2 (2017): vii. See also M. Jacqui Alexander, *Pedagogies of Crossing: Meditations on Feminism, Sexual Politics, Memory, and the Sacred* (Durham, NC: Duke University Press, 2006).

24. Natalie Russell, Huntington Library Curator, interview with author, March 2, 2018. See also Natalie Russell, "Beyond Category: Unpacking Octavia E. Butler," *Huntington Frontiers* (Spring/Summer 2014): 8–12.

25. Shelley Streeby, "Radical Reproduction: Octavia E. Butler's HistoFuturist Archiving as Speculative Theory," *Women's Studies* 47.7 (2018): 719–732.

ENDNOTES

26. Jonathan Swift, "The Lady's Dressing Room" (1732), in *The Poems of Jonathan Swift*, Vol. 2, ed. Harold Williams (Oxford: Oxford University Press, 2014), 530.

27. OEB 3222.

28. Gerard Manley Hopkins, "Pied Beauty," in *The Poetical Works of Gerard Manley Hopkins*, ed. Norman H. Mackenzie (Oxford: Clarendon Press, 1990), 144.

29. Octavia E. Butler, *Parable of the Talents* (New York: Grand Central, 1998), 39.

30. Sami Schalk, *Bodyminds Reimagined: (Dis)ability, Race, and Gender in Black Women's Speculative Fiction* (Durham, NC: Duke University Press, 2018), 2; Walidah Imarisha and adrienne maree brown, eds., Dedication to *Octavia's Brood: Science Fiction Stories from Social Justice Movements* (Oakland, CA: AK Press, 2015); Tananarive Due, "The Only Lasting Truth: The Theme of Change in the Works of Octavia E. Butler," in *Octavia's Brood*, 261; Lynell George, *A Handful of Earth, A Handful of Sky: The World of Octavia E. Butler* (Santa Monica, CA: Angel City Press, 2020), 165.

31. Schalk, *Bodyminds*, 52, 56.

32. OEB 894.

33. Laura R. Barraclough, *Charros: How Mexican Cowboys Are Remapping Race and American Identity* (Oakland: University of California Press, 2019).

34. Madhu Dubey, *Signs and Cities: Black Literary Postmodernism* (Chicago and London: University of Chicago Press, 2003), 64, 68, 72.

35. Carl Abbott, "Pasadena on Her Mind: Exploring Roots of Octavia E. Butler's Fiction," *The Western Historical Quarterly* 49 (Autumn 2018): 329.

36. Veronica Jones, interview with author, January 21, 2021.

37. Dana Jones, interview with author, January 19, 2021.

38. Judy Matthews, interview with author, January 28, 2021.

39. Dana Jones, interview with author, January 19, 2021; Meredith McKenzie, interview with author, January 14, 2021.

40. On "riderless world" see "The Phantom Light of All our Day" by Nathaniel Mackey, *Eroding Witness: Poems* (Urbana and Chicago: University of Illinois Press, 1985). Thanks to Priscilla Wald for this reference.

41. "The Monophobic Response," in Connie Samaras, *A Partial Correction to the Representations of Earth Culture Sent Out to Extraterrestrials on the United States 1977 Voyager Interstellar Space Probes* (San Francisco: New Langton Arts, 1994).

42. Eve L. Ewing, "the first time [a re-telling]," from *Electric Arches* (Chicago: Haymarket Books, 2017), 8.

ENDNOTES

43. Jacqueline Woodson, "grown folks' stories," from *Brown Girl Dreaming* (New York: Nancy Paulson Books, an imprint of Penguin Group (USA), 2014).
44. Gwendolyn L. Brooks, "a song in the front yard," in *Selected Poems* (New York: Harper & Row, 1963), 6. Reprinted by consent of Brooks Permissions.
45. Aimee Meredith Cox, *Shapeshifters: Black Girls and the Choreography of Citizenship* (Durham, NC: Duke University Press, 2015).
46. Christina Sharpe, *In the Wake: On Blackness and Being* (Durham, NC: Duke University Press, 2016), 52–53.
47. Saidiya Hartman, *Wayward Lives, Beautiful Experiments: Intimate Histories of Social Upheaval* (New York and London: Norton, 2019).
48. Quoted in Dr. Jeffrey Elliot, "Interview with Octavia Butler," *Thrust: Science Fiction in Review* 12 (1979): 19.

A is for Alias

1. OEB Box 335, Folder 1.
2. Though she signed most of her schoolwork Estella, she also described being called Estelle. See George, *A Handful of Earth*, 55.
3. Author interview with Dani Patterson (née Black), February 1, 2021.
4. OEB 1262.
5. Author interviews with Bebe Martin-Smith, February 26, 2021; Dani Patterson, February 1, 2021; Sylvia Rhue, June 21, 2018; Romay Pavlick (née Callos), September 8, 2018; Barbara Richardson King, February 2, 2021.
6. OEB 5677–5682.
7. OEB 4.
8. OEB 2713–2714.
9. OEB 5682.
10. OEB 1278.
11. OEB 590.
12. OEB 913.
13. OEB 911.
14. OEB 1276.
15. See also See Gerry Canavan, *Octavia E. Butler* (Urbana: University of Illinois Press, 2016).

ENDNOTES

16. OEB 912.
17. OEB 3172.
18. OEB 2899.
19. OEB 2452.
20. OEB 763.
21. OEB 2728, 2729.
22. For "Lynn Guy" and "Adam Lynn" stories, see OEB 43, 51, 53, 437–438, 2468, 593, 915.
23. OEB 912.
24. OEB 2468.
25. OEB 323.
26. OEB 1250.
27. OEB 1519.
28. OEB 2467.
29. OEB 3111.
30. She also referred to herself as "Shaari, "Shaar," or "Mishaari," perhaps variations on Silver Star. Canavan, *Octavia E. Butler*, 19.
31. OEB 2472.
32. OEB 906. For mentions of *Patternist* names, see OEB 909, 910, 911, 2291, 2818.
33. OEB 455.
34. Octavia E. Butler, *"Wild Seed,"* in *Seed to Harvest* (New York and Boston: Grand Central Publishing, 2007), 14.
35. Butler, 43.
36. Nisi Shawl, "Excerpt 3 from 'A Conversation with Octavia E. Butler,'" in *Strange Matings: Science Fiction, Feminism, African American Voices, and Octavia E. Butler*, eds. Rebecca J. Holden and Nisi Shawl (Seattle: Aqueduct Press, 2013), 129.
37. OEB 1278.
38. OEB 2723.

B is for Bambi

1. OEB 3112.
2. Pasadena Digital History Collaboration, pasadenadigitalhistory.com, accessed 15 January 2021; Bebe Martin-Smith, email to author, February 6, 2021.

ENDNOTES

3. OEB 3111, April 21, 1963 diary entry.
4. OEB Box 325.
5. Movie advertisement, *The Pasadena Independent*, April 6, 1966, p. 19.
6. *They Started Here: Distinguished African-American Alumni*, Pasadena City College (1993), 7. Pasadena Digital History (accessed January 15, 2021).
7. OEB 3112, April 5, 1966 diary entry.
8. OEB 3111.
9. Steven Harper, "An Interview with Octavia E. Butler," *Marion Zimmer Bradley's Fantasy Magazine* 37 (Fall, 1997): 47.
10. OEB 3112.
11. Megan Behrent, "The Personal Is Historical: Slavery, Black Power, and Resistance in Octavia Butler's *Kindred*," *College Literature* 46.4 (2019): 805.
12. Charles H. Rowell and Octavia E. Butler, "An Interview with Octavia E. Butler," *Callaloo* 20.1 (1997): 60. See also Larry McCaffery and Jim McMenamin, "An Interview with Octavia E. Butler," in *Conversations with Octavia Butler*, ed. Conseula Francis (Jackson: University Press of Mississippi, 2010), 21; Behrent, "The Personal Is Historical": 795.
13. *Pasadena City College Catalog*, 1967–1968, p. 254. Pasadena Digital History (accessed January 15, 2021). Thanks to PCC librarian Linda Stewart for this reference.
14. Rowell and Butler, "An Interview with Octavia E. Butler," 60.
15. Nathan Solis, "Author Octavia Butler Dies, Leaves Legacy," *The Courier*, March 9, 2006. Pasadena Digital History (accessed January 15, 2021).
16. See Valerie Smith, "Neo-Slave Narratives," in *The Cambridge Companion to the African American Slave Narrative*, Vol. 1, ed. Audrey Fisch (Cambridge: Cambridge University Press, 2007): 168–185. Ashraf H. Rushdy, *Neo-Slave Narratives: Studies in the Social Logic of a Literary Form* (New York: Oxford University Press, 1999).
17. Octavia Butler, "Loss," in *Pipes of Pan: An Anthology of Student Writings*, vol. 24 (1968), 18. Pasadena Digital History (accessed January 15, 2021).
18. OEB 3112.
19. OEB 441.
20. K-Ming Chang, *dear Bambi: Three Poems by K-Ming Chang*. https://aaww.org/dear-bambi-kristin-chang/. Thanks to Erin O'Malley for introducing me to these poems.
21. Kiki Smith, *Born*, 2002. Bronze (99.06 × 256.54 × 60.96). Collection Albright-Knox Art Gallery, Buffalo, New York.

ENDNOTES

22. Alison Saar, *Rouse*, 2012, wood, bronze, found antler sheds, graphite (90 × 60 × 60).
23. Margaret Cavendish, Countess of Newcastle, *Poems, and Fancies* (London, 1653).
24. Cavendish, Countess of Newcastle.
25. Quoted in Joan Fry, "Congratulations! You've Just Won $295,000: An Interview with Octavia Butler," in *Conversations with Octavia Butler*, 127.

C is for Character

1. OEB 281.
2. Marilyn Mehaffy and AnaLouise Keating, "'Radio Imagination': Octavia Butler on the Poetics of Narrative Embodiment," in *Conversations with Octavia Butler*, 103.
3. OEB 336, Folder 5.
4. OEB 1615.
5. OEB 1615.
6. OEB Box 337.
7. OEB 1623.

D is for Dog

1. OEB 48.
2. Octavia Butler, "Eye Witness: Who Would Have Imagined That When Writer Octavia Butler Gazed into a Dog's Eyes, Her Perspective Would Change Forever? (Aha! Moment)." *O, The Oprah Magazine*, 3.5 (May 2002): 79.
3. John Berger, "Why Look at Animals?," in *About Looking* (New York: Vintage, 1992), 5.
4. OEB 48.
5. OEB 48, Butler, "Eye Witness," and Canavan, *Octavia E. Butler*, 74.
6. Dr. Jeffrey Elliot, "Interview with Octavia Butler," *Thrust: Science Fiction in Review* 12 (Summer 1979): 19.
7. OEB 48.
8. Butler, "Eye Witness," 79.
9. Phone conversation with Sylvia Rhue, June 23, 2018.

ENDNOTES

10. OEB 814.
11. OEB 1270.
12. Butler, *Parable of the Sower* (1993; reis., New York and Boston: Grand Central, 2019), 45.
13. Octavia E. Butler, *Survivor* (New York: Signet, 1978), 15.
14. OEB 3177.
15. OEB 3172, OEB 323.
16. OEB 3218, OEB 2727.
17. OEB 3218, OEB 2727.
18. OEB 1165.
19. OEB 536–537.

E is for Equisetopsida

1. Butler, *Clay's Ark*, in *Seed to Harvest* (New York and Boston: Grand Central, 2007), 529, 541, 606.
2. Butler, *Wild Seed*, 193.
3. Butler, *Mind of My Mind*, in *Seed to Harvest* (New York and Boston: Grand Central, 2007), 280.
4. OEB 455.
5. OEB 3275. See also Introduction.
6. Lena Maloney, email message to author, May 29, 2019.
7. Leslie Howle, phone interview with author, April 27, 2018.

F is for Flash

1. OEB 590.
2. OEB 92.
3. OEB 913.
4. Romay Pavlick, interview with author, Sept 8, 2018.
5. Dani Patterson, email to author, Aug. 8, 2018.
6. OEB 916.
7. OEB 3111.
8. OEB 921. See also OEB 2816, OEB 2470.
9. OEB 2821.
10. OEB 913.
11. OEB 921.

ENDNOTES

12. OEB 2460.
13. OEB 3111.
14. OEB 1555.
15. OEB 1555.
16. Marcia Holmes, "Brainwashing the Cybernetic Spectator," *History of the Human Sciences* 30.3 (2017): 3–24, and Deirdre Barrett, "Hypnosis in Film and Television," *American Journal of Clinical Hypnosis* 49.1 (July 2006): 13–30.
17. OEB 826.
18. OEB 826, OEB 825.
19. See Canavan, *Octavia E. Butler*, 18.
20. OEB 916, OEB 2812.
21. OEB 439, also OEB 2474, 2812, 592.
22. OEB 2813.
23. OEB 11.
24. OEB 2474.
25. OEB 2474.
26. OEB 3111.
27. OEB 2806.
28. OEB 2827.
29. OEB 323.
30. OEB 13.

G is for Ganymede

1. The *Mundus Jovialis of Simon Marius*, trans. A.O. Prickard, *The Observatory* 39 (1916): 380.
2. OEB 3020.
3. "Welcome to 'Octavia E. Butler Landing,'" March 5, 2021, NASA Mars Exploration Program. https://mars.nasa.gov/resources/25701/welcome-to-octavia-e-butler-landing/ (accessed March 8, 2021).
4. Butler, *Parable of the Talents*, 81, 392.
5. OEB 1278.
6. OEB 593.
7. OEB 913.
8. OEB 1628. "The People" is possibly based on Zenna Henderson's 1960s novels about humanoid aliens. See "An Interview with Octavia E. Butler" by

ENDNOTES

Larry McCaffery and Jim McMenamin in *Conversations with Octavia Butler*, 16.

9. OEB 921, OEB 913.
10. OEB 1628.
11. OEB 1628.
12. *Amazing Stories* 14.10 (1940): 144. https://archive.org/details/Amazing_Stories_v14n10_1940-10_-_Ziff-Davis/page/n147/mode/2up (accessed March 2, 2021).
13. OEB 2908.
14. OEB 1543, 1544.
15. Sylvia Rhue, email correspondence with author, December 29, 2020.
16. For an image of the pink notebook, see George, *A Handful of Earth*, 24, 39. The F% symbol is written in pink pen on the outside cover.
17. OEB 1241.

H is for Horse

1. Octavia Butler interview with AnaLouise Keating and Marilyn Mehaffy, "'Radio Imagination': Octavia Butler on the Poetics of Narrative Embodiment," *MELUS* 26.1 (2001): 45.
2. Keating and Mehaffy, "'Radio Imagination,'" 54.
3. OEB 2456, 2457.
4. OEB 2456, 2457.
5. OEB Box 337.
6. Elliot, "Interview with Octavia Butler," 83, 181.
7. Thanks to Alexis Adkins of the California State Polytechnic University, Pomona for helping me track down Pistorius.
8. *Oxford English Dictionary*, s.v. "trace," https://www-oed-com.proxy.library.upenn.edu (accessed September 2, 2021).
9. Dickens, *David Copperfield*, 667.
10. Gina M. Dorré, *Victorian Fiction and the Cult of the Horse* (Burlington, VT: Ashgate, 2006), 82, 101.
11. James Creelman, *On the Great Highway: The Wanderings and Adventures of a Special Correspondent* (Boston: Lothrop Publishing Company 1901), 301.
12. OEB 3111.
13. Dickens, *David Copperfield*, 418.

ENDNOTES

14. Roland Barthes, *Image, Music, Text* (New York: Hill and Wang, 1977), 158.
15. Barthes, *Image, Music, Text*, 159.

I is for "I am"

1. OEB 1517.
2. OEB 13.
3. OEB 1516.
4. Rebecca Wanzo, "Apocalyptic Empathy: A *Parable* of Postmodern Sentimentality," *Obsidian III: Literature of the African Diaspora* 6.2 and 7.1 (2005, 2006): 80.
5. Audre Geraldine Lorde, "A Burst of Light: Living with Cancer," *A Burst of Light: Essays* (Ithaca, NY: Firebrand Books, 1988) 132.
6. OEB 1516.

J is for Junie

1. OEB 3830.
2. OEB 3829.
3. OEB Box 343. Mrs. Butler says she attended school until she was promoted to the sixth grade. By Octavia's account, her mother was ten when she left school.
4. OEB 921.
5. OEB 2288.
6. OEB 2471.
7. OEB 2471.
8. OEB 3825.
9. *A Conversation with Octavia Butler*, in *Parable of the Sower*, 334. Also OEB 3222.
10. OEB 2478.
11. OEB 2463.
12. OEB 924.

K is for Kapok

1. OEB Box 161. See also Amazon notes on trees, OEB 3117, 3118.
2. OEB Box 161.

ENDNOTES

3. Alfred W. Crosby, *Ecological Imperialism: The Biological Expansion of Europe, 900–1900* (New York: Cambridge University Press, 2006), 293.
4. Email correspondence with artist and landscaper Daniel Tucker, daniel@pippinhedge.com.
5. Butler, *Parable of the Talents*, 213.

L is for Lion Girl

1. Rudyard Kipling, *The Two Jungle Books* (Garden City, NY: Doubleday, Doran, 1895), 9. Internet Archive.

M is for Mother

1. OEB Box 325.
2. OEB Box 343.
3. OEB 3298.
4. Josh Sides, *L.A. City Limits: African American Los Angeles from the Great Depression to the Present* (Berkeley, Los Angeles, London: University of California Press, 2004), 43.
5. OEB Box 343.
6. Octavia Margaret Butler, diary entry, OEB 3111.
7. Diary entry, March 2, 1962. OEB 3110.
8. OEB 3220.
9. OEB 3111.
10. OEB 3210.
11. Diary entry, April 6, 1963, OEB 3111.
12. OEB 3111.
13. Sylvia Rhue, "The Hottest Church in Town," unpublished short story via email correspondence, August 26, 2021.
14. Rhue, "The Hottest Church in Town."
15. Rhue, "Hottest Church in Town."
16. Octavia E. Butler, *Parable of the Sower*, 15
17. Jayna Brown, *Black Utopias: Speculative Life and the Music of Other Worlds* (Durham, NC and London: Duke University Press, 2021), 100.
18. Butler, *Parable of the Talents*, 411.
19. OEB 3216.
20. OEB 3216.

ENDNOTES

21. OEB 533.
22. OEB 533.
23. OEB 1542.
24. OEB 3222, OEB 1278. Also published, with slightly different wording, in the essay "Positive Obsession," in *Bloodchild and Other Stories* (New York: Seven Stories Press, 2005), 125.

O is for Ooloi

1. OEB 3227.
2. OEB 395.
3. OEB 567.
4. OEB 3227.
5. OEB Box 83, Folder 1625. See also Aimee Bahng, "Plasmodial Improprieties: Octavai E. Butler, Slime Molds, and Imagining a Femi-Queer Commons," in *The Queer Feminist Science Studies Reader* (Seattle: UW Press, 2017): 310–326.
6. OEB 891.
7. OEB 892.
8. OEB 893.
9. OEB 891.

P is for Public Library

1. OEB 2456.
2. OEB 2456, OEB 332.
3. Note: this is Mrs. Butler's own account of her schooling in OEB Box 343. Elsewhere Octavia wrote that her mother only had three years of schooling. OEB 1278. See also Note 3 in "J is for Junie."
4. OEB 343, OEB 1278.
5. OEB 755, OEB 95.
6. OEB Box 309.
7. "Free Libraries: Are They Becoming Extinct?," *Omni* 15.10 (August 1993): 4.
8. OEB 3222.
9. See OEB 585–587. Quotations taken from essay published as "Free Libraries: Are They Becoming Extinct?".
10. OEB 1278.

ENDNOTES

11. "Free Libraries: Are They Becoming Extinct?". See also OEB 585–587.
12. OEB 4, 5, 5677–5683. For a list of SF authors she read, see George, *A Handful of Earth*, 135.
13. OEB 1278.
14. Kellie Jones, *South of Pico: African American Artists in Los Angeles in the 1960s and 1960s* (Durham, NC: Duke University Press, 2017), 41.
15. OEB 276.
16. OEB 536, 537.

Q is for QWERTY

1. OEB 1278.
2. OEB 271.
3. OEB 2715, July 31, 1963.
4. OEB Box 325 (folder 13).
5. OEB 3110.
6. OEB Box 325 (folder 13).
7. Diary entry from April 21, 1963. OEB 3111.
8. OEB Box 325.
9. Email correspondence from Sylvia Rhue, December 29, 2020 and Bebe Martin-Smith, February 6, 2021. Also phone interview with Dani Patterson, February 1, 2021.
10. OEB 2726.
11. OEB 3824.
12. OEB 3824.
13. OEB 1278.

R is for Rex McDonald

1. Rufus Jackson tribute to Rex McDonald, reprinted in E.A. Trowbridge, "The Missouri Saddle Horse," Missouri State Board of Agriculture, *Monthly Bulletin* 11.10 (October 1913): 10.
2. Herbert J. Krum, *Short Stories about Famous Saddle Horses*, vol. 1, no. 1 (Lexington, KY: Press of Transylvania Printing Co., April 1910), 50.

ENDNOTES

3. Bill Downey, *Whisper on the Wind: The Story of Tom Bass—Celebrated Black Horseman* ([Place of publication not identified]: The Long Riders' Guild Press, 1998 edition).

4. Marguerite Henry, *Album of Horses* (New York: Rand McNally & Company, 1951), 30.

5. OEB 1620.

6. OEB 48.

7. "Rancho Elastico Open House Set Saturday," *Star News*, March 15, 1962. https://newspaperarchive.com (accessed January 28, 2021).

8. Lucie Lowery, "Animal 'Kingdom' Periled," *Star News*, January 22, 1968; Bill Mayer, "Altadena 4-H Club May Lose Animals," December 14, 1967; Margaret Stovall, "Youngsters Promote Friendship Program," July 23, 1965; Margaret Stovall, "4-H Club Stocks Up," May 1, 1959. https://newspaperarchive.com (accessed January 28, 2021).

9. Ken Harris, "Arroyo Seco Stable Horses" (2006). http://animalstories-ken.blogspot.com/2008/12/arroyo-seco-stable-horses.html. See also Meredith McKenzie, "Altadena: A Horse Lover's Best Kept Secret, *Altadena Now*, January 30, 2021.

10. Phone interview with August Simien, Jr., January 29, 2021.

11. Phone interview with Dani Patterson, February 1, 2021.

12. Phone interview with Dana Jones, January 19, 2021.

13. Phone interview with Veronica Jones, January 21, 2021.

14. Zack, *Altadena: Between Wilderness and City*, 62.

15. Frances Barrett White and Anne Scott, *Reaches of the Heart* (New York: Barricade Books, 1994), 191, 134.

16. Phone interview with Meredith McKenzie, January 14, 2021.

17. Anna Sewell, *Black Beauty* (Oxford: Oxford University Press, 1992), 26.

18. Sewell, *Black Beauty*, 20, 110.

19. Downey, *Whisper on the Wind*, 191.

20. Sewell, *Black Beauty*, 157, 11.

21. Karl Marx, *Capital Volume I*, trans. Ben Fowkes (London: Penguin Classics, 1990), 498.

S is for Sexy

1. OEB 11 (Jan. 29, 1963). All other quotes from OEB 3222.

ENDNOTES

T is for TV Western

1. OEB Box 325.
2. OEB Box 336.
3. Butler, *Parable of the Talents*, 127.
4. OEB 2926.
5. OEB 538.
6. OEB 3111.
7. OEB 2893.
8. OEB 3222.
9. OEB 2474.
10. OEB 2296.
11. OEB 2290.
12. Butler, *Patternmaster*, in *Seed to Harvest* (New York and Boston: Grand Central Publishing, 2007), 634.
13. Joan Didion, *Slouching Towards Bethlehem* (New York: Farrar, Straus and Giroux, 2008), 30.

U is for Utopia

1. OEB 3275, August 16, 2001.
2. OEB 3111, diary entry, April 16, 1963.
3. "Letter from W.E.B. Du Bois to Communist Party of the U.S.A." (October 1, 1961). https://credo.library.umass.edu/view/pageturn/mums312-b153-i071/#page/1/mode/1up (accessed May 31, 2022).
4. Stephen M. Ward (ed.), *Pages from a Black Radical's Notebook: A James Boggs Reader* (Detroit: Wayne State University Press, 2011), 85.
5. James Boggs, "Black Power: A Scientific Concept Whose Time Has Come," in *A James Boggs Reader*, 174.
6. OEB 501.
7. OEB 3210.
8. "The Black Panther Party's Ten-Point Program." https://www.ucpress.edu/blog/25139/the-black-panther-partys-ten-point-program/
9. Jayna Brown, *Black Utopias: Speculative Life and the Music of Other Worlds* (Durham, NC: Duke University Press, 2021), 84.
10. OEB 496.
11. OEB 498, my brackets.

ENDNOTES

12. OEB 1163, June 26, 2005.
13. Phone conversation with Leslie Howle, April 27, 2018.
14. OEB 565.
15. OEB 565.
16. The yearlong programming and exhibition at Armory Center for the Arts was curated by Julia Meltzer, with the Los Angeles arts organization Clockshop. *Radio Imagination: Artists and Writers in the Archive of Octavia E. Butler* (Los Angeles: Clockshop, 2018).
17. Lauren Halsey, "and it was a natural extension of my dreaming," *Radio Imagination*, 68–74.
18. Connie Samaras, "The Past Is Another Planet," *Radio Imagination*, 80–90.
19. Author interview with Connie Samaras, June 5, 2018.
20. Stephen Best, *None Like Us: Blackness, Belonging, Aesthetic Life* (Durham, NC: Duke University Press, 2018), 44.
21. OEB 3216, March 2, 1978.
22. Octavia E. Butler, "'Afterword' to The Book of Martha," in *Bloodchild and Other Stories* (New York: Seven Stories Press, 2005), 214.
23. OEB 3177, April 1, 1982.

V is for Victorville

1. See oral histories collected by Richard D. Thompson at https://mojavehistory.com. See also his book, *Murray's Ranch: Apple Valley's African-American Dude Ranch* (Apple Valley, CA: Desert Knolls Press, 2002).
2. Sherryl Vint, "Becoming Other: Animals, Kinship, and Butler's 'Clay's Ark,'" *Science Fiction Studies* 32.3 (2005): 296.
3. Stuart Kellogg, "Life on the Dude Ranch," *Daily Press*, May 25, 2002. www.pasadenadigitalhistory.com (accessed January 15, 2021).
4. OEB 332.
5. OEB Box 343.
6. Jim Lindsay, "The parable of her talents," *Pasadena City College Courier*, March 16, 2000. www.pasadenadigitalhistory.com (accessed January 15, 2021).
7. Email correspondence with Ernestine Walker and Enas Elmohands, October 16, 2019.
8. OEB 894, c. 2000.

281

ENDNOTES

X is for Xenogenesis

1. Notecard on "Cancer Types," OEB Box 161.
2. Cited by Fred Moten, "A common place flaw" in *Radio Imagination*, 31.
3. Notecard on "Oncogene theory," OEB 3014.
4. OEB 2896.
5. Notecard on "Carcinogens—Xenogenesis," OEB Box 161.
6. *World Book Encyclopedia and Dictionary*, s.v. "Xenogenesis," 1963. See also notecard on "Xenogenesis," OEB Box 161.
7. Erasmus Darwin, *The Temple of Nature*, Canto I, l. 247 (1802). https://www.gutenberg.org (accessed July 3, 2020).
8. *Three Gothic Novels* (Hammondsworth; New York: Penguin Classics, 1988), 264, 311.
9. Patricia Melzer, *Alien Construction: Science Fiction and Feminist Thought* (Austin: University of Texas Press, 2006), 78.
10. OEB 3227.
11. Notecard on "Imago," OEB Box 161.
12. Notecard on "Humanicide," OEB Box 161.
13. OEB 413.
14. Interview with Larry McCaffery, in *Across the Wounded Galaxies: Interview with Contemporary American Science Fiction Writers* (Urbana and Chicago: University of Illinois Press, 1990), 67.
15. Butler, *Dawn*, in *Lilith's Brood* (New York and Boston: Warner Books, 1989), 122.
16. Butler, *Dawn*, 16. See also her short story about Hitler, "The Actor," OEB 8.
17. OEB 3227.
18. Butler, *Dawn*, 237.
19. Priscilla Wald, "The Art of Medicine: Cognitive Estrangement, Science Fiction, and Medical Ethics," *The Lancet* 371 (June 7, 2008): 1908–1909.
20. OEB Box 161.
21. Siddhartha Mukherjee, *The Emperor of All Maladies: A Biography of Cancer* (New York: Scribner, 2011), 16.
22. OEB Box 161.
23. OEB 559.
24. OEB Box 161.

ENDNOTES

Y is for Yearbook

1. Butler, *Parable of the Sower*, 287.
2. OEB Box 337.
3. OEB Box 337.
4. OEB 1622.
5. OEB 1253.
6. Phone conversation with Romay Callos Pavlick, September 8, 2018.
7. Phone conversation with Barbara Richardson King, February 2, 2021.
8. Email correspondence with Sylvia Rhue, December 29, 2020.
9. OEB 1623.
10. OEB 1623.
11. OEB 1623.
12. OEB 3114.
13. OEB 1623.

Horse appendix / Appendix of horses

1. Charles Dickens, "The Volante," *All the Year Round* vol. xv, June 23, 1866. www.djo.org.uk.

ACKNOWLEDGMENTS

I am grateful to all the kind people who helped me along this circuitous journey...

Those who shared with me their stories and expertise: August Simien, Jr., Barbara Richardson-King, Bebe Martin-Smith, Connie Samaras, Dana Jones, Dani Black Patterson, Ernestine Walker (and Enas Elmohands), Judy Matthews, Julia Meltzer, Lawton Gray, Lena Maloney, Leslie Howle, Lynell George, Meredith McKenzie, Michael Mims, Pablo Miralles, Richard Thompson, Romay Pavlick, Sylvia Rhue, Veronica Jones, Wanda Poston.

The librarians, library staff, and archivists who generously gave of their time: Alexis Adkins, Anuja Navare, Daria Popousis, Dorothy Espalto, Genevieve Preston, Jean Phillips, Karla Nielsen, Katie Rawson, Linda Stewart, Mina Marciano, Natalie Russell, Nathaniel da Gala, Young Phong.

Those who helped me envision and realize the book's design: Aimee Wright, Amanda Brown, Chi-wang Yang, David Juengst, Dorothy Espalto, Emilio Martinez Poppe, Eric Cho, Katie Rawson, Lesia Mokrycke.

Colleagues and friends who read or discussed with me portions of the project, and those who offered guidance and cheered me on: the two anonymous reviewers of the manuscript, Ania Loomba, Anne Cheng, Dagmawi Woubshet, David Eng, Ellen Singer-Coleman, Eric Cho, Herman Beavers, Jack McNichol, Jed Esty, Jim English, Joon Oluchi Lee, Julia Bloch, Kay McGuffin, Ken Lum, Lorene Cary, Margo Crawford, Mary Ebeling, Melissa Jensen, Nancy Henry, Paul Saint-Amour, Pablo Miralles, Pam Moffat, Pearl Brilmyer, Philip Davis, Priscilla Wald, Rebecca Wanzo, Rosemarie Bodenheimer, Sterling K. Johnson, Suvir Kaul, Tamara Walker, Tavia Nyong'o, Wiley Cunningham, Zack Lesser. A special shout-out to my besties, the constant and brilliant Amanda Swarr and Jerry Miller.

This book would not have been possible without the Yang family, Ellen, Ho-chin, Chi-hui, and Chi-wang, plus Sonia and Rae-An, Emilie and Floyd, and the dear people who offered a lifeline in 2017–2018: Ah-Qiong, Frank James, Guido Marcucci, Jiasong Yuen, Joe Lin, Karen Chien, Katrina Duncan. My deepest thanks go to Eric Cho, who has over the years inspired me in countless ways.

INDEX

Abbott, Carl 259
Adams, Karen 29, 30, 33–34, 38–41, 45, 246
Adkins, Alexis 270
Aesop 52
Alanna 9, 66, 193
Amber 9, 88
Angelou, Maya 124
Ansara, Michael 193
Anyanwu 9, 75, 185
Ayapo, Lilith 1, 3–4, 9, 67, 129, 147–149, 230

Bailey, Moya 258
Bailey, Pearl 216
Baldwin, James 201
Barnes, Bob 258
Barraclough, Laura R. 22
Barthes, Roland 112–113
Bass, Tom 172, 174, 179, 181–182
Behrent, Megan 266
Berger, John 63
Berlin, Ira 58
Best, Stephen 273
Beyoncé 214
Black Beauty 10, 175–176, 179–182, 245
Boggs, Grace Lee 9
Boggs, James 201
Bradbury, Ray 7, 34
Brooks, Gwendolyn L. 25
brown, adrienne maree 19, 259
Brown, Jayna 139
Brown, John 178
Bryan, Paul 186

Butler, Laurice James 63, 148
Butler, Octavia Margaret Guy xiv, 9, 12, 19, 29, 33, 36, 38, 49, 50, 63, 74, 83, 89, 115–116, 118–121, 123, 131, 134–137, 139–143, 145, 148, 155, 158, 159, 166–167, 170–171, 190, 201, 218, 239

Canavan, Gerry 265, 267, 269
Carroll, Lewis 128
Cavendish, Margaret 54–55
Chambers, Whittaker 52
Chang, K-Ming 53–54
Cho, Jorge 16
Clare, John 70
Copperfield, David 8, 103–105, 107–112, 249–256
Cox, Aimee Meredith 25
Crosby, Alfred 128

Darwin, Erasmus 227
Davis, Angela 202
Davis, Bette 111
Defoe, Daniel xi
Delaney, Samuel 33
Dickens, Charles xiv, 103–105, 107–112, 173, 179, 182, 233, 248–257
Didion, Joan 195–196
Disney, Walt 34, 48–49, 52, 191
Doro 39, 44, 58, 74–75, 89, 96, 185
Dorré, Gina M. 110, 270
Downey, Bill 275
Dubey, Madhu 22
Dubois, W.E.B. 200
Due, Tananarive 20, 259

INDEX

Elliot, Jeffrey 260, 267, 270
Ellison, Harlan 33, 169, 170
Emily (Little Em'ly, niece of Mr.
  Peggotty) 108–112, 189, 213, 250,
  256–257
Everett, Tod 52
Ewing, Eve L. 24

Francis, Conseula 266
Fry, Joan 267

George, Lynell 20, 259, 270, 274
Gilmore, Ruth Wilson 225
Greene, Lorne 40, 189
Guy, Edna Estelle Hayward 12, 30, 136,
  141, 148, 201, 204, 209–210, 217–218, 226,
  242
Guy, Lynn 30, 38, 265

Halsey, Lauren 204–205
Harper, Steven 266
Hartman, Saidiya 25
Heep, Uriah 249
Henry, Marguerite 110, 174
Highland Dale 175, 176
Hopkins, Gerard Manley 16
Howle, Leslie 17, 76, 78, 203

Imarisha, Walidah 19, 259

Jackson, Mahalia 50, 167
James, Will 58, 160
Jamieson, Ayana A.H. 258
Jeffries, Herb 213–214
Joetta 37, 240
Johns, Leah-Rae 69–70, 161
Jones, Dana 23, 177, 259, 275
Jones, Kellie 274
Jones, Veronica 23, 177, 259, 275

Kaneshiro, Stephen 67
Keating, AnaLouise 267, 270
Kennedy, John F. 96, 97, 99, 100
Kennedy, Robert F. 51, 240

King, Jr., Martin Luther 50–51, 99,
  124–125, 200
Kipling, Rudyard 131–132

Laffan, Patricia 35
L'Amour, Louis 186
Larkin, Mary 9, 58, 75
Lassie 67–68, 175, 190
L'Engle, Madeleine 205
Lorde, Audre 116

Mackey, Nathaniel 23, 259
Maloney, Lena 76, 268
Marius, Simon 93
Martin-Smith, Bebe 5–6, 7, 31, 49–50, 159,
  167, 236, 242
Marx, Karl 182, 200
(Maslin), Keira 9, 67, 214–216, 233
Matsumoto, Ada 58
Matthews, Judy 177–178
McCaffery, Larry 266, 270, 278
McCue, Marion J. 11
McIntyre, Vonda N. 229
McKay, Gardner 40, 192
McKenzie, Meredith 178, 271
Mehaffy, Marilyn 267, 270
Meltzer, Julia 204, 277
Melzer, Patricia 228
Micawber, Mister (Wilkins) 108, 110, 111,
  256
Mims, Michael 177, 258
Miralles, Pablo 258
More, Thomas 204
Morris, Susana M. 8
Mowgli 130–131
Murdstone, Miss (Jane) 105, 108,
  248–249
Murray, Nolie and Lela 212–213, 216

Nikanj 147, 149, 230

Olamina, Lauren Oya 9, 17, 66, 95, 116,
  129, 139
Ouida 30, 161

288

INDEX

Patterson, Dani Black 31, 82, 241, 268
Pavlick, née Callos, Romay 59, 238–239, 240
Peggotty (Clara) 108, 251
Peggotty (Ham) 108, 251
Peggotty (Mr.) 108, 109, 251
Peter Pan 154, 156, 158, 160
Phillips, Jean 258
Pistorius, Anna 106–109, 248–257
Poitier, Sidney 178
Poston, Wanda 134, 142–143

Ray, Man xiii–xiv
Reagan, Ronald 14, 67, 226, 229
Rhue, Sylvia 64, 99, 138, 167, 241
Rice, Anne 185
Richardson-King, Barbara 31, 241
Robinson, Jackie 5
Roddenberry, Gene 194
Rowell, Charles H. 266
Rushdy, Ashraf H. 51, 266
Russell, Natalie 14, 258

Saar, Alison 54
Salten, Felix 49, 52, 55, 87, 145, 180
Samaras, Connie 205, 259, 277
Schalk, Sami 19, 21
Schoborg, Jeanne Newton 172
Sewell, Anna 179–182
Sharpe, Christina 25
Shawl, Nisi 265
Shelley, Mary 227
Shing, Joseph Li-Chin 67, 149
Shori 8, 9
Sides, Josh 268

Silver Star 23, 30, 34, 35, 39, 41–45, 58, 78, 80, 88, 95, 106, 121–123, 176, 180, 184–185, 190, 191, 193, 203, 214, 216, 222, 233, 245
Simien, Jr., August 177, 179
Sitting Bull 106, 110, 256
Smith, Kiki 54
Smith, Valerie 51, 266
Spenlow, Dora 104, 109, 111, 173, 254
Spot 62–63
Steerforth, Tom 108–109, 112, 179, 254–255
Story, Carrie 212
Streeby, Shelley 259
Superman 82, 97, 123, 145
Swift, Jonathan xi, 15

Teray 88, 195
Topousis, Daria 257
Tory (the dog) 68–70, 190
Trigger 213
Tubman, Harriet 139
Tucker, Daniel 126, 129, 272

van der Straet, Jan 128

Wakefield, Agnes 252, 253, 254
Wald, Priscilla 259, 278
Walker, Ernestine 217, 277
Wanzo, Rebecca 258, 271
Wayne, Bruce 246
Wayne, John 195–196
White, Charles 178
Williams, Guy 50, 191
Woodson, Jacqueline xiii, 24
Wright, Richard 201

Zack, Michele 258, 275
Zeus 93–94
Zorro 18, 50, 167, 189, 190–192, 245–246

Author photo, *c.* 1979 Everson, WA, Main Street Rodeo Parade. Taken in front of my parents' Chinese American restaurant.